Anything For You
(The Connor Family, Book 1)

LAYLA HAGEN

Dear Reader,

If you want to receive news about my upcoming books and sales, you can sign up for my newsletter HERE: http://laylahagen.com/mailing-list-sign-up/

Chapter One
Landon

"You need a vacation," Adam said.

I was pacing my corner office in the high-rise in San Jose, massaging my right temple. I could feel a headache forming.

"I know."

"A real vacation. Not one that lasts forty-eight hours."

I laughed because that was an accurate description of my vacations for the past few years. As my right hand, Adam knew all about it. But now I'd just finished negotiations for a partnership with another important player in the software industry. For the next few weeks, everyone would be focusing on paperwork and celebrating. I wasn't needed for either, and I was exhausted. The months leading to this point had been intense.

"You're right. Taking two weeks off wouldn't be a bad idea."

Adam widened his eyes. "Are you serious?"

I paced the office some more, keeping to the window, which was my favorite place in the room. It focused on work.

"Nah, LA. I want to spend some time with my family."

"That's great. I can count on Val to throw your phone in the ocean if you overdo answering 'urgent' e-mails." Adam nodded encouragingly, making air quotes around the word *urgent*.

"Don't give her any ideas," I warned. My twin sister Valentina had too many ideas as it was. I reached for my smartphone on the desk. "I'll call her right now."

Adam understood the dismissal and left the room. I dialed my sister's number and she answered after the fifth ring.

"Congratulations," she exclaimed before I even had a chance to open my mouth. "You just finalized negotiations, right? How are you celebrating?"

Only Val would remember the exact time I'd seal the deal. She was one of a kind.

"Yes, I did. And as for celebrating… I want to come home for two weeks."

There was a pause, and I wondered if either of us had accidentally ended the call. Then Val exclaimed, "Wait, I think my ears might be deceiving me. Dearest brother of mine, did you actually say you're coming home? For two weeks?"

I could hear the smile in her voice. "Yes, exactly."

"On business?"

"No, I want to take time off."

I heard the change in her voice, the sudden softness.

"I can't wait either, munchkin," I said.

"Don't call me that," Val protested. That had been our father's nickname for her. He used it when he wanted to tease her. It had always made her smile.

"Fair warning, you might have to put up with it for the next two weeks."

"You brute. At least give me a few days to enjoy having you here before you start annoying me."

"I'm not making any promises. See you tomorrow, Val. I want to ask my assistant to buy that airplane ticket before she leaves."

"Sure. Go ahead. See you tomorrow."

After the line went static, I rose from my leather seat, looked out the window, and smiled. I was going home.

Chapter Two
Maddie

I straightened up when Val called my name, then sauntered toward the house, careful where I stepped. I'd transformed her front yard into a mess, but that was how landscaping worked in the initial phase.

"Here, I made some iced tea." She set the tray on the large wooden table in front of the house and poured the tea into two glasses.

"Thanks!" I gulped it down greedily, the liquid cooling my throat. This was just what the doctor ordered. It was an unusually hot afternoon for the end of June in LA. Val's ranch-style house was located on the northwestern side of the city, and the ocean was so far away that not even a wisp of a breeze reached us here.

"How is it going?"

"I'm done for the day, just waiting for the timber posts to be delivered. I talked to the driver a while ago. He should be here in ten minutes."

Val finished her tea, sweeping her gaze across the yard. She'd commissioned me to transform her downward-sloping property into a terraced garden, and the first step involved breaking down the smooth slope into multiple levels. I'd started the project only this week, so right now it looked as if a meteorite had hit it squarely in the center.

"Okay. Landon will arrive from LAX soon. Do you want to join us for dinner? All my siblings are coming." She smiled warmly. Val was an unusual employer. Unusual in the best way possible. I'd landscaped the yard surrounding her office building a few months back, and she'd loved the results so much that she commissioned me again.

She was friendly and fun, and I was more than tempted to say yes. I'd met her sister Lori and her son Milo, and they were fun too. And last Friday I'd been here to discuss the last details of the project with Val and caught a glimpse of the entire family— minus Landon, of course—arriving for dinner, and they seemed very tight.

I only had pizza leftovers waiting for me at home, and no company whatsoever, but I shook my head. I didn't want to infringe on their family time.

"Thanks, but I'm okay."

"Okay." She drummed her fingers on the table, checking the time on her phone, her excitement palpable. When the unmistakable sound of a car pulling up to the front gate reached us, she rose from her seat and skidded down the patchy earth, her dark brown hair bobbing down her back. The house was at the top of the slope, the entrance gate at the very bottom. This place would look like the Garden of Eden by the time I was done with it. Shame it had to be in shambles exactly when her brother arrived.

I rose from my seat too, trying to decide on the best way to make myself scarce so I could offer them privacy. I ended up heading inside the house. I'd deposited my bag and a change of clothes in the foyer this morning, and I could check my e-mails while I waited for the delivery. Even though the bulk of the landscaping business was hands-on, I still spent one or two hours dealing with organizational tasks or finalizing designs for the next project. I only played in the dirt in one project at a time, but I typically completed the design phase for the next project at the same time. Unfortunately, I found my phone was out of battery. It must have died after I talked to the delivery driver. I debated changing out of my work clothes, but there was no point. I'd have to help unload the truck, and I'd just get my good clothes dirty too.

When I stepped out of the house again, Valentina and her brother were just finishing the climb up the slope, and *holy hell. That* was Landon Connor? When I saw the family last week, I gathered that the Connor gene pool was an enviable one.

The women were tall, with delicate and elegant features, the men even taller—over six feet— and very handsome. But in my humble opinion, Landon was the best-looking of all.

Of course, my opinion might have been skewed by the fact that he was wearing a suit right now. Since I worked outdoors, I mostly saw the opposite sex in tanks or short-sleeved T-shirts, soaked in sweat. I was a sucker for a man in a suit, especially one who wore it as well as Landon did. His hair was a darker shade of brown than Valentina's, but their eyes seemed to be the same bright green. They both stopped talking upon seeing me.

"Landon, this is Maddie Jennings."

"I hear you're the one responsible for turning this"—he gestured to the terrain behind him— "unrecognizable."

"Guilty as charged."

The corners of his lips lifted. *Oh my, that smile.* I was wishing I had changed. Bits of earth clung to my jeans, and I'd smeared my T-shirt over the course of the day. My blonde hair was hanging in a limp ponytail. *Not* that I was trying to impress Landon, no matter how swoon-worthy his smile or how well he wore that suit, but I felt out of place between his pristine clothes and Val's crisp pencil skirt and blouse.

Val elbowed him playfully. "Well, if you'd given me a few days' heads-up, I could have told Maddie to start after you leave. There was—" A ringtone interrupted her. It came from the inside of the house, and ceased after two rings.

She groaned. "That could be the supplier's call I've been waiting for all day. I promise I won't be long, but I have to call him back. One of the lavender suppliers jumped ship, and I need to replace him right away."

"I can pull some strings and ask in my circle about lavender producers—" Landon began, but Val interrupted him.

"Landon Connor!" She slashed the air with her forefinger. "You're here on *vacation*. You haven't had one in so long that possibly you forgot what it means. *Yes* to cocktails and fun and lazy days in the sun. *No* to work of any kind."

Landon didn't miss a beat. "I can do whatever I want."

"Oh don't you dare pull the big brother card on me. I'm your twin."

His lips twitched. "Older than you by fifteen minutes."

She shook her head, turning to me. "He seems to have no concept of vacation, so he needs all our help. He'll be staying here at the house, so do me a favor and be my spy. If you see him anywhere near his phone or laptop, I want an immediate report."

I smiled at their banter and felt the need to contribute too. "But you need a supplier, and he can pull strings. Just saying, if I had a brother who could pull strings for me, I wouldn't say no."

Landon whistled appreciatively.

Valentina stared at me. "Whose side are you on?"

"Yours," I replied with mock seriousness. "You sign my paychecks."

"I'm going to check my phone." She narrowed her eyes, then headed inside the house. A few seconds later, I heard a truck come to a stop in front of the gate.

"And that'll be the delivery," I informed

Landon.

"What delivery?"

"Timber poles for the terracing process. To stabilize the earth."

"Who's unloading them?"

"The driver and I. The other guys working for me have gone home already."

Landon motioned with his head toward the gate. "Come on, I'll help."

He shrugged out of his suit jacket, laid it on the wooden table, and strode down the slope before I could say anything to the contrary. On the way, he popped open the buttons of his sleeves, rolling said sleeves up to his elbow, revealing strong forearms. I sighed, shaking my head. I was a sucker for men in suits, but men with rolled-up sleeves and muscled forearms were my kryptonite.

"I can handle this, Landon. It's my job. Go relax!"

He chuckled. "Let's make a deal. You start the spying job for Val on Monday. It'll be quicker if I help."

I couldn't argue with him on that point. I opened the double gate and the driver backed the truck into the yard. He climbed out of it the next second.

"Hiya, Maddie! Sorry for the delay. Traffic's a nightmare."

"Hi, Johnny!" I'd worked with him on my past six projects, and he'd been late every time. But his timber was top-notch, and I liked working with small, local producers.

Landon shook hands with Johnny. "Landon Connor."

I had to admit, the man packed more authority in those two words than others did in entire speeches. The way in which he carried himself radiated confidence and power. I liked that he didn't seem to think he was above physical work.

Unloading still took a long time, even with Landon helping us. I'd quickly surmised that he worked out on a regular basis because he didn't struggle once with the weight of the poles. When we were down to the last three, Johnny went to the front of the truck to bring the papers I had to sign to confirm the delivery. I was standing inside the truck and Landon down on the ground when I suddenly felt something tugging at my foot. Glancing down, I realized my shoelace had come undone, and one end was stuck under a pole. I yanked my foot, hoping to free the end of the shoelace. Instead, I managed to lose my balance. A shriek escaped my lips as I realized there was nothing I could grasp to stop my fall. I'd been at the edge of the truck, which meant I was hurtling directly toward the ground. I made a wild movement with my arms, my chest constricted, and my stomach lurched to my throat. My shoelace came free with a tiny pop, and then I felt two strong hands grip my shoulders, stopping my free fall just as I planted one foot firmly on the ground, then the other.

"Oh God." I clung to Landon for dear life,

my breath coming out in pants. I was still unsteady on my feet.

"You're okay. Just breathe," he said.

I did just that, feeling a little foolish, and a lot hot. I realized the latter was because Landon had me tucked against his chest. He smelled like wood, and something else. Something masculine and potent. Landon was looking down at me with a mix of concern and reassurance, and I melted a little under his intense scrutiny. It had been a while since anyone except my younger sister, Grace, worried about me. The green of his eyes seemed even more intense up close. His arms felt so impossibly good around me, strong and steady, that it took me longer to wiggle out of his arms than it should have. My face was burning.

"Thanks," I muttered.

"Maddie! What happened?" Johnny stepped into view, jaw slack, papers crumpled in his hand as he took in the sight of me, all flustered and disheveled.

"Fell out of the truck, but I'm okay. My shoelace caught under a log and I lost my balance."

Johnny was distressed despite my reassurance. "Is your ankle okay?"

"Perfect. Let's just finish unloading."

"Johnny and I will do it." Landon's tone was polite but commanding. I imagined this *polite bossiness* had gotten him very far in the business world, but I was more than a little tempted to contradict him just to see how he'd react to being challenged. Ah, I was getting feisty. This man had a strange effect on me.

But truthfully, my ankle was a little unsteady as I stepped on it, so I decided not to push my luck. Instead, I signed the papers Johnny handed me. I also watched Landon flex those muscles I was now more intimately acquainted with, what with the side of my face slamming right into them. They looked fine times a million, the ridges visible through the shirt.

Once all logs were safely rolled on the ground, Johnny bid us goodbye, pulling the truck out of the yard. I quickly closed the gates, aware that I was alone with Landon. Though the space around us was immense, it suddenly felt too small.

"I'm going to change out of my work clothes, shower, and then I'll be on my way," I said.

Landon nodded, but his gaze flicked to my ankle. "Are you sure you don't want to have that checked out? You wince when you step on it."

He was perceptive. Had he been watching me that closely? A wave of heat spread through my limbs at the thought. When he snapped his gaze up to meet mine, I felt on fire.

"I'll ice it and it'll be golden. Don't worry." I motioned to the house. "Up we go before Val finishes her call and realizes I failed my spy job on the first day."

Landon's grin was contagious. "We agreed that you'll only start your spy job on Monday."

"But she doesn't know that, does she?" I had no idea why I felt so at ease around him. I'd just met the man. But maybe because I knew Val, I felt like I knew him by association too.

"You catch on fast, Maddie. We're going to get along just fine."

I climbed the slope up to the house, slower than usual, with Landon in tow. When my step faltered under my banged-up ankle, Landon brought his hand to my back, steadying me—and making my entire body sizzle at the contact. *Cold shower, here I come!*

Val had won me over the second she said my team and I could use a personnel bathroom to shower in at the end of the day. In her office building, she had small amenities on the ground floor. Then she had extended us the same courtesy of cleaning up when we started working here, insisting the house had enough bathrooms that we weren't inconveniencing her in the slightest.

I left Landon on the front porch, took my backpack from the foyer, and headed straight to the shower. Fifteen minutes later, I stepped out of the bathroom feeling reborn. I was wearing a knee-length red dress made out of cotton and black ballerina shoes. I spent so much time in jeans and rugged T-shirts at work that my free-time wardrobe consisted almost entirely of dresses. I'd rinsed my hair too, and blow-dried it. Now it was hanging in loose waves down my back.

On my way out of the house, I heard Val still talking on the phone. There was no point waiting to tell her goodbye. I found Landon on the porch. He was downing a glass of the iced tea Val had made earlier, even though the ice had long since melted.

His eyes widened when he noticed me, and then his gaze traveled down my body before quickly snapping back up to my face. I felt a sudden surge of feminine pride, congratulated myself on applying lipstick and mascara.

"See you on Monday, Landon."

"Do you want to stay for dinner? Everyone else should arrive soon."

It was official. It wasn't just Val; the Connors were a friendly bunch. And I was even more tempted to say yes than when Val asked. Something about Landon's deep voice made the offer seem a little sweeter, a lot hotter—courtesy of the muscle-roped forearms, I was sure, since his sleeves were still rolled. But this was his first night home with his family. If Val's enthusiasm was anything to go by, he hadn't been home in a while. I didn't want to interrupt their time.

"Thanks, but I can't."

"See you on Monday, then."

He held out his hand, and I thought it was strangely formal that he'd want to shake it, but when I put my small hand in his much larger and firmer one, he surprised me by lifting it to his mouth and kissing it. A bolt of energy ran through me when his lips touched my skin. I shuddered. *Literally*. Landon exhaled sharply, training those gorgeous green eyes on me.

"Have a nice evening, Maddie."

I nodded, tiptoeing past him after he let go of my hand.

When I arrived home, I tried focusing on the pitch I was drafting. I was determined to finish it tonight. I was looking forward to spending tomorrow on Venice Beach with my sister, possibly drive to Malibu to our favorite seafood restaurant. The promise of a lazy weekend should have improved my concentration, but a certain handsome man kept hijacking my thoughts.

Chapter Three
Landon

"Where's Maddie?" Val asked when I entered the foyer a few minutes later.

"She just left. We didn't know how long you'd be on the phone."

"Oh, okay. What happened to your shirt?"

I glanced down. There were some dirt smears from the poles.

"A little incident. Comes with the territory when the entire property looks like a minefield."

A button was missing too, probably dislodged when Maddie slammed into me. Seeing her tumble out of that truck nearly gave me a heart attack. She tried to put up a brave face in front of Johnny, but I knew she was still shaken. She'd been trembling against me just moments before, when every delicious inch of her upper body had been pressed against me.

"Oh, okay. Pity Maddie couldn't stay for dinner."

"I asked her too, but she looked like she had plans."

Val cocked a brow. "What does someone who has plans *look* like?"

"You know, dressed up. She looked nice."

She was a knockout in that red dress, with those red lips.

"Hallelujah, hallelujah," Val exclaimed, joining her hands as if praying, holding them up to her chin, looking mockingly at the ceiling.

"What's that supposed to mean?"

"You're noticing women."

I groaned. "Can I at least have dinner before we start this conversation?"

Val narrowed her eyes as if considering my suggestion. "No, no. We'll have it right now. Hard truths are easier to swallow on an empty stomach."

I smiled. My sister had inherited our dad's habit of dishing out nonsensical sayings. This actually had been one of his sayings.

"You should date again," she informed me.

"Munchkin, we've been through this."

"Don't call me that." Val hesitated, then added, "It's been four years since Rachel died."

"I'm aware of that," I said coolly. "If you were in my place, I wouldn't push the point."

"Yeah you would. You know you would. And I'd push back, just like you're doing, but you wouldn't give up. So I'm not giving up either. That's what family does." She sniffed the air, narrowed her eyes. "Do you want to take a shower before dinner?"

"Yes. Wasn't expecting you to drop this so quickly."

"I think our food is burning. I'll circle back to it. Don't worry, preferably after you've had some bourbon. I bought your favorite, by the way. Make yourself at home. I'm going to check on the food."

I jogged up the stairs and headed to the room Val usually put me in when I was visiting; the bedroom overlooked the back of the property. Through the window, I saw the terrain was intact there, which meant the terracing project was only encompassing the front. My thoughts returned to Maddie. Of course I'd noticed her. I'd noticed her even before she changed. Those gorgeous blue eyes and smooth skin were impossible to miss. Plus, I liked her sense of humor.

Contrary to what Val thought, I wasn't blind to the opposite sex. But when Rachel died, a part of me died too, and it would be unfair to any woman to offer just what was left of me. What woman would be happy with that? And the risk of loving and losing someone—I couldn't expose myself to that again. I chose not to.

I showered quickly, and by the time I returned downstairs, the entire family had arrived.

Val, sitting cross-legged on the couch, was chatting with our other sisters, Lori and Hailey. My brothers, Will and Jace, were standing near the dining table, each holding a drink.

"Uncle Landon!" Milo exclaimed when I entered the living room, running to me and wrapping his arms around my waist.

"Look at you. You've gotten taller since the last time I saw you."

Milo stepped back, looking proud. "I'm a

young man now."

I bit back a smile. He'd turned six earlier this year.

"You are. Now, let me say hello to my brother, young man," my sister Lori said, sidestepping her son and hugging me, a few hairs sticking out of her long blonde mane tickling my face.

Once she stepped back, Will held out a hand. "Much more manly than hugging."

"Yeah, we haven't missed you that much to warrant a hug," Jace chimed in, shuddering as he uttered the last word. I'd missed these two.

Hailey rolled her eyes. "Well, *I* want my hug. So out of my way."

Hailey was a bit shorter than Lori and Val, but her grip was firm. She favored Mom's side of the family, having inherited Mom's dark brown eyes and hair.

"Uncle Landon, did you bring presents?" Milo asked the second Hailey let go.

"Of course I did. Wouldn't dare show my face around here without any. What kind of uncle would I be?"

I brought his present from the foyer, and watching Milo unwrap it was as satisfying as ever. I loved this kid.

"Whoa!" he exclaimed, holding out the soccer ball for everyone to see. "Thank you, Uncle Landon. I promise I won't lose this one too."

Laughing, we all headed to the table, where

Val proudly pointed to the stuffed turkey. "I know it's not Thanksgiving, but I was feeling festive. Made it just like Mama's recipe."

Jace rubbed his hands together. "Val, I'll be an honest man. I don't even remember how Mama's tasted, but yours is the best turkey. Took me being poisoned by well-wishers to fully appreciate your cooking talents."

Jace had been nine when our parents died. Young enough not to remember such details. Val and I were ten years older. We'd just started our first semester at Harvard. Our parents had been so proud of us. We'd both received a soccer scholarship, and our coach used to say we'd be drafted to play professionally.

But our parents died in a car accident just before Christmas our sophomore year. Val and I dropped everything, came straight home. We hadn't even had time to mourn our parents before we realized there was no one around to look after our siblings except us. Will was the second oldest, but still three years younger than we were and not of age.

My father had opened a pub upon emigrating from Ireland, and it had been the bread and butter of our family. My mother had been selling homemade cosmetics, but they had never rendered a profit. There was no way Val and I could return to Harvard. We dropped out and ran the pub while also taking classes at a local college. That hadn't even been the hardest part. Raising our siblings and helping them through their grief was.

Sometimes I looked at them and still couldn't believe they were all adults. Jace was playing pro soccer. Hailey was a business consultant. Will was a detective, and Lori ran a popular event-planning agency, while also solo parenting her son. Val was at the helm of her own cosmetics and fragrances company.

Once we'd both graduated college, we dropped the pub in favor of corporate jobs—both the income and the prospects were much better. Val started toying with the idea of making cosmetics. She'd always loved helping Mom. We started the business on the side, and in three short years, it was making enough profit for us to both quit our jobs and focus on the company. My passion and talents lay in software, but I liked working with Val, so I stayed with the company until it was stable enough that she didn't need me. I started my own company, a software firm that revolutionized payment transactions, at around the same time I met Rachel. We'd moved together to San Jose so I could be right in the heart of the software industry.

"So just to confirm," Will said, "you're staying here for two whole weeks? Val says so, but there's always the risk that she just daydreamed about it."

"I'm staying for two weeks, so I'll be here for the Fourth of July too," I confirmed. "Which means you're stuck with me."

Jace waved his hand. "Pfft, Val's stuck with you. We'll just drop by for dinner from time to time to take advantage of her cooking skills. You don't mind if we take advantage, sister dearest, do you?"

Val pointed her fork at him. "As long as you keep bringing dessert, we're good."

I turned my attention to Milo. "I heard you're on vacation, Milo. Would you like some soccer training?"

"Really? Every day?"

Lori put a gentle hand on his arm. "Not every day. I'm sure Uncle Landon has other plans too."

"I don't," I said truthfully. "We'll see how it goes, buddy, okay? I'm a strict coach, so you might not even want me every day."

"But I will," Milo sputtered.

Despite not pursuing soccer professionally, I still had the bug, and I played every Sunday morning in San Jose. Jace was training with Milo regularly, but the boy still loved to play with me.

"Well," Hailey said slowly, leaning her elbows on her table, training her almond-shaped eyes on me. "Just so we're clear, I'm monopolizing you on weekends. It's the only time I'm in town."

As a business consultant, Hailey traveled to her project locations from Monday through Thursday and was back in LA on Fridays. Both Val and I ran an ongoing campaign to convince Hailey to work with either of us, but we'd been unsuccessful. Every time we brought up the subject, she reminded us that we can hang up our older siblings cloak now that everyone's an adult. As if. I felt as responsible for them at thirty-four as I did when I was nineteen.

Hailey was smart as a whip, but from our long phone calls, I'd surmised her efforts weren't appreciated the way she deserved.

"Lori, how's the event-planning business coming along?" I asked, listening intently to her answer, gauging if she needed any help, whether financial or just picking my brain. I was in LA on vacation, but that didn't mean I couldn't do what I did best: take care of my family.

Dinner lasted long into the evening as we laughed at old memories and poked fun at each other. It felt good to be home, surrounded by my family. Back in San Jose, I had some family too: the Bennetts, cousins on my mother's side, who lived in San Francisco. They'd adopted me, especially on holidays, and I liked spending time with them, but I'd missed my siblings.

When we finally called it a night and rose from the table, Hailey said, "If you don't have plans tomorrow, I'll make some for you. Wouldn't want to leave you to your own devices too much. You might resort to your old tricks… like working."

I threw Val an exasperated glance. "What did you do, munchkin, put the entire family on alert?"

"Don't underestimate me. The entire neighborhood. Plus Maddie. Asked her to keep an eye on him while she's here," she informed our siblings.

Lori clapped her hands. "Good."

I looked at Jace, then at Will. "Any of you

plan to back me up here?"

Will pretended to think hard about it, then said, "I'm staying out of it."

"Me too. You're toast, brother," Jace exclaimed. "Not tying myself to a sinking ship."

Growing up, it had always been brothers versus sisters, but I sensed a shift at the table. Now it was Connors versus Landon, and I was losing by a decent margin.

An image of Maddie popped into my mind, wearing that red dress with her hair falling in luscious curls around her. She'd shuddered when I'd kissed her hand, and I'd barely resisted the urge to do it again.

Considering how quickly she'd sided with me today when it came to Val's supplier, I had full confidence that I could win Maddie over to my side. I was looking forward to it.

Chapter Four
Maddie

I loved LA. I loved the endless beaches, the San Gabriel Mountains in the distance. I loved how you could drive from one side to the other and feel like you were in a different city altogether. Cosmopolitan and ever changing, LA had a life of its own. I'd fallen hook, line, and sinker for all it had to offer (including the occasional celebrity sighting) ever since I moved there.

There were also things I didn't like about it, such as the traffic or the minor vandalism acts—especially when I had to face them at six o'clock. On Monday morning, I found my beloved Chevy truck with the windshield broken. Since there were no parking opportunities in front of my bungalow, I always parked on the adjacent street, where two of the three streetlamps were broken. I supposed the semidarkness invited such acts. I cleaned the driver seat of glass as best I could, then climbed in and drove straight to the car repair shop.

The mechanic tried to sell me on a small Prius as an exchange car while my truck was in the repair shop, but I wasn't having any of it.

"Lady, this isn't a car rental. You get what we

have."

I crossed my arms over my chests, leveled him with my stare.

"I run a landscaping business. I carry supplies with me and need space to deposit tools and plants. If you can't give me any truck, I'm taking the Chevy and giving my business to someone else."

I was only half bluffing. I did need a large vehicle, but I also didn't have time to find another repair shop. In the end, I got my way and drove out a battered, old truck with a faulty transmission.

I arrived at Val's forty minutes later, but the boys I worked with, Sevi and Jacob, were already there and had started with the first patch of land that would become a terrace. Since my company was a one-person show, I only hired guys on a project-by-project basis. Not the best option since sometimes they bailed on me midproject, but hiring a full-time team wasn't in my budget right now. The extra profit went toward Grace's tuition at law school. I didn't want her to be in debt up to her eyeballs when she graduated.

If everything went according to plan, I'd be able to hire people full-time in eighteen months.

But for a one-person company, I was proud of how fast I'd made a name for myself in this business. For two years in a row, I won the Best Garden award granted by one of the most prestigious LA design magazines.

"Hey, Maddie!" they greeted in unison. I waved back, heading up to the house to drop my backpack in the foyer as usual.

"Good morning! How's your ankle?" I jumped at the sound of Landon's voice. He stepped through the open front door into the foyer. My God, was he gorgeous or what? He was wearing jogging pants and a shirt that molded perfectly to his chest. The short sleeves confirmed what I'd guessed on Friday when he'd held me to him—his arms were corded with lean muscles. Judging by the sheen of sweat on his skin, he must have just finished his run.

"Morning, Landon. My ankle is as good as new. Is Val here too?"

"Already left."

"Oh, okay. I wanted to explain why I'm late. Someone broke my windshield, and I had to take it to the mechanic."

"How did that happen?"

I shrugged. "Vandals, I suppose."

"Did you already file a police report?"

"No, that takes too much time and usually leads nowhere."

"Will is a detective. I'll call him up and ask him to look into it for you."

A warm feeling sprouted in my chest and I smiled up at him, remembering how he'd offered his help to Val on Friday. Landon Connor had a white-knight complex, and it was totally doing it for me. Not that I was a damsel in distress. I didn't need saving, and even if I did, I could be my own knight. But it was sure good to know that chivalry wasn't dead.

"Thanks, Landon, but I don't want to waste your brother's time. These things usually don't lead anywhere."

Landon stepped closer. So close, in fact, that I could see the contours of his six-pack. I snapped my gaze up to his face, praying that by some miracle he hadn't realized I was perving at him. Landon was gazing down at me with an intensity that made my entire body strum.

He studied me, and being on the receiving end of his attention was making me squirm. "Does this happen often?"

The concern in his voice endeared him to me.

"This is LA. My neighborhood is okay, but these things happen from time to time. No biggie."

His shirt was becoming more transparent by the second as he continued to sweat. And even though I usually found sweaty men unappealing, everything about Landon was beckoning to me, even his smell—a clean, manly deodorant scent.

Maybe the testosterone oozing off him was simply messing with my senses. I really had to quit staring. When I met his eyes again, I realized this time he'd caught me staring.

"I'll give Will a call," he insisted.

"You're not used to being told no, are you?"

He grinned. "Is it that obvious?"

"Yeah. And I *am* saying no. I appreciate the concern, Landon, but I don't have time to file complaints and whatnot. I should get started on work," I said, finally remembering I was here to work on Val's yard. Landon kept those beautiful green eyes trained on me until he took my breath away. Eventually, he relented.

"I'll leave you to it. I'm going to hop in the shower."

I tried very hard to push away any thoughts of a naked Landon only feet away while I started my workday. It was no small feat. I barely knew the man and he already had a spell on me, but I was determined to fight it. He was here on vacation, and I was here to work, nothing more.

I still had some scars from my failed engagement, even though it had been eight months since Owen and I broke up. I'd followed him to LA and didn't regret moving because I loved the city. But when the relationship imploded, it shook me to my bones. I'd come to LA with dreams of building a life together, and after the breakup, I'd felt as if my life plan had been erased and I was standing in front of a whiteboard. I was still working on drawing up a new life plan. I had the professional part figured out, but my personal life needed work.

I focused on scooping the earth out of the first terrace level for the better part of the morning, only stopping when I saw Lori enter the yard with her son, Milo.

They both greeted me, and Lori said, "He'll hang out with Landon for a few hours. Soccer practice." Turning to her son, she added, "Come on, Milo. I think Landon's waiting for us in the backyard."

The fact that Landon liked spending his vacation training his nephew endeared him to me even more. Lori and Milo disappeared inside the house, and a short while later, Lori left.

I started laying the foundation for the makeshift wooden trail that would serve as the main path for the next couple of weeks. Transforming the slope into terraced levels involved dislodging bits of earth, and the old path up to the house would be caught up in the process. At the end of the project, I'd bring in a specialist in masonry to build stone steps, but for the moment, the makeshift trail would do.

By noon, I was halfway done with it when I heard an ear-splitting cry echo through the yard. *Milo.* Heart leaping in my throat, I sprinted up to the house.

My glutes and thighs were burning in protest by the time I nearly bumped into Landon.

"Do you know here Val keeps the first-aid kit?" he asked.

"I've got one in the car. What happened?"

***

Landon

"Minor cut under his knee."

"Minor, huh? I heard him scream from the front." She gave me a stern look I found adorable.

"I'll bring the first-aid kit from my car and wash my hands."

"Okay, come directly to the backyard afterward."

I soothed Milo until Maddie arrived, her hands clean, carrying the first-aid kit. Milo was sitting in the hammock, closely inspecting his leg.

"Hey, Milo, let me take a look at that." She crouched over him, splaying her palm just under his cut. "Okay, that's not a big deal. We'll just clean it up and put a Band-Aid on it."

She glanced at me out of the corner of her eye, and I didn't hide my smile.

"But I'll need stitches," Milo muttered. "It splits open, look."

Maddie flinched as Milo proceeded to pull at both sides of his leg and the wound parted.

"It's not as deep as you think, Milo."

"Are you sure?"

"I am sure. It's going to pinch a little when I clean it, but you're brave, aren't you?"

Milo nodded solemnly and gritted his teeth as Maddie worked on the cut. The tenderness in her gestures stirred something inside me. She kept talking to him, distracting him, her voice calm and soothing.

Milo only loosened up after the Band-Aid was in place. He stepped down from the hammock, placed his foot tentatively on the ground.

"Hey, it doesn't hurt at all. Let's get back to playing."

I laughed. "We're done for today, buddy.

We're meeting your mom in two hours. We should go if you want that ice cream."

"Okay, I'll go change."

After he went inside, Maddie asked, "How come you can play soccer?"

"Wanted to play pro. Even got a college scholarship for it."

"Nice. So how come you didn't go pro?"

"Moved back here after my parents passed away and focused on other things. I still play as a hobby."

"Wow, aren't you full of surprises?"

"You haven't seen anything yet."

Her eyes widened and she sighed, a cute little sound I wanted to eat up. Her lips were perfect: pink, plump, with a sweet bow in the middle. This woman was seven levels of tempting, and I hadn't been tempted in years. I didn't *want* to be tempted. But Maddie had been in my thoughts all morning. The broken windshield still bothered me. She didn't seem to need or want my protection, but I wanted to give it to her anyway.

"Well, I'd better get back to work," she said.

She went past me inside the house and I caught a whiff of her body wash, sweetly floral but fresh somehow. She smelled delicious. With a shake of my head, I resolved to put Maddie out of my mind.

I managed to keep my resolve for about twenty-four hours. Since I'd grown up in LA, my oldest friends were all here, but they only had time to meet after work. I'd arranged for some breakfast get-togethers next week, but this week, I'd reserved my mornings for Milo. Since it was the end of June, he was on his summer vacation, so he had as much time to fill as I did.

The next day, Lori dropped off Milo for practice at eight o'clock and picked him up at ten. I went for a run afterward and finished my tour at the front of the house. Maddie was a few feet lower on the slope, bending over, securing one of the logs. Her ass was sticking up in the air, and the sight was glorious. When she finally straightened up, her breasts bounced with the movement, and her face was flushed; half her blonde hair had fallen out of her bun. She looked a little wild, and that prompted an image in my mind—a flash of Maddie's entire body reacting on a thrust, calling my name. I'd fist her hair while burying myself in her to the hilt.

She met my eyes and smiled sheepishly, smoothing one hand over her hair. Her smile was amazing. I couldn't tear my eyes from her, and I kept her gaze, watching the flush extend to her chest, her teeth gnawing at her lower lip. Still, I didn't break eye contact. She did, but I looked at her long after she averted her gaze.

Distraction. I needed a distraction from Maddie. Luckily, distraction was always one phone call away.

Chapter Five
Maddie

My cheeks were burning. Could he tell? I hoped he couldn't. My blood had rushed to my face earlier anyway from staying crouched for so long. How could I get so flustered just because he was looking at me? I redid my bun for the hundredth time today. Damn hair! I went to get a haircut yesterday. My ends were split, and I told her I just wanted a trim.

"Oh, honey, of course. I'll just shave off a few," the hairdresser had assured me.

No clue what she was referring to by few, but clearly not inches, because she cut off a lot from the front. Now the front was at that weird length between bangs and random strands, and it fell out of my bun. It was the last time I'd trust anyone with her roots died blue and her ends pink to come near my hair with scissors. I liked wearing a bun on top of my head, not at the base, but I'd have to use pins until my hair grew back, and I didn't like feeling scraps of metal or plastic on my scalp.

I spent half the day with my ass up in the air, walking along the horizontal base the guys dug for the timber pole, checking it was the right width and depth. The smell of freshly turned earth filled my nostrils. I stopped and took out my earbuds around midday, when Sevi and Jacob went on their lunch break. My ears popped a little. In the eerie silence, Landon's voice echoed through the yard.

"No, we agreed on the KPI targets already. There's no negotiating now."

I groaned. It was my second day on my spy job, and I was already failing. How long had he been working?

I laid down my hand trowel and skittered to the porch to police Landon. He was sitting at the wooden picnic table, deep lines marring his forehead, his jaw set. I moved until I was right in front of him, placed my hands on my hips, and narrowed my eyes, giving him my most stern, no-nonsense look, which had the unexpected effect of making him grin.

"I'll call you back later," he said into the phone, then clicked off.

"What do you mean, I'll call you later? I believe you meant 'I will not be calling you over the next two weeks. Forget I exist.'"

Landon shrugged, his grin still in place. "I relaxed all morning. I thought I'd take a break from taking a break during lunch."

"Val was right. You really don't know how to vacation, do you?"

"I'm out of practice, that's all. I have a competent team, and an acting CEO I'd trust with my life, but it's hard to disconnect."

"Well, I suppose business empires aren't built

by taking vacations often. When's the last time you had a proper vacation?"

"Four years ago."

His answer tugged at a memory. Val had told me Landon's wife died four years ago. Now I understood Val's determination to make sure he relaxed. I was determined not to fail at my spy job again.

"Are you eating lunch with your crew?" he asked.

"No, I don't eat lunch."

He drummed his finger on the wooden table. "Why not?"

"I mostly forget. It's inconvenient eating on site. My hands are dirty, and packing lunch is a drag."

My stomach churned loudly at that exact moment.

"Your stomach seems to disagree," he said.

"It usually does."

"Have lunch with me today. Come on, you're starving."

"The work won't finish itself."

"Maddie, you need to have lunch. And I'd love your company."

Ah, his tone held that polite bossiness from the first day again, and poof, my resolve vanished.

"Oh, I don't know. Even though, if I do eat with you, I might distract you from calling back your business partner."

The corners of his lips twitched, as if he were laughing at a private joke.

Landon rose from the bench and motioned with his head toward the house. "By all means, go ahead and... distract me."

The way he said it, in a lower, huskier tone, made it sound dirty. I parted my lips, exhaling. Was Landon flirting with me? Or was my mind playing tricks on me because I'd been perving at him since he arrived? That look he gave me earlier, though... I thought he'd been doing some perving too. In any case, the smart course of action was to remain outside, work through lunch.

Instead, I wanted to follow him inside. Everything about him beckoned to me; the pull I felt toward him was almost magnetic.

"You win. What are you feeding me?" I asked.

"Something delicious."

He wasn't lying. We ate heated-up roast beef leftovers at the kitchen table, and it was the best thing I'd eaten in a while. The meat was tender, and I thought I tasted a hint of cinnamon in the gravy. I'd somehow managed to get gravy on my fingers too.

"Val is an excellent cook," I exclaimed.

"Always has been. She picked up the best tricks from Mom."

"I can't imagine how hard that must have been, raising your brothers and sisters."

"It wasn't easy. We knew how to be their oldest siblings, but parenting them was an entirely different thing. You should've seen Val and me giving them an earful when we caught them sneaking out of the house. Guess who'd taught them the trick?" He pointed with both thumbs at himself, laughing.

"Did you ever regret giving up college and soccer? I think you were at Harvard, right? Val mentioned it once."

"Yes, it was Harvard. I never regretted it. I was needed here," he said simply, and I believed him. Nothing in his body language contradicted his words. I admired him for not shunning responsibility and commitment.

"How did you manage financially?" I asked.

"Val and I ran Dad's pub for a couple of years while we took classes at a local college. We gave it up as soon as we got decent job offers. We wanted to keep it because it reminded us of our parents, but it wasn't feasible. Dad opened it when he came over from Ireland," he said with a melancholy smile.

"Wait, are you lot Irish?"

"Half Irish. The Connor part didn't tip you off?"

"Not really. Neither of you has that Irish brogue."

Thank God he didn't. One thing Landon didn't need was more help being sexy as hell, and the brogue was *hot*.

"That we don't. But we did inherit a solid work ethic, an interminable list of oddball sayings my dad insisted were Irish—though I've never found proof of that—and a tradition for Friday night dinners. Dad always told us he got together with his folks every Friday before moving across the ocean, and we adopted that tradition. My siblings get together every week. I was part of it before moving to San Jose." The melancholy was mirrored in his eyes.

"And you miss it."

"A lot. I think coming here reminded me just how much. But enough about me. Tell me about your business," Landon said. "Why landscaping?"

"I studied architecture, but after I got my degree, I realized that I like transforming outdoor spaces. So I branched into landscaping, and also took courses about plants and flowers. I mostly work on people's personal yards. I like putting together beautiful spaces where they can come home and relax, you know?"

Landon had drawn his chair nearer to mine, and our thighs were touching under the table, which sent my senses into a tailspin.

"That's great thinking. Everyone needs a place to disconnect and recharge."

"Exactly. And I love it when I have a huge space to work with, like here. There's so much I can do. We moved around a lot when I was a kid, and since my parents knew we wouldn't permanently live there, we rented small spaces. During summer holidays, we traveled in a trailer. It was very claustrophobic, and the outdoor space was always a parking lot."

"Why were you moving around?"

"My parents traveled to music gigs across the country, and there was no one they could leave me and my sister with." That nomadic existence had been exhausting. It had been hard to strike any meaningful relationships at school since we moved so often.

"Do they live in LA now?"

"No, they're still traveling around. But I set up roots here. My sister's in town too."

I wasn't sure how much he wanted to know or if he was just being polite, but suddenly I was feeling very chatty. Usually I was the exact opposite, especially around men I'd just met. But Landon made me lower my guard.

"Why LA?"

I shrugged. "I moved here with my ex. The relationship didn't work out, but I'm happy here. I lived in Miami before, went to college there, but I like it here much more. Less humidity."

He grinned. "No alligators."

I grinned back. "Always a plus. In Miami, every time someone who lived near the water asked me to landscape their property, I kept looking over my shoulder."

"Did you own your own business there too?"

"Yes. I like the independence, even if the income varies so much, especially in between projects. Do you ever turn off your business brain?"

"Ah, that's a definite no." He smiled, and damn if I didn't want to keep this man smiling.

As I chewed on my last bit of beef, a strand of hair caught at the corner of my mouth. I moved my hand to push it away, but I had a little gravy grease on my fingers, so I only managed to stick the strand to my fingers.

I groaned, and Landon laughed.

"Had a haircut disaster yesterday. The front is too short for a bun. I had it in my face all day."

"Wait, I'll unstick you."

He brought a wet cloth from the sink, rubbing my fingers clean and then the corners of my mouth. The gesture felt intimate, especially because Landon was looking closely at my lips. I licked them almost unconsciously, and he drew in a sharp breath, snapping his gaze up. We were so close that I felt his breath on the skin above my upper lip. It electrified my entire body. His right hand was still touching my cheek as he rubbed the right corner of my mouth clean. The way he looked at me... *God*, I was buzzing with awareness. When he pulled away, returning with the cloth to the sink, I felt cold.

"Thank you for feeding me. I'll help you clean up."

He held up a hand. "Nothing to help me with. I just have to put the plates in the dishwasher."

"Okay, I'll let you get back to relaxing, then." I emphasized *relaxing* with a wiggle of my finger. The corners of his lips tilted up. I loved making him smile. It was a good look on him. Scratch that—it was a drop-dead-sexy look that made his mouth even more appealing. *Oh, that mouth.* I bet he could do delicious things with it.

"I plan to relax, don't you worry about me. I'm meeting some old friends this week, but always in the evenings."

"Oh, you should stop by the bar where my sister works. They have live music every Tuesday and Thursday."

"Band any good?"

"They're really good. I sometimes go too. Gives me a chance to catch up with her."

"Where is the bar?"

I told him the address, and he jotted it down on his phone.

"Will you be there this week, Maddie?"

"Yes, on Thursday."

"Then I'll stop by too, with my friend."

I clapped my hands, then rubbed them together. "Excellent. You'll have fun."

He wiggled his eyebrows. "You promise?"

I swallowed, feeling a little light-headed. Oh, what those gorgeous green eyes and those tempting lips did to me.

"I promise."

Was I imagining the chemistry between us, the hot look from before? I had my answer when Landon's gaze traveled up and down my body. Tingles spread through me. It was a *scorching-hot* look.

Chapter Six
Landon

I saw her the moment I stepped inside the bar. Maddie was impossible to miss. Her blonde hair was once again pulled up in a messy bun, several strands dangling around her face. She was also behind the counter, pouring a draft beer.

I made my way through the patrons, inspecting the location. Whenever I went to a new bar, I automatically compared it to the pub Val and I ran years ago. It had been all black wood and shades of green, and had an air of general shabbiness.

This one was all warm tones, the dim lighting casting a pleasant glow on the brown wood. The place was packed with patrons standing around the high, round tables. A few servers milled around, and at the far end of the room was a makeshift stage, but it was still empty.

"Fancy seeing you here, stranger," Maddie greeted me playfully when I reached the counter. "Where's your friend?"

"Couldn't make it after all."

"And you came anyway because…?"

"You promised fun, Maddie. Why are you behind the bar?"

"My sister has the flu, so I'm filling in for her." A frown marred her forehead as she reached to the rack above our heads where wineglasses were hanging. "She gets sick a lot lately. I keep telling her it's not normal, that she should go to a doctor, but she doesn't listen. Calls me a nag."

I grinned, plunking my forearms on the bar. She filled the glass of wine, handing it to the redhead next to me. Then Maddie pointed at me. "Don't make fun of me. I know she's a grown-up, but I can't help myself."

My grin widened. I recognized the behavior. "Far from me to make fun of you. I'm the same. I call it eldest sibling syndrome. Nice to find a kindred spirit. So, you know the owner, or how come you can work instead of your sister?"

"I used to work here. When I first moved, my business wasn't bringing in much income, so I was supplementing it with bartending. So now, if my sister has to miss a shift, I cover for her so she still gets the money. What can I get you, Landon?"

I looked at the blackboard hanging on what I assumed was a fake-tile wall to our right. Several cocktails were scribbled on it in white chalk. "I'll take the house specialty."

She made a come-here motion with her finger, and I leaned in over the counter. Even though alcohol fumes were swirling around us, I still caught a clear whiff of her perfume. I barely refrained from leaning in even closer.

"It'll give you a really nasty hangover

tomorrow. Several people already complained about it, including yours truly. I don't recommend it. You look like a bourbon type of guy anyway."

I pulled back, laughing. "I look like it? Is that translation for Val talking about me?"

"She might have said a few things. So, bourbon?"

I nodded, watching her prepare my drink. I'd been watching her more often than I wanted to admit over the last days. I'd talked her into eating lunch with me every day. I brushed her fingers when I took the glass, and she drew in a sharp breath, jumping a little as if the contact electrified her. What would she do if I trailed my mouth up to her neck, tugged with my teeth at her earlobe? An image of Maddie arching her hips and back into me filled my thoughts. Her scent was still fresh in my mind, as was the feel of her skin under my fingers. I could practically *feel* her pressed against me.

"I want my goddamn drink."

We both looked in the direction from where the voice had come. A surfer, by the sorry look of him. He raised his brows at Maddie, tapping his hand on the counter.

"Come on, how hard can it be to make a mojito? Fucking get to work already."

"Apologize to Maddie, or you'll be out on your sorry ass in ten seconds." Maintaining my calm, I shifted closer, straightening up.

He hunched slightly when he realized I towered over him. His eyes darted to Maddie, then back to me, and he raised both hands in surrender.

"Okay, I'm sorry."

Maddie smiled sweetly at him while working on his cocktail. "Rule number one. Never be disrespectful to the person serving your food or beverage. You never know what they might put in." When she slid his glass toward him, the guy looked down at it as if afraid to touch it. I held my glass up in her direction, grinning. Her sass was contagious.

She tended to the other patrons as I enjoyed my bourbon, perched on one of the barstools. The servers milling around the room prepared the orders they received themselves, but Maddie still had her hands full.

A band climbed on the stage soon after and performed covers of well-known songs, as well as some of their own. Maddie was right; they were very good. Several of the patrons started dancing. So did Maddie behind the counter. She was wearing a blue dress with a black belt around her tiny waist. Her shoulders were bare.

"You're a very good dancer." I drank up the sway of her hips and thighs, the sensual-as-fuck yet classy way in which her ass arched up rhythmically. I had a very sudden and very clear vision of me holding those hips, pressing her against me. Jesus, I hadn't felt such a pull toward a woman in years. I couldn't tear myself away.

"Thanks. I typically dance the entire time they perform, but house rules forbid me leaving the bar. But there are no rules saying I'm not allowed to dance behind the bar."

"What time does your shift end?"

"I'm closing, so three o'clock."

"And you're working on Val's yard tomorrow?"

"Yeah. Coffee will be my best friend."

"I'll talk to Val. I'm sure she won't mind if you take the day off."

She shook her head. "No can do. I don't like skipping work for personal reasons."

Stubborn woman. I didn't like the fact that she'd only get a few hours of sleep, but I respected her work ethic.

"My place is just five blocks away. I'll be home in twenty minutes tops," she continued.

"You're walking?"

"Of course." Motioning to my empty glass, she asked, "Another bourbon?"

"No." I wanted to keep a clear head, so I glanced at the menu, choosing the first nonalcoholic drink that caught my eye. "I'll have a mint lemonade with ginger and strawberry."

"You must be very secure in your masculinity. Women usually order that."

"I'm very secure in my masculinity, Maddie."

Her lips parted, forming a small, delicious O. I was affecting her, in the same way she was affecting me. I didn't take my eyes off her as she prepared my drink. She glanced up at me every few seconds, and I enjoyed immensely the way she bit into her bottom lip after every glance.

"Here is your drink!" She sounded breathless.

I stuck to the bar for the next few hours, listening to the band, ordering almost everything from the nonalcoholic side of the menu, and fending off any men who came on too strong on Maddie.

"Stop scaring away the customers," Maddie admonished me after I caused the third male customer to cower away.

"He was more interested in you than the drink."

"I know, but you still can't scare off customers."

"But you can put them off from the house specialty?" I challenged.

"I don't put everyone off. Just the people I like." She winked at me and continued to dance while mixing cocktails, pouring drinks. She was an unquenchable well of energy and sinful moves. The more I watched her, the more I wanted to know how she'd feel against me. I wanted to dance with her—another new impulse for me.

She chitchatted with other patrons too, and annoyance twanged inside me whenever a man asked her for her number. She declined every time, which was when it dawned on me that she might be seeing someone. Why hadn't that occurred to me before? Surely a woman like her wasn't single. She was smart, sassy, and hardworking. She'd mentioned an ex, but that didn't mean she didn't have someone in her life at the moment. Fuck, that thought bothered me. Even though I didn't have a right to be bothered.

As three o'clock neared, the patrons shuffled out one by one, even though the band kept playing as if they had a full house. Fifteen minutes before closing time, there were just two other people besides us. Maddie had dismissed the servers on the shift, saying she could close up by herself.

I watched her dance become wilder, more passionate, and I couldn't take it any longer. I leaned over the bar and said, "Come out here and dance."

She jutted out her lower lip. "Can't. House rules."

"Come out here."

"Landon—"

"Break the rules with me, Maddie. Dance with me."

She swallowed hard, glanced at the clock, at the last two patrons who were headed out the door, then nodded. She stepped from behind the bar, smiling shyly as she walked closer to me. It was her first shy smile. Her blue eyes were beautiful.

I looked at the band, who'd started to gather their things as the patrons left but now began playing just for us. It was the kind of music I wanted. I didn't want a slow dance; I wanted a wild one. I took her hand, twirling her once before lowering my hands to her hips. She had her back to me, and I stepped closer until her spine was pressing against my chest. Maddie put her hands on top of mine but didn't push them away. I kept us both still for a moment. I had to ask first. I had to know.

"Maddie, are you dating someone?"

She shuddered in my arms, pressing her back even closer to me. "There is no one in my life, Landon."

"Then be mine for this dance."

I heard her sharp intake of breath, and then her hair tickled my face. Half her bun had come undone again. I pulled the elastic band. Her hair was silky and soft.

"Let's get rid of that, shall we? It's just in the way."

She nodded wordlessly, taking the elastic band from my hand, shoving it in a small pocket in her dress. I pushed her hair to one side, baring the back of her neck to me. I lingered with my fingers on her skin longer than necessary, pressing my thumb where her hairline ended.

"Are we going to dance or what? I'm breaking the rules with you, Landon. You'd better make it count."

I was breaking some rules of my own. It was the first time I'd let myself come this close to a woman in years. But that didn't matter right now. This moment was all that mattered. Maddie was all that mattered. She had wanted to let loose and go all wild the entire night, but she hadn't been able to behind that bar. I was going to give her what she needed.

Lowering my hands to her hips again, I moved us both to the rhythm of the music. She gave herself to the music, to me, the sway of her body smooth and inviting. Her scent was driving me insane, and I knew the intoxicating flower sweetness would be branded in my memory for a long time. Taking her hands, I twirled her, catching the feral glimpse in her eyes.

"You're good at this, Landon."

I spun her again, once, twice, until she lost all sense of space and swayed right into my arms. Laughter tumbled out of her, and I could hear the reverberations of her guffaws against my chest. It was contagious. I joined in on her laughter, but then she let the music take her over again, and I pulled her to me. I wanted to soak up all her sensual energy. Our hips were aligned, our chests touching. Heat was building inside me, and when I felt her frantic breath land on my jaw, lust shot right under my belt. A drop of sweat dripped from her temple, making its way to her earlobe. I wanted to lick her there.

When the music stopped, we both glanced at the stage questioningly. I didn't want the moment to end. Judging by how tightly Maddie was holding my hand, neither did she.

"Sorry, guys, we already played fifteen minutes extra for you. But we really have to go."

Maddie jumped, slipping her hand away. "Oh, I have to close up. I lost track of time. I…."

As the band gathered their instruments, Maddie wiped the bar surface with a wet cloth, put the remaining glasses in the dishwasher.

"Landon, you don't have to wait for me."

"Yes I do. I'm walking you home."

Maddie straightened up, scrutinizing me like

she was seeing me for the first time. "I live just a few blocks away."

"It's not up for negotiation. It's late, and your car was vandalized. It's not safe."

She laughed softly. "I just met you last week. How do I know *you're* safe?"

"Val can vouch for me. Give her a call."

"At three o'clock in the morning?" She tilted her head, her eyes holding a challenge.

"The owner shouldn't let a woman close up the bar. I never let Val do it. He should have asked one of the guys who worked as server to do it. A lot of drunkards hang around in front after closing time, and most people you meet on the street at this time are looking for trouble."

"I walk home alone every time I'm here."

"Not this time."

"You're intense."

I laughed. "You could say that."

"That's why you hung around the entire night? To walk me home?"

"That and I wanted to dance with you. So the matter's settled."

"No it's not."

"You can't get rid of me, sweetheart. I'm walking you home."

***

Maddie

I gave in to him, because how could I not? I had the shrewd suspicion that it wouldn't have mattered—he'd have walked me home anyway. He seemed the kind of man who wouldn't be deterred by a no, and I liked it, a little too much. I also liked that he was so protective of me. Did that make me a little nutty?

Truthfully, I appreciated his offer, because with the wave of tourists that summer brought in, you could never be too careful. Grace always drove after a shift because she lived farther away.

He had a point about my car being broken into. And I had to admit to myself that I wanted his company for a few more minutes. The way he'd danced with me... My insides were melting just remembering it. My entire body was still wound up tight from all the sensations he'd stirred inside me.

"It's a lovely night," I exclaimed as we left the bar.

"Great for a walk," he replied. Judging by the sheer number of people out and about, you wouldn't have thought it was almost four o'clock in the morning. LA was just as alive and vibrant as ever, though summer seemed to be an especially crowded time.

I wrestled with the million questions I had for him. I didn't want to pry, but at the same time I wanted to know more about him, and I wanted to know things directly from the source, not from Val.

Maybe I was imagining things, but while we were dancing, I felt a connection—something that went beyond the spark between us. In the throes of dancing, he seemed to let loose in a way I hadn't seen him do since he arrived.

"Can I ask you something?" I tried.

"Sure."

"Did something happen to make you decide to take time off?"

"We just finalized talks for a partnership with another player in the industry. We have a lot of synergies between us, and it makes sense. But I've been working sixteen-hour days for the last six months to make it happen. I needed a break. And I missed my family. It's been years since I spent more than a few days at a time with them." He smiled at me, a smile that made my insides flutter. Damn my traitorous insides. They had no business fluttering. "But if my brothers ask, my official story is I needed a proper break from everything. I'll never hear the end of it otherwise. Plus, I did need a vacation during which I don't wake up to check sales numbers and go to bed making projections."

"Instead you unload timber poles and walk women home in the middle of the night."

"Just one woman. And I'll gladly do it again. I had a great time tonight, Maddie. I loved dancing with you."

My skin sizzled, and I nearly melted into a puddle when he cocked his head and trapped my gaze with his.

"I loved it too."

"Worth breaking the rules?" he challenged.

"One hundred percent."

"Tell me about your sister."

"Grace is the smartest person," I piped up. "She's in law school right now on a partial scholarship and works at the Lucky Bar and a few other places."

"And that's enough to pay the rest of the tuition fees?"

"No, I'm paying them. She works to cover her living costs."

He smiled. "You're a great sister."

"Thanks. I don't want Grace to graduate with a ton of debt. That puts a lot of pressure on you as a young professional."

We arrived on my street faster than expected. When had time flown by? Tiny bungalows were crammed into each other along the street. I had no yard to speak of, but living alone in LA came at a cost.

I wasn't ready to say good night, but I wouldn't invite him in either. Our dancing had been fun and a lot more explosive than I expected, but I wouldn't cross that line.

I stepped up on my porch but Landon remained with his feet on the concrete, not making any move to follow me. I liked that a lot—that he knew when to push and when to respect boundaries.

"See you tomorrow, Landon. Thanks for walking me home."

"Anytime, Maddie."

He pulled out his phone and asked, "What's your number?"

"Why do you need it?"

His eyes were focused on his screen, but the corners of his mouth tilted up. "You'll see. Number?"

I rattled it off, watching him closely. My heart was pounding against my rib cage as I tried to read the situation. When he shoved his phone back in his jeans, he bestowed a smile upon me and I felt a hot sizzle slither down my spine, followed by a cold shiver. I had no idea why this man had such an impact on me. That issue was only more aggravated when he took my hand in his and raised it to his mouth, just like he'd done on that first day. He brushed his lips on my knuckles, and this time the heat his lips brought spread throughout me, concentrating low in my body. Another rush of heat shot right between my legs when he looked up and I saw his pupils had widened. He let my hand go the next second. Thank heavens. If he'd held my hand longer, I might have done something crazy. Like kissing him. Oh, scratch that. I would have jumped him.

"See you tomorrow, Maddie."

I felt his gaze on me while I unlocked and pushed my door open. Once inside, I hurried to the window and saw him heading away with purposeful strides. I was overcome by the impulse to head back out, ask him to come inside.

It dawned on me that he hadn't told me what he needed my number for. But I got my answer a few minutes later when my phone chirped with an incoming message.

Now you have my number too, beautiful. Anytime you need someone to walk you home, give me a call.

I looked at that message for a long time, smiling like a fool.

Chapter Seven
Landon

"Well, well, someone's up to no good."

I nearly jumped out of my skin at the sound of my sister's voice. Lori was in Val's living room, curled in the armchair near the window, the light from her e-reader illuminating her features. Val invited her and Milo to spend the night here since I was taking them to a festival near Venice Beach tomorrow. I felt up the wall until I reached the light switch of the lamp in the nearest corner and flicked it on.

"Why did you do that?" Lori raised her hands in a dramatic gesture, covering her eyes.

"Not all of us have cat eyesight, Lori. What are you doing here?"

She held up her e-reader. "Have this fantastic book I can't put down."

I didn't buy it. "Still have trouble sleeping?"

"Yep." Lori usually followed that by saying she and I inherited our mother's sleeping affliction, but I begged to differ. Mom once told me she couldn't sleep because she had too many thoughts and worries. "So where were you?"

"Out."

"Come on, Landon. Indulge me a little. Do you know how often I fantasized about being the one to catch you sneaking in?"

"Let me guess. Every time I caught you?"

"You got it."

I smiled down at my sister, deciding to torment her. "Must keep my secrets."

"You are impossible."

"But you still love me."

She sighed. "I do."

I fought a yawn. I was tired, but I strongly suspected my sister could do with some company. As a troubled sleeper myself, I knew just how boring those hours of non-sleep were, or how dark, depending on the type of thoughts fighting for headspace. But somehow, positive thoughts never struck in the dead of the night.

So even though I knew this was one of those occasions in which I'd fall asleep right away, I dropped in the armchair next to Lori. My sister put the e-reader down and watched me. No, scrutinized was the word I was looking for. I felt as if my sister was holding a magnifying glass over me, looking for clues.

"I was with Maddie."

Lori narrowed her eyes and her lips became so thin, I was instantly reminded of our mother, even though she looked nothing like Mom.

"And you what, had your way with her and then left her in the dead of the night? I love you, brother, but that's a dick move."

I winced. "Jesus."

Lori wasn't smiling anymore. "I'm serious."

I shook my head. I'd always been close to my siblings, but talking about what constituted a dick move with my sister in the dead of the night was a first.

"You don't have anything to worry about, Lori. I was at the Lucky Bar with Maddie. She was covering a shift for her sister. She had to stay until closing—"

"And you waited so you could walk her home." Lori sighed with relief. "So glad Momma made sure you boys carry on Dad's chivalry."

I was surprised at her remark because I didn't remember such details about our father. He'd been a good husband and father, that much I knew. But certain details hadn't registered, or I'd forgotten them—which was even more frustrating. Lori was five years younger than me, but I always did think women were more perceptive than men. Mom had taken manners very seriously.

"I never liked the idea of Val closing the bar," I said.

"Yeah, I remember."

"Didn't think it was safe back then, and I don't think it's safe now."

"You did the right thing. But now that I know you haven't pulled a dick move on Maddie, I *can* bring up the subject of your dating life."

"Lori, it's been six years since that ass left you and Milo, and you're still single. Don't lecture me about dating."

She stiffened and I regretted my words, but then I also didn't. We rarely touched the subject of her personal life. "You know nothing about my dating life."

She had a point, but her defensive reaction spoke volumes. Also, I would have known if she'd been dating seriously. One of my brothers would have told me.

"It's been six years, Lori," I tried again. "Don't you get lonely?"

"Of course I do. And you think I wouldn't want to go out, try to chase that white-picket-fence dream again? I plan weddings for a living. But I can't parade men in and out of my son's life. The dating world is a lot like seeing a fin in the water and thinking it's a dolphin, only to later discover it's a shark. It takes trial and error to get to the good ones. I don't want to give Milo whiplash, having him think he'll finally have a father figure in his life only to pull the rug from under him."

"I understand."

"Will is going to have your ass for this. You should see the stern looks he gives any guy who so much as comes in sniffing distance. Like I'm sixteen or something."

I hid a smile. I knew for a fact that Will thought he was being so smart about it that Lori couldn't tell.

"I can deal with Will."

Lori laughed. "You're out of practice,

Landon."

"High time to get back in the saddle, I'd say."

"I couldn't agree more. It's so good to have you here. Who else would stay up and talk to me even if he was dead tired?"

"Charming. You're making me feel really special right now."

She leaned back on the headrest, yawning. "Thanks for pampering Milo like this, training him. It means a lot to him."

"You're changing the subject."

"I don't have anything more to say on the topic."

I was tempted to push her more but decided not to. Besides, she looked sleepier than when I'd arrived, and as a fellow insomniac, I knew she should head to bed right now. As if on cue, she yawned again.

"I think I'm going to bed," she said.

"Good night, Lori."

It looked as if at least one of us was going to have a good night's sleep, and it wasn't me. Though I'd been ready to fall asleep when I came in, I felt wide-awake now, watching Lori climb the staircase.

My thoughts flew to Maddie. There was no denying that I was attracted to her. Everything about Maddie beckoned to me. When she smiled, she lit everything up, and I wanted some of that light. I wanted her. I liked her smile, her laughter, the way her eyes warmed when she talked about Grace. Her fierce determination that her sister should have the best.

The only reason I hadn't kissed her good night was that I couldn't have stopped at one kiss. I wanted more. Taste her skin, make her moan. All new impulses that should have made me want to pull away. I'd fought hard to piece myself together after losing Rachel. I'd promised myself that I wouldn't let myself care for someone so deeply again, that I wouldn't even let myself *want* to care. But when it came to Maddie, all I wanted was to get closer.

When I climbed the staircase, I took out my phone and noticed a message from her from about half an hour ago.

Maddie: Made it home all right?

Even though she was probably asleep by now, I answered anyway. She'd see it in the morning.

Landon: Cab dropped me off a while ago, and I chatted with Lori for a bit.

She answered a few seconds later.

Maddie: Does insomnia run in your family? On my first day on the job, I returned at two o'clock in the morning because I'd forgotten to shut off the power to one of the machines, and Val was on the porch, typing on her laptop!!

Will you look at that? And Val was calling *me* a workaholic. I hovered with my thumb over the keys, but I didn't want to type back. I wanted to hear her voice. I needed it. Jesus, it had been less than an hour since I dropped her off, and I already missed her. I headed to my room and dialed her number as soon as I closed the door behind me.

"Uhhh, the answer is so long it deserves a phone call?"

"I like talking more than typing." Not strictly true, since I thought e-mails were more efficient than calls at work, but just hearing her voice made me smile. "It does run in the family. Mom was like this, and Lori's just like her. Why aren't you sleeping?"

"I have too much energy. Dancing usually has that effect, especially with a partner who knows what he's doing. And you certainly kept your promise."

I sat on the bed fully clothed, trying to make sense of the tightness in my chest. The thought of Maddie with other partners drove me crazy. Fucking hell! I had no right to feel possessive of her.

"What did you talk about with Lori?" she asks.

"Her, Milo. She asked where I was tonight."

"I can tell her the entire story, vouch for your excellent dancing skills."

Her last words came out shaky, and they sent a shock straight under my belt. A gurgling sound came from her end, like someone trying to stifle a yawn.

"Go to sleep, Maddie. You're tired."

"Hmm, I know, but I like talking to you. So much better than sleep. Tell me about your life in San Jose."

"I wake up at five, reply to all outstanding e-mails, then go to the gym for one hour. When I arrive at the office, I go through the schedule with my assistant. A typical day consists of back-to-back meetings, both internal and external. I head home at about eleven."

"At night? Wow. Are you even human? How can you concentrate for so long?"

"Habit."

"What do you do on weekends?"

"On Saturday I Skype with Milo for an hour or two before heading to the office, and on Sunday I work in the morning and play soccer in the afternoon."

A pause, then "Wow."

I imagined Maddie lying in her bed, just like I was. Did she sleep naked? With an old shirt that reached just to the middle of her ass? My dick strained in my pants, and I undid the belt and button to relieve some of the pressure. It wasn't enough, especially when more images flooded my mind.

"What's the most outrageous thing you've done?" I asked out of the blue. I wanted to know everything about her.

"Wow, you're hitting up the big stuff, digging deep already. You go first."

"During a frat party at Harvard, I ran naked through the campus when it was freezing outside."

"That's not outrageous. It's stupid."

"I know. Your turn."

"I skinny-dipped on a dare. At night, on a beach in Malibu."

An image of Maddie naked in the ocean slammed into my mind.

"To be a fly on the wall. Well, the sand," I

said and heard her catch her breath. "What else do you like, Maddie?"

"Lots of things. Burritos with extra cheese and guacamole, curling up with a good book and hot cocoa, lying in the sun on an empty beach."

"What else?"

"Dancing with someone who can make my entire body feel awake." Her last words sounded throaty. I lowered the zipper of my jeans, freeing my erection. A groan tore from me, and I knew I had to end the call before she realized how far gone I was.

"That's quite a list," I said in a strained voice.

"You sound tired."

"We should call this a night."

"I'll see you tomorrow, Landon."

"Sleep tight."

I dropped the phone the second the line went static, and another groan tore from me as I fisted my dick, imagining Maddie here with me. I moved my hand faster and faster until I was spent, but my hunger for Maddie still wasn't satiated.

Chapter Eight
Maddie

I didn't sleep at all. After finishing the conversation with Landon, I realized I had to get up in two hours because I wanted to check on Grace before heading to Val's, and two hours of sleep would just make me groggy. So instead, I made soup for Grace, stopped by the pharmacy because I was sure she'd be out of medicine for her cold, and headed to her apartment building. The weird thing? I had so much energy, you'd think I slept a full eight hours and ingested caffeine pills upon waking up.

Maybe I was still high on my conversation with Landon. I was sure I'd crash eventually, but maybe sight of a certain Connor brother would be enough to fill me with this weird, giddy energy again.

My sister was awake when I arrived in her tiny apartment. Her roommate was away this week.

"What happened to your hair?" she shrieked instead of saying good morning. She was sitting cross-legged on her bed, leaning with her back on the headboard, heaps of used napkins surrounding her. Grace looked a lot like me, and people often mistook us for twins, even if she was seven years younger.

"Haircut disaster. Went to a new hairdresser

because I desperately needed a trim."

"I'd give you a better haircut blindfolded."

"I know. How are you feeling?"

Her nose was red and puffy, as were her eyes.

"Not good. I'm going to the doctor today. You were right. I should have gone sooner."

I pressed my lips together to keep from saying I told you so. There was a time for gloating my general older-sister wisdom, and this was not the time.

"I brought you chicken soup. I left it in the kitchen. Do you want me to bring you some?"

"Nah, I'll eat later. Thank you, Maddie. You're so good to me."

I ruffled her hair and she pushed my hand away, pretending to be annoyed. I loved doting on her. Ever since I was tall enough to reach the stove, I cooked her favorites. Our parents were always gone, either performing or rehearsing. Growing up, I'd missed the warmth of a parent doting on me, and I hadn't wanted Grace to feel the same way.

I couldn't protect her from the instability of a musician's income. She'd worn hand-me-downs from me her entire childhood, and there were Christmases when we couldn't even splurge on a festive meal, but I was determined to compensate where I could.

"How was the Lucky Bar last night?" she asked.

I fidgeted in my spot at the end of the bed, weighing the pros and cons of telling her everything about the shift. I hadn't told her about my attraction to Landon, but now I was bursting to share everything with her. So I sat at the edge of her bed and poured my heart out, describing every tiny detail about the dance, the walk home, the phone call.

"Wait, wait, wait a second. Which one's Landon?"

"The one who lives in San Jose."

She held up her finger as if telling me to wait, picked up her smartphone, and typed something in it.

"Holy guacamole on a spike! Landon is like... all my favorite movie stars combined. I mean, this is just a headshot, but I can't imagine a man with his face not having a body to go with it."

I grinned. "He's hot. Saw him in jogging clothes a few times. Doesn't leave anything to the imagination, trust me."

Grace blew her nose loudly, then adopted a dreamy expression. "And he's a good dancer, huh? You know what they say about good dancers."

"Oh, I do." I'd thought about it the entire night. The way his body moved... I imagined he'd be just as excellent in bed as he was on the dance floor. When he'd asked me if I was seeing someone, I thought he might flip me around and kiss me. But then I realized why he'd asked. He wouldn't have danced that way with me if I were seeing someone else. In some ways, our dancing felt more intimate than kissing.

Grace tilted her head, studying me. "Something's not right. You're usually not this open about liking a guy. Not since—"

"Don't say his name."

"I was going to say He-Who-Must-Not-Be-Named. Since him, you've been more... guarded."

I'd tried dating after Owen, but it didn't amount to much. I shrugged, fiddling her bedsheet with my fingers. "I know, but Landon's so out of my reach, it's almost like crushing on a movie star. It's safe, you know? Because it's all in your imagination."

"That dance was not in your imagination."

"I know, but it was just a dance."

I couldn't explain to Grace the conundrum that was Landon, mainly because I didn't understand him completely either. But even though he was fun, and even a little flirty, I could feel that emotional barrier he'd put in place. I wanted to reach out to him, break it down, but didn't know how. Like I was an authority on breaking barriers or something. I had erected some walls of my own after Owen. I didn't want to start unbricking my heart for anyone. But damn, I loved the way Landon smiled at me last night. I wanted to see him happy. Was that crazy?

"Do you want me to drive you to the doctor?" I asked.

"Nah, it's okay. I can drive."

"I should go. If I arrive early at Val's, I'll be done quicker, and then we can catch up this evening."

"Take care."

On the way to Val's, I drank the entire coffee I bought at the Starbucks opposite Grace's building, but I could feel the tiredness setting in already. And it was just eight in the morning. I had a silver lining, though. This was the time of day Landon went for his run, unless Lori was dropping Milo early for training. In any case, my chances of seeing him in workout gear were excellent.

I switched on the radio, hoping for some music beats to chase away my drowsiness. Three songs in and I was sleepy as hell. Then the stream of music was interrupted by the news bulletin.

"A storm will be rolling in from the coast today. We're expecting heavy rain and the wind can reach up to one hundred miles an hour."

Fantastic. I'd been listening to the weather report yesterday, and they'd said the storm would not reach LA. Just my luck. I groaned as traffic on La Cienega Boulevard slowed almost to a standstill. Not unusual, but not what I needed, especially with this news. It meant I had to shop for supplies to cover Val's yard. Rain brought the risk of erosion when the terrain was a slope. I grabbed my phone and checked where the nearest shop was. Then I groaned again. I'd be a million years late to Val's. I needed a semipermeable ground cover and spikes to fasten it. The reason I didn't have them in my pack of supplies was that it rarely rained in summer. A storm on the last day of June was very unusual.

When I finally had the supplies, dark clouds had already rolled in and the wind was chilling. This storm was going to be a sucker, but between the boys and me, we'd manage to secure the entire front yard before the downpour began.

The space in front of Val's gate was emptier than I'd expected it. Val was probably at the office, but when I'd left yesterday, Lori's car was in the drive too. I remembered on the spot Milo telling me they were going to the festival on Venice Beach today, and they'd be leaving at eight. But then I realized what else was wrong with the picture in front of me. Only Jacob had arrived to work, and he wasn't working. He was leaning against his car... waiting. A familiar dread knotted in my stomach. This was not happening. Not today, when there was a storm rolling in. I was instantly jolted awake. I climbed out of my car.

"Hey, Jacob! Where's Sevi?"

He looked at me apologetically. *Crap, crap, crap.* I knew what was coming.

"Sorry, Maddie, we got an offer yesterday. Today's the first day of work. Sevi's already there. I just wanted to tell you in person."

This was the part of my business I hated. People just up and leaving because a newer, bigger, better construction site needed workers. I was pissed to no end, but I fought to remain calm.

"Jacob, be reasonable. You can't quit midproject. I pay you the market price."

He shrugged. "This project's bigger, Maddie. Will last until the end of the year."

"Stay today, so we can secure the yard before the storm comes in." I couldn't keep my voice down any longer. It was the last day of June, and I'd already paid them for this month, so I didn't have anything to hold over his head.

"Can't, Maddie, I'm so sorry. We start today. I have to be there so they don't give the job to someone else."

He gave me another shrug, then climbed into his car and drove away. I wanted to scream, and kick, and maybe even cry a little. Why were people so undependable? There was no way I could find someone to help me secure the yard before the storm kicked in. With trembling hands, I pulled out my phone and started posting job offers in all the groups I knew. This would only get me temporary workers for next week, but they'd have to do until I found permanent replacements for Jacob and Sevi. There was a real possibility I'd complete this project late, and I hated that. I knew Val wouldn't mind, but I liked keeping my word, meeting my deadlines. It was why I'd made it this far.

There was only one thing to do.

I had to kick ass, and pronto.

Chapter Nine
Landon

Venice Beach was exactly as I remembered it, bustling with people. The festival was organized along the promenade, and the vendor booths with wooden toys looked at odds with the palm trees and the people carrying surfboards or cocktails. Will was meeting us here too.

"If we hurry, we'll be able to stop by every booth before the storm starts," Lori said. "I can't believe it. A storm."

She looped an arm through mine as we walked straight into the madness, Milo bouncing from one booth to the other.

"I forgot what it was like to walk with you," Lori said with a chuckle. "I feel like we're in a parade. I caught ten women checking you out. And that's with me on your arm. They don't know I'm your sister."

"I thought you wanted me to date?"

"Oh, I do. But here's a tip for survival. If a woman's lips look as if they were sucked off with a faucet, or she keeps checking her phone and looking at you, run in the other direction. Many would like to nab a tech mogul. Your net worth is more than anyone's whose handprints lie on the Walk of Fame. Your face has been on enough magazines to be recognizable. But don't worry, I have your back."

"I'm the oldest brother. That's not your task."

Lori scoffed, scooting tighter to me. "Just reminding you how to play your cards in our dear City of Angels. You don't have a ring on your finger to keep the sharks at bay."

Even when I was a married man, a ring never deterred those who were out to catch a big fish, but I'd never been interested. I wasn't now either. My mind was on Maddie.

Will joined us fifteen minutes later, clasping a hand on my shoulder.

"Seriously? You have to boast that badge wherever you go?" Lori challenged. "You're off duty."

"The badge comes with advantages. People think twice before trying any funny business."

Lori's gaze followed Milo from one booth to the other, and then she looped her other arm around Will's. Some days I still couldn't believe Will was part of the police force. It had come as a complete shock when he'd announced his career choice. Growing up, he'd had a healthy disregard for rules, even a few encounters with the police. Talk about contradictions. Val had cracked so many jokes about police officers when he told us that I knew for sure something was off. The moment he'd left, she'd started sobbing.

"He's going to have a gun. He's going to be around

bad guys. What if something happens to him?"

Secretly, I agreed with her, but if that was what he wanted, there wasn't anything either of us could do. Val had hoped it would be a *phase*, but I knew better. Will was determined, and when he decided on something, he went through with it— which he did. I was proud of him even though he skirted too close to the danger line for my peace of mind.

When dark gray clouds gathered above, my thoughts flew to Maddie and her determination to keep the project on track. Did she account for bad weather when she drew a timeline for a project? Or would she stubbornly work through the rain? Somehow, I felt I already knew the answer.

"They weren't kidding about that storm warning," I said.

"Storm warning?" Will asked.

Lori nodded. "They announced it this morning. I wonder if it'll have an impact on the whole terracing business."

"I'll check with Maddie when I get home," I assured her. Lori cocked a brow and failed to disguise a knowing smile.

"So, what other plans do you have today, Landon?"

She didn't say "besides checking on Maddie" out loud, but I picked up the gist of her question.

"I'm meeting Craig and his wife before dinner." Craig was one of our oldest childhood friends.

"So you're free after dinner? Maybe I should take you out," Lori teased.

"Ah, you didn't get enough big-brother teasing from me?" I volleyed back smoothly, fighting a smile.

She narrowed her eyes, looking at me with mock menace. "So that's how you're gonna play it?"

I held up a hand. "This is fair game. I only use underhanded tactics for people who don't share our blood."

"So you keep saying," she muttered.

"I can help with that," Will offered. "What were you teasing her about? I fall into the older brother category."

"Buddy, you're the third oldest in the family," Lori said. "That in no way qualifies you to be in the *older* category. Or the youngest. You're in the wishy-washy middle with me."

That was true. Jace was the youngest, followed by Hailey. Then came Lori and Will. But I knew why Will felt part of the older gang. When Val and I were at the pub, he'd often cooked dinner for Lori, Hailey, and Jace, and helped them with homework.

I'd missed bantering with my siblings after moving away.

"Val and Landon are twins. Technically, I'm the second oldest," Will said.

Lori wrinkled her nose, directing us all toward Milo, who had skipped two booths ahead. "Technicalities don't work for me, just like your

81

badge doesn't."

"You seem to find it useful when you ask me to come up with bogus rules for Milo. Remember the time you made me tell him I could arrest him for eating too many sweets?"

"It's so easy to pawn that off on you, though. *He* is a big believer in badges. And I'm a big believer in chocolate fudge." She smiled, pointing to a booth. "I'll treat all of us."

"You don't have to—" Will and I began, but she cut us off.

"My treat. No negotiating. As a thank-you to both of you for coming here today."

Half an hour later, the downpour began. We'd managed to take cover under a tarp just in time. We waited and then waited some more, but it showed no sign of stopping. I'd texted Maddie once, but she hadn't replied. I was growing restless with worry. Was she out in the rain?

When it became clear the downpour would continue, I bid Lori, Will, and Milo goodbye and hailed a cab. I texted Maddie again, but she didn't answer. The rain was so thick you could barely see anything out the window. The traffic was a nightmare. It took me *hours* to reach the house.

When I stepped out of the cab, it seemed to me that only Maddie's car was parked here. I stepped through the front gate and scanned the grounds. The rain soaked me in seconds. I had to use my palm as protection over my eyes to keep the rain from stabbing my eyeballs. The entire yard seemed covered in some sort of plastic tarp. Only the wooden trail was uncovered. I didn't see Maddie, and my shoulders felt lighter. But as I finished scanning the front yard, movement on the far left caught my attention.

I groaned. There she was, her hands maneuvering the end of the tarp. And she was... arguing with herself? I couldn't tell, but she was talking and shaking her head, and there was no one around. I headed straight toward her.

"What are you doing out here?" I tapped her shoulder, but she still startled, whirling around.

"I need to secure the cover with spikes," she explained.

"Where are the guys?"

"They quit."

"Maddie, let's go inside. You can finish this when the rain eases a bit."

She shook her head. "If I don't secure this, there's a risk the rain will dislodge the earth."

As far as I could see, there were spikes at regular intervals. The cover looked pretty fucking secure to me.

"Maddie, you're soaked. I'm soaked."

"Then go inside. I need to finish this."

She kept fumbling with a spike, and I gripped both her wrists, looking straight at her.

"Maddie, stop being so stubborn or I swear I'll throw you over my shoulder and take you inside."

She wiggled a hand out of my grip, then held the finger up warningly. "You just don't get this."

Except I did. I knew that feverish need to keep fixing what you could when a problem escalated until it was out of your control. I found myself in such situations at least twice a month at the office, and working through it always got me to the other end. But I wasn't about to let Maddie give herself pneumonia.

She tried to wiggle her other hand out of my grip, but I tightened my fingers on her skin. I was scanning her body, weighing what the easiest way would be to toss her over my shoulders when she exclaimed, "Oh my God, you're seriously going to throw me over your shoulder."

"Yes."

She dropped the spike she was still gripping in the hand I held captive and started marching toward the house. I walked next to her, releasing her hand but keeping my eyes trained on her in case she changed her mind. When we stepped out of the rain and onto the porch, I took a good look at her. Her gray shirt was soaked and transparent, and I could see her black bra, the swell of her breasts where the fabric gave way to skin. Longing thrummed through me, to touch her, taste her. I wondered if she was wearing matching panties, but I didn't have to wonder for too long. Her pants—not jeans, but some thinner fabric—were as transparent as her shirt. She was wearing a black thong, the thin scrap of fabric at the back running right over her crack, leaving her round ass cheeks in plain view. My fingers itched with the impulse to remove that thong, touch and lick all the places it had covered.

"You are unbelievable." She took the elastic band out of her hair and squeezed the water out of her blonde tresses before whirling to face me. Stepping closer, she poked my chest. "Unbelievable. Who does that?"

"Who stays out in a torrential rain?" I countered, trying to ignore the bolt of heat her touch had sent through me.

"Someone who wants to finish a job." She poked me again, and I caught her wrist because if she touched me one more time, I couldn't be held responsible for my actions. Her mouth was *so* close. Pink and plump, and I knew she'd be soft and sweet. She licked her lower lip, her own gaze pinned on my shirt. When our eyes met, she brought her free hand to my chest, and I exhaled sharply.

I leaned in and captured her mouth. She parted her lips with a sigh, allowing me entrance. Her taste! I could get addicted to it, to the way she gave herself to me, without restraint or reservations. I let go of her wrist and moved one hand to her waist, fisted her hair with the other, angling her head so I could explore her mouth better. Slipping my hand down from her waist, I cupped her ass, pulling her flat against me. She groaned in my mouth when my erection pressed along her belly.

I was going to kiss her until her legs shook.

***

Maddie

The contact was electrifying, jolting every nerve in my body. His lips fit perfectly against mine. The scruff on his jaw lightly scraped against my skin, but I liked it. I liked it even more when he pushed me back until I felt a solid wall behind me. Talk about being between a rock and a hard place. Eh, I could always do with more of such delicious hardships. I loved this—being trapped by his strong body, with no other choice but to fully surrender to his kiss. And oh, what a kiss this was. No one had kissed me like that, not ever.

He explored and probed, our tongues clashing in a wild dance until I felt liquid fire coursing through my veins. He deepened the kiss, demanding more, and then he intensified the rhythm as if he was making love to my mouth. Heat pooled low in my body. When a deep groan reverberated in his chest, my knees weakened. As if sensing this, he gripped my waist with both of those strong and steady hands. I had a hunch he was that type of man who would be strong and steady no matter what, who'd never let me fall.

"Maddie," he whispered, once he'd pulled back so we could take a much-needed breath. I stared up right into his eyes. His pupils were dilated, his eyelids hooded. Desire was written all over him, making it hard for me to think.

In this second, nothing seemed more important than feeling his lips on mine again. When he leaned in again, I grabbed his collar, pulling him all the way toward me. The second our lips touched, I felt exhilarated, caught up in his magic once more. This time, we took it a step further, kissing more furiously, with more passion. He moved his hands under my ass, scooping me up. When my center collided with his erection, I fisted his hair. We were grinding against each other, the tension we'd built up last night begging to be released. Even through all the layers of clothes, the friction was unbearable. I was slick between my legs. When he pushed the tip of his erection against my clit, I nearly came. With my clothes on.

But then something snapped in my mind, and I tore my mouth away from his. I looked to my right, and Landon leaned his forehead against my temple, his hot breath landing on my ear. Despite my soaked clothes, I was on fire. He lowered me to the ground, and we stood entwined like that, breathing heavily, until the cold crept up my spine again, making me shiver.

Landon stepped back, running a hand through his hair. Small drops of water splattered all around. Without the proximity of his body, cold blasted through me. I ran my hands up and down my arms, but it didn't help much.

"You should change out of the wet clothes."

I sighed. "I only have one change of clothes. I don't want to get that soaked too."

"I'm not letting you go back out there until the rain stops."

"What are you going to do to keep me out of the rain, kiss me some more?"

His eyes snapped fire. "Don't think I won't."

I swallowed hard, trying to figure out my next steps. I really did need to change out of these clothes.

"I'll go find you something in Val's room if you don't want to change into yours," he said.

"That's not appropriate," I countered.

Something flashed in those green eyes. "Let me make this clear. You're changing into either Val's clothes or your own because I won't let you give yourself pneumonia. So, what's it gonna be?"

Needing to move, I paced the front porch. The cold was seeping into my bones.

Landon cleared his throat. "Your clothes are completely transparent."

I stopped pacing, looked down at my chest, and immediately crossed my arms over it. Oh, crap. This explained why he'd been looking at me like he wanted to eat me up before kissing me. He still looked at me like that. Embarrassment clouded around me. I felt naked.

"Why didn't you tell me that before? I'd have come out of the rain sooner."

"I didn't realize you'd ditch your work ethic for anything."

Landon smiled, and laughter bubbled out of me.

"If the price was flashing you my boobs, I would. I have priorities."

"You're flashing more than that." He

swallowed hard, and I remembered with a pang that I wasn't wearing jeans. I looked down at my pants. They were transparent. Since I was wearing a thong today, I'd been parading my ass in front of Landon.

When I looked up, I couldn't meet his eyes. "I'll go shower and put on my spare change of clothes."

He nodded, and I felt his eyes follow me as we entered the house. I retrieved my backpack from the foyer and swung it over my shoulder, making a beeline for the bathroom.

I took a long, hot shower, but my entire body was still buzzing with adrenaline. My mind was so full of Landon and his kiss that I couldn't concentrate on anything else. I wondered if he was also taking a shower right now. He'd been all wet too, after all. The mere possibility that we might be naked at the same time was messing with my senses.

I stepped out of the bathroom in fresh clothes, keeping my old ones in front of me with both hands. I'd wrung them out, but they were still wet. I needed a plastic bag to wrap them in before stuffing them in my backpack. As I approached the living room, I heard Landon's voice.

"Adam, forward me the entire e-mail exchange, and I'll make up my own mind." A pause, then "Of course I trust you, but I don't like making decisions knowing only half the conversation."

I slowed my pace, not wanting to walk in on him mid-phone call. Leaning against the wall, I closed my eyes, smiling as I replayed the kiss in my mind, and all the passion it held. It was the result of all that tension we'd built the night before during our dance. We'd both needed to release it. Now I could go back to daydreaming about him in that off-limits sort of way you daydreamed about a movie star.

When I couldn't hear him talk anymore, I went to the living room. He'd changed too, and a vision of him in the shower flashed in my mind. *Crap.* Maybe I could go back to safely daydreaming about him on Monday, when the memory of the kiss subsided, when I couldn't still feel his taste on my lips. For now, I had to put some distance between us.

"I need a plastic bag for the clothes or I'll get my backpack all wet," I said.

"Sure. Let's go to the kitchen and find one."

While he searched and crouched to check the lower drawers, I did my best *not* to perv at his ass. On second thought... why not? I'd already established today was an exception. Why not get a good look at Landon's backside while I was at it? It was muscular, strong....

Unfortunately, he found a plastic bag all too soon. I took it from him, careful not to touch his fingers. I was already on a slippery slope with my wandering eyes; who knew what his touch might prompt me to do.

"Well, I'd better get going." I clutched the full plastic bag to my chest. "I checked the weather report and the rain won't stop soon. I fastened the cover to the ground, so there shouldn't be any problems."

"So why were you so adamant to stay in the rain and finish whatever you were doing?"

"Ah, I was being a bit overzealous, wanting to double on the spikes in a few places, but this isn't a tornado, just a storm, so it's not really necessary. I can get a little… lost in my own head when things go to hell. Thanks for pulling me out."

"I do that too when the shit hits the fan. Get trapped in my mind."

"Who pulls *you* out?"

"No one." Landon shrugged, and I could imagine him in his office until the late hours of the night, his brilliant mind working incessantly on finding a solution. He was so intent on saving everyone else, but maybe he needed a little saving himself.

"Maddie, tell me you're not leaving because we kissed."

"Of course not! I don't run away from problems."

But I did avoid temptations… especially when they came in the form of Landon Connor. Some might call this cowardly. If they had better tactics to keep from wanting to jump a man's bones after he'd just kissed you like his life depended on it, I was happy to take notes.

He grinned. "I'm a *problem*? No one's called me that."

"You've got everyone pussyfooting around you?"

"I call it strong leadership."

"Some might go with dictator."

"Depends on who you ask." He laughed softly, opened his mouth again, but then his phone rang. I used that as my way out.

"Will you tell Val that I left early because of the rain? I promise I'll be back with a full crew on Monday. And I'm going to borrow one of her umbrellas."

"I'll relay the message."

I pointed to the phone he was clutching in his hand. "And that needs to stop. Don't make me fail at my spy job. I can't keep it a secret from Val forever."

Grinning widely, he stepped closer. "Oh, I think you can. We're good at keeping our secrets, aren't we, Maddie?"

He was much too close, and the scent of soap fresh on his skin was clouding my thoughts. I blinked a few times, then stepped back nonchalantly. Not knowing what to reply—or if to reply at all—I waved at him. *Waved.*

"I'll see myself out. I know where the umbrellas are."

He nodded as his phone rang again. His voice reached me as I hurried to the foyer, picked up a pink umbrella with silver stars sprinkled on it, and let myself out. On the porch, I instinctively looked to my right. Just seeing the wall he'd kissed me against sent tingles up my fingertips. I could still remember every little detail about that kiss.

I had a feeling I wouldn't forget them until Monday.

Chapter Ten
Landon

Adam was tiptoeing around me, and it was pissing me off. The only logical conclusion was that things weren't going as smoothly as we'd hoped, but also not serious enough to warrant my return. He'd called to give me the rundown of this week's events, including how Sullivan, the owner of the company we were partnering with, was dragging his ass on signing the papers.

He wasn't sticking to our terms and was making additional requests. Adam said he hadn't cc'd me on any of his e-mails because he could handle it all and didn't want to spoil my vacation. I trusted him, but I didn't want to be left out of conversations.

It took two more semi-threatening phone calls until Adam finally did send me the entire e-mail exchange with Sullivan. Sitting in the armchair under the window, I scrolled on my phone, analyzing every word. It was frustrating and would prolong the process by a few weeks, but it was what it was.

With no choice but to admit Adam had been right, I set the phone on the small ottoman next to the armchair. Adam could handle this. It didn't warrant my interference, much less a quicker return to San Jose. Thank God.

Rachel and I had had big dreams for DBC Payment Solutions. Even though she had been working as a teacher and hadn't been part of the company, she'd always cheered for it. So far, I'd surpassed our dreams, but all the success felt... empty. For the first time in years, I wasn't looking forward to heading back to San Jose. I wanted more time here. More time with Maddie. My mind was so full of her. Jesus, how she'd surrendered to me! I could still feel her warmth. Her delicious taste and sweet moans were branded in my memory.

I rose to my feet and headed outside. It was still raining, so I paced the porch, half hoping Maddie would step through the front gate. Even though I was here on vacation, even though I wasn't really soul mate material anymore, or any kind of mate material, I wanted Maddie. I wanted her badly. It was like allowing myself to taste Maddie had opened a door for other wants I'd denied myself.

"Fucking hell, is the great flood upon us?"

I blinked up to see Val hurrying up on the porch. The rain had covered the sound of her steps. She shook her umbrella, shuddering.

"Can't leave this out here to dry, the wind will blow it away," she mumbled. Taking in her yard, she added, "Oh, Maddie covered the ground."

"Yeah, she said this should keep the earth from dislodging. She left a while ago."

Val nodded. "I hope she didn't get soaked, poor thing." Ah, what a sight that had been.

"Everything okay, Landon?"

I schooled my expression so I didn't seem too eager or too guilty.

"Yeah, sure."

She folded her arms, leaning against the exact same spot where I'd kissed Maddie. If I got through this conversation and didn't give myself away, I deserved an Oscar. So much for humoring Maddie about being able to keep a secret when I was the weak link. Val was my twin. We'd always had a strong bond. Growing up, we often banded against our parents like the pair of marauders we were. We'd mastered the trade of sneaking out when we were eleven, and it required seamless cooperation. We'd passed that trade to our siblings, which came back to bite us when we were the ones in charge of them. That required even more banding together and cooperation between Val and me. Telling each other everything had been a way to unload, as well as a necessity. It was common for our siblings to tell me one story and another to Val, with the hope of wiggling their way out of a sticky situation. Since we'd been the inventors of the tactic, we caught on pretty soon.

I wasn't used to employing a filter around Val.

"You look different today." She narrowed her eyes, pointing vaguely at my face. "Did you get good news from the office or anything?"

"No, the opposite. There's more trouble with the merger than I anticipated. Looked over some e-mails—"

"Aha!" She unhitched herself from the wall, placing her hands on her hips, the umbrella under one arm, her purse hanging on the other. "You answered e-mails? That's a rabbit hole."

At least she hadn't caught on to the other thing. You win some, you lose some. But I wanted to make one point clear.

"I'm not a kid, Val. I don't need you to police my vacation."

She walked up to me, patting my cheek. "Yes you do, Landon. That's the whole point of having a sister who knows you like the back of her hand. You used to love your work-life balance. You used to lecture me about it. Would I be wrong to assume you're tipping that balance in favor of work so you don't feel how empty your life has become?"

I blinked at her. There was no hiding from Val.

"You're not wrong."

She nodded sagely. "So don't do that while you're here. Take some time out. You need it. Trust me, I'm not being a nag for no reason."

I chuckled. "So as long as you have a reason, you think you can just nag away?"

"Well, I *am* your sister. That means I can nag by default, and I'll get away with it." She gave me a devilish grin.

She sat on the small bench between two windows, looking at the rain.

"Why are you home so early?"

"I have a phone conference this afternoon

and figured I could do that from home too." She frowned, looking out onto the yard.

"Anything wrong?"

Val shrugged. "No, I'm just a bit nervous. Remember the potential client I told you about?"

"The one who wants you to develop an exclusive line of fragrances and lotions for his stores?"

"Yes. His team is flying in on the fifth of July for my pitch. I have to win him over. This would be a big deal, Landon. The biggest yet."

"I know."

The client she was talking about had high-end department stores all over the world. It would make her company an international player.

"I can look over that pitch with you if you want, give you some feedback."

She straightened, excitement dancing in her eyes, then shook her head. "No, I can't do that. You're on vacation."

"This is a once-in-a-lifetime opportunity."

I barely bit back a laugh as I watched her struggle with herself. "I'll show it to you tomorrow." She looked at the property. "I can't wait for the yard to be ready."

"You said Maddie landscaped the yard in your office building too?"

"Yep. And it's the best thing I ever did. Whenever I feel like my head will explode, I go for a walk there. It's amazing."

"These are big projects for a one-person

company, even with the occasional workers," I said. I stepped back from the edge of the porch because the wind had changed and the rain was pelting my face.

"She said she plans to hire a full-time team as soon as her sister finishes law school."

Because she was paying the tuition fees, of course. That was why she was doing the job of several people. I wanted to take care of that woman, make sure she didn't have a worry. And she wasn't even mine. I was determined to change that.

Chapter Eleven
Maddie

I spent my weekend pampering Grace, who'd been told by her doctor that she'd better stay indoors and rest a lot while taking flu medication. On Monday morning, I showed up at Val's house with two workers in tow. I had taken one look at them and knew they were in for the very short-term only. I estimated they'd work for me for a week, at most, but I had already cast my net wide, and I was confident I'd find the right people soon.

"Ben, Derek, I'm going to give you a rundown of the project, and then tell you about what we'll be working on today." Even though tomorrow was the Fourth of July and we wouldn't be working, I'd wanted them to start today so I could show them the ropes.

Ben smiled. "Sure. This is a great place."

Derek was inspecting the ground cover. "Good thinking, covering this up, or we'd have a serious problem on our hands."

After instructing them on their tasks, I set out to inspect if the storm over the weekend had done any damage. I also kept peeking at the house out of the corners of my eyes. There was no movement whatsoever, and when I entered to leave my backpack, there was no sign of Landon. I couldn't help the twinge of disappointment. I'd gotten used to my daily dose of gorgeous-man appreciation. I'd especially counted on it to kick-start the week.

This was a suckier Monday than usual, and a girl had to do what she could to get through the day. Just to be completely sure he wasn't around, I went to the backyard too. Nope. I'd missed my chance to see Landon out for his daily run. Maybe he'd come back later for his training with Milo.

It was for the best that Landon wasn't here, I told myself. Was I attracted to him? Hell yes. Not only because he was sexier than any man I'd seen, but because I genuinely loved being around him. He made me laugh. I liked making *him* laugh. But he wasn't the man for me for about a million reasons.

I concentrated on those as I started peeling away the tarp.

My line of work was usually unsexy, but unhitching wood spikes from a moderately dry earth made this Monday especially messy. By ten o'clock, I was pretty sure my boots were full of mud. Two hours later, I was convinced I'd find mud even in my teeth.

"Boss, we're going on our lunch break," Ben announced sometime later.

I stood up, stretching my neck. "What time is it?"

"Almost one o'clock. Wanna join us? My girl packed enough sandwiches to feed three of me."

"No, thanks. Enjoy your lunch."

"We'll be just outside the front gate in my car," Derek said.

After they left, I sighed, trying hard not to think that Landon and I had lunch at one o'clock on the dot every day since he'd arrived.

I'd just turned my back to the front gate when I heard it open. I knew without looking it was Landon. It was as if my body reacted to his mere presence. My heart began to hammer, my pulse quickened. I didn't look up until he was right next to me. Wow. He was wearing a suit, and it fit him so well I could swear it was custom-made.

He held up a takeout bag. "Lunch?"

Drawing on every ounce of self-preservation skill, I took a step back. But not before I caught a whiff from the takeout bag.

"Are those burritos?"

"With extra cheese and guacamole, just the way you like it. You can't say no."

"Oh, but I can," I teased, even though I couldn't believe he'd bought burritos, that he'd paid such close attention to our conversation. "You're not the boss of me."

He gave me a smile so perfect, I could swear my underwear caught fire.

"Eat with me, Maddie."

Oh goody! He was using the same tone as when he'd told me to break the rules with him that night at the Lucky Bar. I knew without either of us saying it out loud that this—our need for togetherness—was breaking yet another rule.

I seemed to be even more susceptible to him after our kiss. But the man was wearing a suit and bringing my favorite food. I could indulge in my daily session of sexy man appreciation and enjoy a burrito at the same time. How could I say no?

"Let's go in the kitchen," I said.

I took off my shoes before stepping inside the house and followed Landon to the kitchen. The second we entered it, I felt the walls press in on us, forcing us closer together. I was aware of Landon's every move. He shrugged out of his suit jacket, draping it on the back of a seat. The sleeves of his shirt were rolled up to his elbows. What the sight of those muscle-corded forearms did to me....

"I'll get us some plates," I offered, opening one of the overhead compartments from which I remembered Landon taking out plates last week. My memory was playing tricks because I was facing glasses.

"This is the one with the plates." Landon came up behind me, reaching to the compartment to my right, retrieving two plates. When he lowered his arm, his elbow brushed the side of my breast. A sizzle bristled through me, stoking a fire deep inside. I felt Landon's sharp exhale against the side of my head and realized I was gripping the counter for no reason at all. I let go as Landon stepped back, and we headed to the small kitchen table. I sat opposite Landon, careful so our legs wouldn't touch under the table. The room seemed to have shrunk in size in the past few seconds, but I suspected any space would feel small when filled with so much sexual tension.

"So, when are you training Milo today?" I asked.

"I'm not. He's at a friend's house."

"Oh, I see. What were you up to today?" I bit into my burrito, savoring the rich flavor.

"Met up with an old school friend."

I swallowed the mouthful quickly. "You meet your friends wearing a suit?"

"Might have doubled as a business meeting, so I went business casual."

"Which is the casual part?"

He pointed to the rolled sleeves with a smile.

"What's the dress code for strictly business?"

"Cuff links."

Well, I hoped I'd never be privy to *that* sight. Nothing spelled sex appeal like cuff links. Not every man could pull them off, but I suspected Landon wore them very well.

We chitchatted about his friend while we ate. He'd married his high-school sweetheart and they were now about to have their third child.

"That's the fairy tale come to life, huh? Lucky them, finding each other so quickly. No kissing frogs to discover the prince... or princess."

"Why are *you* still single, Maddie?"

"More than half the population is."

"I don't care about them. I want to know about you." Landon rested his elbows on the table, a twinkle in his eye. "Come on, you know all my deep, dark secrets. Share some of your own."

"Well, technically Val told me all of yours."

"So you prefer I ask her?" he challenged, luring chuckles out of me.

"I don't have any deep, dark reasons for being single. I came close to getting married to that ex I told you about, the one I moved to LA for."

"What happened?"

I felt his gaze on me as I bit into my burrito again, chewing carefully.

"He was an architect too. We studied together. He specialized in buildings, I in landscape. He was very successful. All that success turned him into an ass. He was working on a lot of high-profile buildings, even worked with Warner Bros. on a few movie sets. He got snippier with me as time went by, making snide remarks here and there. I thought it was just all the stress from work getting to him. Turns out he just thought I was beneath him."

"What?"

"Yeah. One evening I kept rattling about a new project, and he just blurted out that I'd wasted all that time getting my architecture degree to be a glorified gardener. He felt I wasn't ambitious enough."

Landon's eyes turned hard. "He told you that?"

"And more. Said that when he took me to whatever awards he received, he felt... ashamed. That it was clear I didn't want more from life, and I'd drag him down. I called off our engagement right away. He seemed almost… relieved."

"Why hadn't you dumped his ass before?"

My body warmed all over at the indignation in his tone. "No one's perfect. I thought if we put a lot of effort into it, we could make it work."

"Being in a relationship shouldn't feel like pulling teeth, Maddie."

A question popped up in my mind, but I wasn't sure if it was appropriate. In the end, my curiosity won. "Was it always easy for you and Rachel?"

I'd expected him to tense at the name, but he merely dropped his head back, as if recalling memories. "We had our fights, like every couple, but it definitely didn't feel like pulling teeth."

"Did you meet here or in San Jose?"

"Here. I met her in the early days of setting up the software business, and we hit it off right away. We had a few beautiful years together before she got sick."

"What happened to her?"

"Brain cancer. It's a cruel disease. We found out late, but doctors said they couldn't have done much even if they had found it earlier."

"I'm sorry."

"Thank you. Sometimes I can't believe it's been four years since she died." He looked into the distance, then shook his head. "But back to your ex. That guy sounds like a douchebag. He didn't deserve you, if he looked at you and all he saw was someone who'd drag him down. Do you want to know what I see?"

"What?" I whispered.

"A hardworking woman who's built a business doing something she loves and is damn good at it."

"Oh, Landon. How can you say that? You caught me having a mini breakdown because my employees quit."

"And today you showed up with new ones. The key to running a successful business isn't *not* having problems, it's finding solutions for them, which you did. I've had plenty of breakdowns myself. Don't be so harsh on yourself. You're doing a great job."

"Thank you." My mood skyrocketed. I *was* proud of myself and my business—at least on days that didn't include breakdowns. But it felt nice to be appreciated by him. "I do love my business."

After a few seconds of silence, he asked, "How is Grace feeling? Still sick?"

"She's much better. Went to the doctor on Friday."

"What are your plans for the Fourth of July? Spending it with her?" Landon asked. I couldn't believe it was already tomorrow.

"Nah, Grace's going to celebrate with her study buddies. Two of my friends moved near Desert Hot Springs a few months ago, and they invited me. I'd love to catch up with them, but driving so long just for a day trip is putting me off. Traffic will be a nightmare for sure. I think I'll just work on some designs for my next project."

"Join us. We're having a small party here."

"Thanks, but I'm not sure it's a good idea. It's a family gathering, and…."

I glanced at the kitchen counter, where we'd shared that heated moment. When I looked back, our gazes crossed. Landon touched my ankles under the table, and energy zipped from the point of contact up between my thighs, which I pressed together. Heat rose to my cheeks. The way he looked at my mouth made it clear he was all too aware of the sizzle between us. The weight of this unspoken thing between us only fueled the tension. My entire body was wound up tight just from sitting across from him, and our ankles touching.

"I'd love for you to be here, Maddie."

"Thanks. I'll think about it."

I rose from the table and carried both our plates to the counter. I'd barely placed them on the wooden surface when I became aware that Landon had come up right behind me.

"Now that's not a good enough answer."

"Is that so? Not to your liking, Mr. Connor?" I challenged. He brought his mouth to my ear.

"Not at all, Ms. Jennings. You need more convincing?" He cupped one of my hips in his large hand and whirled me around to face him. He was only a breath away from me. "What if I add another kiss to the mix? Would that tip the balance?"

"Landon!"

His leather and wood scent enveloped me. It

wasn't fair. Why did he have to be so attractive?

"Was that supposed to be a protest?" He gave me a devilish grin. I was fully aware I'd sounded breathy and needy. "I can't stop thinking about you, Maddie." He brought a hand to my face, splaying his fingers.

Oh, Landon, Landon, Landon.

"Just say yes," he said.

"You're not leaving me much of a choice."

"I know."

Those green eyes grew even more determined. His entire body language reminded me of the way he'd looked when he'd pulled me out of the rain, when he'd announced he'd carry me over his shoulder if I wasn't being reasonable. An image flashed in my mind, of Landon breaking into my bungalow and carrying me over his shoulder to the party if I didn't agree. I grinned. Why did that idea amuse me so much? I liked being on my own two feet, in control of my life. But standing here, merely a breath away from Landon, I realized I wouldn't mind being whisked away by him.

"Okay, I'll be here tomorrow for the party," I relented.

"Good. After that, I'd like to take you to watch the fireworks. Just the two of us."

I narrowed my eyes, even as my heart thundered in my chest. "Landon," I whispered.

"Still didn't sound like a protest."

"You're using dirty negotiation tactics on me."

"Oh, beautiful, I can get much dirtier than this. Would you like proof?"

I cleared my throat. "I'll take your word."

"Go out with me. You know you want to."

"Oh, you can read my mind too, in addition to playing dirty?"

He tilted his head forward until our foreheads almost touched. "No mind reading needed. On Friday, you kissed me back like you wanted me to make you mine on that porch. And I nearly did."

Holy crap. Testosterone was oozing off him, and my defenses were no match. Maybe it was a good thing he was here on vacation. Surely my heart couldn't get involved *too much* in a matter of days? He was leaving in a week, after all. My mind was racing, but having him this close was messing with my ability to remain rational.

"We have chemistry. It's more than chemistry. Go out with me, Maddie."

"Fine, Mr. Connor. You can take me to watch the fireworks."

He tipped his head a little lower, almost touching my lips. "I can't wait."

The sound of the front door opening cut through the sexual tension.

"Landon, are you in the kitchen?" Val's voice filtered to us.

"Yes. Coming right out," he said, without taking his eyes off me.

I drew in a deep breath, watching that gorgeous ass of his as he left the kitchen. Both

Landon and Val were on the porch when I stepped out a few minutes later. They were sitting on the small wooden bench, hunched over a laptop. I made no noise as I put my shoes back on.

"But won't that seem like I don't have enough production capacity?" Val asked.

"No, it'll make him understand you're in high demand," Landon replied.

What was happening? I placed my hands on my hips, stepping right in front of them. "What's this? Val, you made me spy on your brother and now you're the one corrupting him?"

Val winced. "You're right. He offered to look over a pitch I prepared for a potential client I'm meeting on the fifth. He was just supposed to glance at it last weekend, but it kind of spiraled into... this. His fault entirely."

I would have argued, but I'd just had firsthand experience of Landon's convincing prowess. I turned my glare to Landon, who winked at me.

"Landon tells me you're joining us tomorrow."

I eyed the two of them. "Yes. You're sure I won't be intruding on your family time?"

Val glanced at her brother. "Gee, now that she asks, maybe we should change our minds."

Landon crossed his arms over his chest, flashing a grin that bore an uncanny resemblance to his sister's.

"Everyone's required to bring a homemade dish," Val informed me.

I dropped my jaw in mock shock. "First your brother coerces me into joining you, and now you tell me I have to cook? Sneaky."

"That's my middle name," Val confirmed. "How do you think I convince everyone to do my bidding all the time?"

Chapter Twelve
Maddie

I groaned when I pulled into Val's street the next morning. I'd borrowed Grace's tiny Volvo for the occasion, anticipating that parking my Chevy, which I'd retrieved from the mechanic's shop yesterday evening, might be a challenge. Everyone had guests over for the celebration. I glanced along the street, and it was clear I had more chances of hocus-pocusing the car into thin air than parking it anywhere.

I was just about to call Val and ask if there was a nearby parking garage when Landon stepped into my view, walking at a brisk pace along the row of parked cars. I tried not to shimmy in my seat as we made eye contact, but I lost the battle. Landon was affecting me on a visceral level, in a way no other man ever had.

"Hi, Maddie," he said, climbing into the passenger seat and throwing his thumb over his shoulder. "Reverse the car. There's a field we've been using as a parking lot a few streets away."

"You don't have to ride with me. Just give me instructions."

"Trust me, it's easier this way."

One hand on the wheel, I grabbed the stick with the other, moving it into Reverse, glancing in the rearview mirror as I backed away. Out of the corner of my eye I saw Landon's gaze trained on me, and a current of awareness zinged me.

I followed his instructions. He'd been right. If he'd just explained it to me, no way would I have found the field. It was a vast open space between two fence-surrounded parcels atop of which sat ranch-style homes. A few cars were already parked there. I pulled next to a black Chevrolet.

"I have cake in the trunk," I explained as we climbed out. When we reached the rear of the car, I bit my lip, looking around at the parcel. "Are we allowed to park here?"

"Don't worry about it."

I stood on my toes, inspecting my surroundings for any "No Trespassing" signs. When Landon leaned in slightly, I nearly lost my balance.

"Maddie, seriously. Don't worry." On a huskier, playful note, he added, "I only break the rules on special occasions."

Oh, and I remembered said occasions in such vivid detail.

"I don't want to risk the car getting towed away."

"I own the parcel."

I felt my eyes widen. "Oh, okay."

"I bought it at the same time Val did. It was a good investment. Relatively cheap when we bought them, but prices skyrocketed."

"It's a great neighborhood. I have my eye on it too, even though prices are ridiculous. But who knows... maybe in a few years. I like the small-town feeling of it, even if it's far away from the ocean." My landscaper's eye inspected the area. The terrain was sloped too, but less than Val's. Oh, the things I could do with this place. "It's a great place to build a house, raise a family."

Way to overshare, Maddie. We hadn't even gone on a date and I was already talking about a family. I'd shelved those dreams after the engagement fiasco, but Landon was bringing out my romantic side. All that maleness was overpowering.

I focused on opening my trunk. I'd packed the cake in a round, huge plastic form, which was designed especially for transporting cake... but the lid had fallen off, and my entire trunk was smeared with frosting and lemon cream.

"Oh, no, no, no!"

"Maddie, it's no big deal."

"Val said everyone has to bring something. I don't want to show up empty-handed."

"There's enough food anyway."

"I worked on this the entire morning. I don't want to show up with nothing."

"There's a bakery on the way."

"It's open today? That's great. It won't be homemade, but at least I'll bring something."

"That's a plan. What kind of cake was it?" he asked.

"Lemon."

He dipped a finger into the mess, then brought it to his open mouth. I saw half an inch of tongue before the side of his finger disappeared into his mouth, and I licked my lips. Landon grimaced.

"What?"

He shrugged. "I'm sorry but that's... terrible."

"You're pulling my leg." I dipped one finger and tasted it too, and nearly puked. "Crap. I should have stuck to the carrot cake I made when I finished Val's project. She'd seemed to like it, even though she didn't eat much." I was a good cook, but cakes were challenging. "Not that it matters, considering the Tupperware disaster."

After I closed my trunk, we walked side by side down the labyrinth of streets, coming to a halt when we reached a delicious-looking storefront. Felicia's Sweets.

"Yummm," I exclaimed, rubbing my palms together as Landon held the door open for me. The shop was small, just an L-shaped display containing goodies, but no sitting area.

"Happy Fourth of July," a woman greeted us. "What can I get you?"

"Do you have lemon cake?" I asked.

She shook her head. "No. We only have what you can see here in the display."

I squinted at the small labels under each cake, my mouth already watering. Landon pointed to an apple cake with a small American flag made out of whipped cream on top.

"This looks more homemade than the

others."

I straightened up, scandalized. "Landon Connor, are you suggesting I pass a store-bought dessert for a homemade one?"

"That's exactly what I'm suggesting."

"Wouldn't have occurred to me."

Leaning in, he whispered, "Always happy to save your honor."

I wondered what other honor-saving techniques he had in his arsenal, and if kissing me against the wall was among them, but I kept the question to myself.

"Can you take out the apple cake?" I asked the vendor. "I want to take a closer look."

My stomach rumbled when she put it on top of the glass case, right under my nose. Landon was right.

"It does look homemade... except for the whipped cream flag. It's too perfect."

He grinned. "We can mess it up. Can we have a spatula?"

The vendor was looking at us as if worried we were unhinged. "So you're buying it?"

"Yes," I assured her.

"I'm going in the back to bring you a box," she said, handing me a spatula.

Landon and I both laughed once she disappeared through the door.

He held out his hand. "I believe I should do the honors. Since it was my idea."

I pretended to consider this, tapping a finger

against my chin. I loved the boyish enthusiasm lighting up his face.

"I didn't peg you for a mischief maker." I was still playing with the spatula between my fingers, and Landon was watching my every move. I wondered if he was making plans to snatch it away from me. Then I wondered if said plans included kissing me. I bit the inside of my cheek.

"Ah, that would be a correct impression. I was a mischief maker growing up. I just started taking myself too seriously in… recent years. You have an interesting effect on me."

"Honored to claim that praise."

I was slowly piecing together an image of who Landon had been over the years, and I was glad to help him rediscover bits of himself. Handing him the spatula, I pondered the effect he had on me. Usually, I wasn't so open with people. It was as if Landon had dislodged some bricks off that wall I'd erected around myself on the day he kissed me. I wasn't sure if it was because he'd pulled me out of the rain despite my manic stubbornness, or because being in his arms had felt so perfect. He maneuvered the spatula around the flag, messing up the whipped cream until it looked like an amateur chef had poured it.

"You're good at this," I said.

The multicolored cream on the edge of the spatula was beckoning to me. Which was why I was appalled when Landon brought it to his mouth without even offering it to me.

"Hey!" I gripped his hand after he'd had just one lick. "I want some of that too."

"You'll have to fight me on this, Maddie, because it's so good, I don't plan to leave you even a lick of it." He took another swipe. "Come to think of it, Val might not buy it that you made this. It tastes too good."

The nerve of him! That was it. I refused to be called out on my atrocious baking skills while he licked the spatula clean. I lunged at him, but he held his arm up, out of my reach. I was debating how ridiculous I'd look jumping up when I realized I didn't have to. His armpit was ready to be tickled. He was wearing a rather thick cotton polo shirt, and the fabric was covering the sensitive area, but I was confident I could do some damage anyway. Landon shrieked when I ran my fingers over his armpit, his entire body coiling forward. He jerked his arm down, but then quickly raised it again. Damn, his reflexes were too good.

"You know how to play," he teased.

"You're standing between a woman and her whipped cream, Landon. That's a dangerous place to be."

"How dangerous?"

Lowering the spatula, he offered it to me. And then watched as I licked the frosting off. I went up in flames when I realized his mouth had been on it moments before. I didn't know who leaned forward first, but suddenly his mouth was on mine and we were kissing like there was no tomorrow. He brought a hand to the small of my back, pressing me against him. I relished the contact, wanted even more. I didn't want to let go. I wanted him to kiss me for hours. I hoped he planned to do that tonight after the fireworks. Or during the fireworks. I didn't mind, really.

"Ahem." The sound reached me as if through a haze, but it was a while until I realized it was the vendor clearing her throat. Landon and I stepped apart.

"Is the cake ready for packing?" she asked.

"Yes," Landon and I answered at the same time. We watched in silence as she packed, then left after I paid. Landon's phone buzzed when we stepped onto the street. He pulled it out, frowned, then shoved it back in.

"That looks like trouble," I said.

"The partnership isn't going as smoothly as it should."

"Why not?"

"The owner of the other company keeps going back on points we'd already agreed upon."

"Negotiations are your strong suit, though."

"Yeah, but negotiations were supposed to be over. That's why I took this vacation. I'm not looking forward to going back to deal with stuff I've already spent months on. It's a waste of everyone's time." He shook his head, smiled. "But I don't want to waste my time *now* thinking about it."

"Wow. Who are you and what have you done with Landon Connor?"

"I think the more appropriate question is what have *you* done to me?"

Me? I could take credit for this? He definitely looked more relaxed than the evening he'd arrived, or even the next day, when having free time seemed to make him uncomfortable.

"I can't wait for this evening," he said, bringing a hand to my waist, tucking me into him. I warmed up all over. After having had his mouth on me, I was sure my body would combust if he kept touching me. But he seemed to have no plans to let me go. And I didn't make any attempt to wiggle out because he felt amazing against me. I could get used to this, which I absolutely couldn't do. I looked at the cake I was carrying and sighed. I wasn't so sure my heart was safe.

Chapter Thirteen
Landon

In the time I'd been away, my brothers had already set up a bonfire, where everyone was welcome to skewer meat, or s'mores, or whatever else they wanted. We'd brought the picnic table and benches from the front yard to the back, and all the plastic chairs Val kept in storage for outdoor parties.

I loved these gatherings. In San Jose, I often joined my cousins. Celebrations with the Bennetts were fun. There were nine siblings. All of them were married and most had kids, so it was always a full house. I was particularly close to Sebastian, the oldest cousin. He was the founder of Bennett Enterprises— the most successful jewelry company in America. I valued his business knowledge. But as much as I loved the Bennett gatherings, nothing beat being with my siblings.

"Okay, I couldn't help myself and stole a bite of the apple cake from the fridge," Val exclaimed as I passed her and Maddie. "I need that recipe."

"Oh, it's… I don't know it by heart," Maddie mumbled. We'd told Val that Maddie had baked the cake.

I headed to Jace, who was roasting chorizo on

the bonfire. I took another skewer and followed his lead. Mid roasting, I snapped my head up and searched for Maddie… and found her sitting next to Will at the picnic table. He had an arm around her shoulders. She didn't attempt to push it away. In fact, she seemed comfortable, almost as if they were… familiar with each other. My throat tightened, jealousy coiling inside me, twisting my guts. I couldn't believe I was jealous of my own brother. One hand was on her arm, the other around her shoulder. Time to break up that party. I handed the skewer to Jace and walked over to Will and Maddie. I glared at my brother, and he had the good sense to take his hands off Maddie. He gave me a cat-got-the-cream grin before he joined Jace at the bonfire.

"You two ever gone out?" I asked Maddie without further ado. Her eyebrows shot up to her hairline as she stood up, looking around. My sisters were far enough away not to be within earshot.

"You're seriously asking that?"

"Yeah."

She narrowed her eyes. "You're jealous of your brother?"

"Apparently so."

Maddie bit back a smile. "Will *does* have that whole hot-cop thing going on."

I cleared my throat. She pointed at me.

"Did you just growl?"

"Maddie," I said warningly.

She gave in to that smile now. "You *did* growl. Wow. That was *hot*. Relax, Landon. I like a man who can rock a set of cuff links. Cuffs, on the other hand, aren't really my thing." She looked past me, frowning. "Val and Lori are looking at us."

"They're probably having a blast trying to read our body language."

"Did you all have spy training or something?"

"Sort of. We cut our teeth on spying on each other to report to our parents."

"Who was spying on whom? Were there teams?"

I didn't miss a beat. "Teams changed according to interests."

Hailey stepped up to us, looped an arm around Maddie's waist. "Maddie, I need you. Val and Lori are teaming up against me, and I need someone on my side." She turned to me and informed me, "We're discussing shoes. Pumps versus peep toes."

I grimaced. "I'll steer clear of you."

"You do that." Leaning closer to Maddie, she whispered loud enough for me to hear, "Last time he decided to contribute to our shoe conversation, he proclaimed they all look the same to him."

Maddie gasped. "He did not."

As Maddie and Hailey joined the rest of my sisters, I headed to the bonfire to my brothers.

"Landon, you just lost me five bucks," Jace said, then turned to Will. "He really does like her."

Will grinned. "I knew it."

I stared between the two of them. "What's going on?"

"I had a hunch you liked Maddie. Jace

disagreed. Thank you for proving me right." He turned his attention to Jace again. "He turned green with jealousy, I'd say."

"He was choking on it," Jace continued.

"You made a bet?" I asked.

"Gee, you're slow today," Will said. "Yep. You do remember what a bet is, right? You used to bet with us all the time."

I did. It was the most surefire way to motivate him to do something he didn't want to do, to help him get out of his comfort zone.

Jace took a bite out of his chorizo. "We should fly out to San Jose more often. He's losing his touch without us around to give him a hard time."

"All that trouble just to give me shit? You can do that via FaceTime."

Jace pinched his nose, as if considering it. Will shook his head. "Impact's better if we do it in person. But seriously, you should listen to our advice from time to time. You raised us to be well-adjusted individuals."

"It's like listening to your younger self," Jace added helpfully.

Hailey walked up to us, rubbing her belly. "Maddie is a deserter. She sided with Val and Lori on the shoe debacle. Mmm, fire looks ready for roasting some goodies. Will any of you tell on me if I start with some marshmallows?"

I pointed to our nephew, who was loading his plate at the buffet table we'd set up a few feet away from the fire. "After Lori gave Milo an earful about doing the exact same thing?"

"You're right. She'll scalp me." Hailey looked at the skewers in my brothers' hands, then narrowed her eyes as she took in our expressions. "Will, Jace! You've been messing with him."

Jace nodded. "That's our job."

"Stop it or he'll visit us even less." Hooking an arm around mine, she nudged me. "Do you want to go to the buffet with me?"

"I thought you'd never ask."

We went to the buffet, and I loaded my plate with steak, guacamole, and Val's famous veggie burger with quinoa buns. There were so many different dishes that the blend of spices caused an aroma overload.

"Let me guess. Tuna salad is your dish?" Hailey asked.

I schooled my features in a serious expression. "Yes. Fish is healthy. Salad's healthy."

"Really, Landon?"

I shrugged as we made our way to the plastic chairs, which were far enough from the picnic table that I couldn't overhear the conversation between Maddie, Val, and Lori. Milo had joined my brothers at the bonfire.

"Your tuna salad is not as bad as I remember. Sad you haven't expanded your range, though," Hailey said.

"Cooking's never been my forte."

"Oh, you don't need to remind me. We'd all make contingency plans when it was your turn to cook. They mostly consisted of stuffing our faces with sweets when Val wasn't looking."

"Ouch! Some things I don't need to know, Hailey. I was really making an effort there."

Her face fell. "I'm sorry! I didn't mean to sound ungrateful. I know you were doing your best, and you were doing great. I just—"

Chuckling, I held up a hand. "I was messing with you. I knew my cooking was shit, but I didn't want to leave it up to Val and Will all the time."

"Still, that wasn't a nice thing to say."

I kissed her forehead. "We're good, kiddo."

"So, what did Will and Jace do to mess with you?"

"Just the usual."

"They went ahead with that bet, didn't they? I told them not to."

Was everyone in the family five steps ahead of me? I bit into the veggie burger.

"But it worked, huh?" she asked.

"Oh, there was a purpose to it?"

"Well… thinking their territory is under threat usually makes alphas react."

"Territory?"

She waved her hand away. "It's a figure of speech."

I continued to chew on my burger, aware that Hailey was nearing exasperation waiting for me to talk.

"We all want you to be happy, Landon. It might be easier than you think… if you tried. You're not really trying, though."

"We're really having this conversation?"

"Hey! I'm eating your tuna salad. The least you can do is listen to me."

I inspected her plate, noticing the careful way in which she'd pushed my salad to one side, as if to make sure it wouldn't contaminate the rest of the food.

"It is as terrible as you remember, isn't it? You were just buttering me up."

She looked down at her plate, then smiled sheepishly. "Possibly. So, we noticed you've been spending time with Maddie."

"You've all talked about this?"

"We simply exchanged information," she said with a straight face. "And my analytical mind immediately saw a pattern. So, care to explain yourself? I'm here. You'd better take my amazing sisterly advice."

"I can't stay away from her." I knew Maddie deserved more than I could offer her, but I still couldn't stay away. "We're going out tonight."

"That's so great, Landon." Hailey sighed, but instead of dishing *sisterly advice*, her gaze followed Val as she moved from the picnic table to the buffet, and she said, "Is it just me or does Val look like she's carrying a hundred-pound weight on her shoulders?"

"She's got an important meeting tomorrow," I explained. Val had told me that she'd try her best to relax today, and she'd go into the office early tomorrow to go through her pitch one last time. I could relate to the worrying. I had a partnership going from bad to worse waiting for me in San Jose, but I was determined to enjoy these last few days here.

"I know. But it's the Fourth of July. I love how Val preaches to you all about how you should relax on your vacation, and she's just as bad. I'm going to try to get her to relax. But don't think you're off the hook," she said.

"Wasn't dreaming of it."

I spent the afternoon chatting about everything and nothing with my family, the way we always did when we got together. Maddie fit in so well that I couldn't help but wonder what it would be like if she was part of my life permanently. I had a hard time keeping my hands off her. Every time she was within my reach, I touched her. Christ, I needed to be alone with her.

When the sun began to set, she headed to the bonfire, skewering marshmallows and holding them over the flame. I didn't take my eyes off her, and every few seconds, she glanced my way, which might have something to do with all her marshmallows melting off their stick. I watched her melt off six before heading to her.

"You're distracting me," she said.

"How is it my fault?" I challenged.

"You sit there, looking at me, and looking all... *you*."

She stared at me like I was supposed to understand what she meant. I didn't, but she was adorable, all flustered.

"Here, I'll show you how to get it just right."

She impaled another marshmallow on the skewer and I gripped her hand, guiding the marshmallow over the fire.

"Keep turning it so the flames don't burn one spot constantly."

"Okay." She sounded breathless. I trailed my fingers over her bare forearm and felt her shudder against me.

"I love your skin, Maddie."

"Landon... is this okay?" she asked, moving her hands the way I'd explained. "Am I doing it right?"

A vision popped into my head: Maddie spread-eagled on a bed, touching herself at my command, following my instructions to a T, those gorgeous eyes looking straight at me when she'd double-check if she was doing it just the way I wanted.

"Yeah. You're doing it just right. We need the right heat point."

"Are we still talking about marshmallows?"

I grinned. "I am. You weren't?"

She became even more flustered.

"Whatever you were imagining, it's nothing compared to how good I'll make tonight for you. That's a promise, Maddie." Her cheeks were tinted red as I moved the skewer out of the fire. The marshmallow was roasted to perfection.

"We should get going if we want to see those

fireworks," I said as she blew cold air over the marshmallow.

"Let's do that. But we have to stop by my house first. I want to change."

"As you wish, Ms. Jennings."

Chapter Fourteen
Maddie

I couldn't believe Landon was in my living room. Through the cracked door of my bedroom, I could hear him moving around, pacing. My heart rate picked up every time I thought he was coming closer. I'd wanted to change because I'd gotten all sweaty from being near the fire. I inspected my dress in the floor-length mirror. Was this enough? Was it too much? It reached down to my knees, hugged my waist nicely, and ended in a heart-shaped trim over my chest, showing a smidge of cleavage. Spaghetti straps ran over my shoulders. I couldn't believe I was fretting so much over an outfit. Having Landon in my living room was messing with my mind.

Rubbing my hands, I tried maneuvering my zipper again. When I'd tried to zip it earlier, it got stuck in the middle of my back.

"Come on," I urged, pulling and pushing, and pulling some more. It didn't budge. I debated just walking out like this, but one glance at my back in the mirror confirmed my suspicion that I couldn't pull off edgy. I'd just look... unzipped.

I tried unlocking the zipper some more, crying out in frustration. A knock at my partially open door made me jump.

"Everything okay, Maddie?"

"Zipper's stuck," I muttered through gritted teeth, red in the face from the effort. "I give up. Can you help?"

I sucked in a breath when he stepped inside. His presence seemed to fill the entire room. I immediately became conscious of the small space, the simple white furniture. I imagined he was used to luxury.

"If you can't zip it up, try in the other direction so I can at least change."

Landon stepped behind me. I was still in front of the mirror, so I could see his expression of intense concentration as he worked my zipper. It looked hot as all get-out. Everything about him was just so masculine—the set of his jaw, the angle of his cheekbones. Inwardly, I was clenching and contracting every muscle, feeling every cell light up as his fingers moved on my spine, then touched the back of my neck, as he pulled at the fabric. Then they brushed down my spine again.

Ziiiiiiip.

The zipper finally budged, only not upward. Landon had pulled at it with such force, that the momentum carried the movement a long way down, so now my entire ass was on display, the tip of Landon's thumb resting on one cheek.

I sucked in a breath. He groaned—a deep, primal sound that weakened my knees.

"You're so beautiful, Maddie. So beautiful."

In the mirror, I could see him looking down at my ass. When he snapped his gaze up to mine, I saw the feral glint in his eyes, the way his Adam's apple dipped on a swallow. I knew we wouldn't be leaving my bedroom tonight.

He brought his other hand to my shoulder, brushing my hair away from my neck. I instinctively tilted my head to the other side, giving him better access. I needed his lips on me, his touch. I craved it so much that I felt I was going to break out of my skin.

He kissed my neck, and my pulse skittered.

"I want you so much, Maddie." His voice shook, as if he was using all his restraint to keep from ravishing me and couldn't spare even an ounce of it to control his voice. "I wanted to talk first, but... I want you too much. I want to taste you. All of you. I want to make you moan my name when I'm buried inside you. I want to feel you come around me."

Ohmygod.

"We can talk tomorrow," I whispered.

I didn't even want to think about tomorrow. Right now, no reason was good enough to pass up the deliciousness that was Landon Connor.

"Tomorrow," he repeated. And then he slipped his fingers under the spaghetti straps and pushed my dress down. My bra went next, landing at my feet with a soft thump. I was naked except for my thong. Usually, standing in front of a mirror brought on self-conscious thoughts, but seeing the desire in Landon's expression chased away any self-doubt. He draped those strong arms around me, one hand flicking my nipples, the other traveling south, slipping into my thong.

"Oh, God!"

He ran his middle finger up and down my slit slowly. Up, and down... up again, teasing my clit... down again. He was driving me crazy. I pushed back on reflex and felt through his jeans that he was hard.

"I'll make you scream my name tonight, Maddie. Right here, in your bedroom."

"I already did. After our first kiss, when I came home...," I confessed, the words feeling deliciously sinful.

He bit on my earlobe, then licked that spot. "You made yourself come, thinking about me?"

I became slick between my legs at his dirty words.

"Yes."

"I did that the night we danced." His voice had become raspier. "I started touching myself while we were still talking on the phone." He started circling my clit faster, pressing harder. I writhed against him, feeling my nerve endings dance with pleasure already.

"I will make you come like this, Maddie."

It was too much, feeling his erection push along the crack between my cheeks, his dirty words in my ear, his fingers on my nipple, and my clit....

I came so fast and hard that my breath was knocked out of me. My entire back arched, and for a moment I was sure I'd crumple to the floor, but

Landon held me until I rode out my climax. I'd barely regained my breath when he lowered himself to his knees behind me, pushing my thong down.

"Step out of them, Maddie. Then put your hands at the edge of the mirror and spread your legs for me. I want to taste you."

I leaned slightly forward, bracing my hands on the wooden frame of the mirror. Through my parted legs, I saw Landon bring his mouth closer to my center. I cried out at the first swipe of tongue.

"Landon!"

He licked me until I went up on my toes, no longer able to control the energy coursing through me. Watching us in the mirror magnified every sensation. Then his face disappeared from between my legs. I barely had time to wonder what would come next when he parted my cheeks and drew his tongue between them. I gripped the frame so tightly I was surprised the wood didn't crumble.

Then he kissed each of my ass cheeks, rose to his feet, and spun me around. Through the haze of lust, the only thing I could concentrate on was getting him naked. Up with his shirt, down with his pants and boxers. The man was a work of art. His muscles were even more defined, more sculpted than I'd imagined. And I'd spent a lot of time imagining.

"Maddie, I don't have condoms with me."

"I have some. I'll be right back."

I went to my bathroom and found an unopened box in cabinet. I checked the package for an expiration date, because I'd had it for months, but didn't find anything. Whatever. They'd have to do.

When I returned to my room, Landon was standing at the edge of my bed, touching himself.

I sat on the bed facing him, ripping the foil of the condom. But before I sheathed him, I took him in my mouth, going down as much as I could.

"Maddie! Maddie!"

He fisted my hair, moving my head up and down his length exactly twice before pulling out.

"Lie on your back," he said.

We rolled the condom on his erection together, and then I crawled to the center of my bed, lying on my back.

Landon moved on top of me, settling between my legs. He didn't push inside me, though. Instead, he cupped my face and kissed me so tenderly that I nearly cried from the beauty of it. After all our dirty confessions, his sweet exploration of my mouth was unexpected. He pushed inside me slowly. Even though I was sopping wet, he was so thick that I needed time to adjust. He rubbed just the head of his cock inside me, until I cried out for him.

"Landon, I need you all the way inside. Please."

He obliged, sliding inside me to the hilt. My inner muscles twitched and pulsed as he stretched me, adjusting.

"You feel so perfect," he said.

He wrapped his arms around me, resting his head in the crook of my neck. Emotion welled up in my chest, and I was shaking with the effort of containing it. When I realized that his chest was shaking too, I ran my hands down his arms, my heels on the back of his legs, needing to touch as much of him as possible. Keeping me tightly to him, he started driving in and out, every thrust deeper and faster. I thought he might split me in half. Then he changed the position, moving his arms away. On one, he pushed himself slightly up, the other he slipped between us.

"Landon!" I gasped as he took one of my nipples in his mouth, then the other. I missed the full-frontal contact, but I loved his tongue around my nipple, his thumb on my clit. It was all becoming too much again. Tension was building inside me, spurred by his tongue, his fingers, his cock.

I dug my heels in the mattress, lifting my ass up and meeting his thrusts with fervor, until my muscles were burning.

"Fuuuuuck!" He widened inside me, and the realization that he was about to come sent me right over the edge. I cried out, bracing my hands on his shoulders, writhing until he climaxed too.

We lay like that, entwined in all ways, wrapped up in each other until our pulses returned to normal.

"Are you okay?" he whispered. I nodded, still lost in him. He was cradling me in his arms, peppering my neck with kisses. "I didn't mean to be so rough."

"I loved it."

He cradled me even closer. We were both sweaty, but I loved the closeness, the way he held me as if I was so precious to him that he couldn't let go.

Emotions engulfed me again, and all I could do was hold on tight to him. Landon let go of me just long enough to take care of the condom, then spooned with me, flattening his chest against my back. He skimmed one big hand over my breasts, flicking my nipples. A shot of energy coursed straight between my legs. Landon didn't miss it, and he lowered his hand, nudging my thighs apart. I bit into the pillow when his thumb flicked my clit.

"I'm still tender," I whispered.

"Which means you'll come faster." He flipped me on my belly the next second. He braced his thighs at my sides, trapping me beneath him. My heartbeat pounded in my ears as he kissed up my spine, then moved over to one shoulder. His tongue traced a spot on my right shoulder blade.

"Birthmark," I whispered.

"Mmm...." He readjusted his thighs on the mattress as he trailed his mouth farther down.

"What are you doing?"

"Searching for other birthmarks."

"Will you take my word that I don't have others?"

I felt the corner of his lips lift in a smile against my lower back. "I'm a thorough man. I like to check everything myself."

I grinned into the pillow, flicking my toes against one another in excitement. Landon explored every inch of me, touching my skin almost in reverence, as if I was all that mattered to him. He kissed, and licked, and touched until I was trembling beneath him.

"I'm not done making you come tonight, Maddie. Not nearly done. I will love you all night long. I promise."

He kept his promise, loving me tenderly, then fast and hard again, until we were both spent and fell asleep together.

Chapter Fifteen
Maddie

I hid my head under a pillow when the alarm clock went off. Every inch of my body protested at the mere idea of climbing out of bed. I felt like sleeping for a week. Reaching blindly to my nightstand, I snoozed the alarm, stretching out on the entire bed.

I didn't have time to be lazy this morning, because I had to go downtown and pick up some permits for my next project before going to Val's. I should have set my alarm clock fifteen minutes earlier so I could cuddle with the man responsible for the delicious ache in my body. It took me a second to realize that Landon wasn't next to me. Wiping the haze of sleep from my eyes, I peered around. The door to the living room was open, and the smell of coffee filtered in. *Did Landon make coffee?*

I threw on a robe and headed out to my living room. Landon was standing at my kitchen island, fully dressed. He had his back to me, and I had a prime view of his ass. Now that I knew how it looked naked, I found it even more irresistible. I didn't know what to say, or how to act, but I took it as a good sign that he was here, in my kitchen. The floor creaked under my feet, and he whirled around.

"Morning, beautiful," he said.

The tension melted away from my limbs, just from hearing those two words. He had a great voice. Strong yet sweet, and somehow seemed to say, *I wouldn't bolt in the middle of the night. You're worth more than that.*

"Morning."

"I made coffee." He handed me a mug, which I took with both hands. Landon stepped closer, watching me intently as I sipped from my cup. "Let's go have breakfast, somewhere on a beach. I want to spend this day with you. The morning at least."

My insides melted. "I really want to, but I can't."

He kissed my right temple, murmuring, "Here's a little secret. I'm related to your client. I can pull strings for favors."

"I know, but I actually have an appointment to pick up some permits. It's taken ages for them to be processed, so I don't want to miss the chance."

"I can pull strings with people who aren't related to me too, you know. You need anything done, tell me."

"Thanks, you're very generous."

"You just have to say what you need, sweetheart. I can't guess that. Yet."

I sucked in a deep breath. He smelled amazing, all man. I rested my chin on his chest, peppering his Adam's apple with kisses. If it weren't for that appointment I could soak up all the deliciousness that was Landon this morning. He swung his arms around my waist, hoisting me close to him. Surrounded by him like this, I couldn't help but wonder if Landon was the kind of man who'd always be on my team.

"You have great arms," I murmured. "And a great voice."

He laughed. "I like where this is going."

"I'd go on, but I really have to hop in a shower."

"I'll see you at lunch and we'll talk some more."

"Okay. Will you bring something delicious?"

"Of course. I'll bring food. And myself."

"Whoa! You have a cocky side. I wondered when it would show up." I stepped back, folding my arms over my chest and tsking.

"You assumed I have one?" he challenged.

"Landon, be serious. Looking the way you do, and doing what you do for a living, I expected your cockiness factor to be somewhere around a million, give or take."

He grinned. "Looking the way I do?"

I grinned back. "Well, I mentioned your voice and arms. I'd rattle off the rest, but the shower is waiting for me. You have something to look forward to at lunch. Can't tell all my secrets first thing in the morning."

***

As it turned out, the few minutes I had with

Landon were the best part of the morning. The clerk in charge of signing my permits seemed to doubt I was qualified for the job.

"You're working alone, yes?" he asked. His office was small and stuffy, and he smelled like he'd worn that shirt since Christmas.

"I hire people on site for every project."

"Schools are of public interest. Are you sure your... company can handle it?"

"The scope of the project is limited. I could do it myself if necessary. And it's a private school, not a public one," I countered.

"But you still need permits from us. I need more time to look into it."

I drew in a deep breath, forcing myself to remain calm. I knew what would happen if I gave him *time*. He'd take so long that I'd never get my permits on time. I was slated to start this project right after I finished Val's. I promised my clients an all-in-one solution, and I intended to deliver.

I hadn't gotten to where I was by waiting for things to happen. I fought tooth and nail to *make* them happen. Straightening up, I smiled and laid on the charm thickly, pimping myself like there was no tomorrow. Ten minutes later, I left with my permits.

On my way to Val's, I switched on my phone. I'd turned it off during the appointment.

An unread message popped up.

Landon: Val had an accident with a drunk driver. Call when you see this.

Oh my God! I checked the time—he'd texted

an hour ago. I was too petrified to call him, or do anything except hope and pray that Val was all right. She had to be. Taking a few deep breaths, I finally called Landon. He answered immediately.

"Hey!" he said.

"Hey! How's Val doing?"

I held the wheel of my car tightly with one hand. My stomach was churning already.

"Three broken ribs, and her right leg's broken too."

"Oh no."

"She's going to be in the hospital for a night, and then she'll need to take things slow for about six weeks."

"What happened?"

"She had a big meeting today and drove to her office to prepare for it. A drunk idiot slammed into her car." His voice was so tight, I wanted to reach out through the phone and wrap my arms around him.

"You're at the hospital now?"

"I was there earlier, but I left because she asked me to attend the meeting in her place. I'm on my way there."

"You're joking, right?"

Landon laughed. "I'm not."

"How can she still be thinking about the meeting?" I hoped that meant she wasn't in too much pain.

"She's been preparing for it for a month. It's a big deal. We talked about it a few times, and I did work at the company years ago, so I know the bare bones."

"Wow."

"The meeting will last the entire day, so I can't make it to lunch. But I'd like to take you out this evening."

"Landon, you're going to have a hellish day. You don't have to take me out."

"I want to. After the meeting I'll stop by to see Val, but afterward, if you don't have plans...."

I shook my head, then realized he couldn't see me. "No plans."

"Great. I'll text you when the meeting ends."

"All right."

"That's settled, then. I'll see you tonight. I have to go over the briefing for the meeting now."

"Go get 'em. You'll knock them off their asses."

"Thanks for the vote of confidence."

"Are you wearing cuff links?" I asked, remembering he'd told me he wore those whenever he meant business.

"I am. Went home from the hospital to change."

"Pffft, you already got the deal in the bag, then. No one can resist cuff links."

"Ouch! I take back my thanks." He laughed, and I was so happy I'd managed to cheer him up despite everything going on. "I can't wait to see you tonight, Maddie."

Oh, what those words did to me. They awoke

butterflies inside me. I might have even swooned a little, though I wouldn't admit it out loud. I hadn't realized how much I'd hoped to hear them until now. Adrenaline zipped through me, and I couldn't keep my emotions in check.

"Back at you."

After I clicked off, I was grinning like a fool. I didn't want to get all dreamy and romantic, but I couldn't help it. I decided to start the day by visiting Val. I realized I didn't know which hospital she was at, so I texted Landon.

I wanted to see with my own eyes that she was okay, as much as one could be okay with three cracked ribs and a broken leg. I'd bring her a mozzarella and tomato sandwich too. On second thought, I added M&M's to the mix. As far as mood lifters went, M&M's were at the top of my list, and I had a feeling Val could use all the mood lifting she could get.

Chapter Sixteen
Landon

It was six o'clock in the evening by the time I left my sister's office. My right temple was throbbing, my mind spinning. Though I'd called Val periodically during breaks, I headed straight to the hospital to give her a blow-by-blow account of the day and to check on her.

"You look better," I said.

She was lying in bed, one leg in a cast, her torso bandaged up. Her right side had taken the brunt of the collision.

She smiled. "Oh, yes. Please lay it on thick with the charm. I really need it. I haven't seen myself in a mirror, but I can't look better than I feel, and I feel like crap. I've already been spoiled with apparently all the goodies money can buy in LA, but my twin's charm is always welcome." She pointed to the hospital table next to her. It was buried under mountains of sweets and food. She sighed. "My head feels messed up. Tried to read some e-mails today and nearly got sick."

The doctors said she had a concussion, which meant she'd be unable to focus on reading for some time, plus she'd get headaches and become tired quicker, but ultimately there would be no permanent damage.

"This is a disaster," she said.

"It could have been worse," I said quietly. When Will had called, he'd explained everything in one breath. But in the seconds it took him to add, "It's not life-threatening" after saying, "A drunk driver hit her car," my mind had already jumped to the worst-case scenario. I blamed the negativity on having lost so many people already: our parents, Rachel. The thought of losing Val had paralyzed me.

"I know, Landon. We've been through enough that I can appreciate I'm alive. But the timing sucks. Not that there's any good time to be sick, but now with the deal…. Thank you for meeting with them today." She fiddled with her cover, and I sat on the bed next to her good leg. "They're going to jump ship. I could hear it in their voices, even if they didn't say it out loud."

I'd put her on loudspeaker during a few crucial moments, and I couldn't lie to my sister.

"I had that impression too. They think your team won't prioritize the project with you in recovery mode for six weeks."

"And they're right. I might be able to work from home once the headache subsides, but it's not the same thing. A new project requires my presence at the office, to motivate and lead the team. This project was my baby. I was going to oversee the entire development of the line. If I were them, I'd jump ship too."

She shifted her good leg a little to the right, then back where it was.

"I want to run an idea by you," I said.

Val stopped in the act of rearranging her leg. "I'm all ears."

"I could stick around for the next six weeks, get the project rolling, at least until your cast comes off. I know the business inside out. You've streamlined many processes, but I'm a fast learner. I think if we bring this offer to the table, it'll swing things in your favor."

Val looked too stunned to answer, which was saying something, because nothing stunned her into silence.

"Are you sure?" she asked finally. "Can you take so much time off?"

"I have an acting CEO. He's gonna have to up his acting. And I won't be taking time off anymore, just working remotely."

Adam would give me hell, but I didn't care. I'd thought about this nonstop since I realized Val's deal would be slipping through her hands. I was needed here more than in San Jose.

"Landon, are you sure?"

"Yes. We can call Livingston right now and make the offer."

She nodded vigorously, then winced. I whipped my phone out and dialed Livingston's number, putting him on loudspeaker. The conversation lasted less than five minutes. He bought it hook, line, and sinker.

"I'd hug you right now, but I can't," Val said after the line went static. "Thank you, thank you, thank you. You're my hero."

She reached with her left arm to the cornucopia of sweets, taking a bag of M&M's from its midst. Then she narrowed her eyes at me, as if she just realized something.

"Wait a minute. Is your heroic decision one hundred percent about me? Or does Maddie have something to do with it?"

I grinned, stealing some M&M's. "Does it make me less of a hero if I answer yes to the second question?"

Val threw her head back, laughing, then winced, touching her ribs. "I knew it. Oh, Landon, what am I going to do with you?"

"I'm a grown man, munchkin. Don't need your blessing."

"Just as good. I'm not in the habit of dishing blessings. Kicks in the ass, on the other hand... I'll start right away with those once my leg's out of the cast."

"Good to know."

"I'd throw a pillow at you if I could move." That was Val's way of expressing her joy—and it had annoyed the hell out of me for as long as I could remember.

"I'd help you move, but can't, since the pillow would be aimed at me. Conflict of interests and all that."

"You big oaf. I'm so happy for you. I thought

something was going on, but I didn't want to raise my hopes up too much. Just… be careful, okay? You two still have separate lives at the end of the day."

My smile fell. "I know."

"Did you talk to Maddie about this? Does she know you're staying longer?"

"No, but I'm meeting her after I leave here."

"Last night, did you two—"

"I'm not discussing my sex life with you, sister."

Val grinned like a Cheshire cat, holding up the M&M's bag. "I'll take that admission. She brought me these this morning. Had this glow about her, kept smiling. Now I know why. And you should go. You've gone above and beyond your brotherly duty for today. Go have some fun."

"You sure I can't do anything else?"

"I'm sure. And Jace texted me to say he'll be dropping by. I bet he'll be here within ten minutes."

I kissed Val's forehead, then let myself out of the room. Knowing I was the reason for Maddie's smile made me happy. My thoughts had drifted to her so often today that I phased out of the meeting a few times.

I ran into Jace at the end of the corridor, which was deserted otherwise.

"Landon, hey! How did the meeting go? Val was stressed about it."

"It went about as good as it could have gone without her there. I've decided to stay in LA until her cast comes off, oversee the project for her."

"You've.... You can do that? With the whole partnership going on in San Jose?"

"I'll manage. And I'll see about arranging for her to be comfortable at home. She'll need help moving, so maybe a live-in nurse—"

"I'm going to handle that, Landon. There's no stopping you when you go into doing-shit mode." He gave me a shit-eating grin. "Take a breather. You don't have to do everything by yourself. Focus on the business, leave the rest to us. Now, elevator's behind me. Get in before you start discussing the details with me."

I grinned back, because he was right. We had a lot of details to go through, but we could deal with all that in the morning. Right now, I needed to see Maddie.

Chapter Seventeen
Maddie

I looked in the mirror for the millionth time, wondering if my outfit was appropriate. Landon had texted me earlier, saying he'd come straight to my house after he visited Val. Considering I had no idea what the plan was for the evening, I'd opted for a dark green top, which fit me snugly with straps crisscrossing on my upper back, and a black skirt that flowed to my knees.

When I heard a car pull in front of my house, I hurried to the entrance, skidded on the tiles, and lost my balance, nearly pelting headfirst into the front door. *Whoops.*

Straightening up, I pushed my hair out of my face and opened the door. My tongue stuck to the roof of my mouth as I took Landon in.

Sweet heavens.

His suit had to be custom-made. There was no other way it could fit him so perfectly over his shoulders and muscular arms yet be tapered at the waist.

He'd meant it when he'd said the suits he wore over the past week were business casual. This... this wasn't casual. He looked one hundred percent the CEO he was, and one thousand percent handsome. Landon had dressed to impress. And while I knew he'd put the suit on for the meeting and not for me, well… count me impressed.

It wasn't his suit that spurred butterflies in my stomach, though, nor his smile. He was carrying a bouquet of orange lilies and roses.

"I didn't know what your favorite flowers were, but these looked beautiful."

When I took them from him, my fingertips brushed his nails, but the small contact was enough to make my skin tingle.

"Are you going to invite me in?" A lazy smile spread on his face.

"Yeah, of course. Come in. I'll put these in a vase. Thank you so much. They're gorgeous."

My voice sounded strange even to my own ears. A little high-pitched, but also gruff. I busied myself finding a vase, which took some time, because I was too scatterbrained to focus. When I finally did find it and held it up under the running faucet, I felt Landon come up behind me.

"Maddie, did I read this wrong? Do you not want me here?"

In the time it took me to inhale, he moved his hand from the edge of the sink to my waist, as if he couldn't help touching me, even though he wasn't sure if he should.

"No, no, I want you here. I do." I placed the vase on the counter, arranged the bouquet in it. Only then did I turn around to face him. I didn't like the creases on his forehead, much less that I'd put them there.

"I'm sorry. It's just... been a while since I received flowers. They make me feel special."

He studied me, bringing a hand to my face, caressing my cheek with the back of his fingers.

"You are special to me, Maddie. It's been a while since I bought flowers, but I wanted to do this for you. I want so many things with you. Buy you flowers, take you out, make you laugh."

His words reached so deep inside me, I knew they'd take root there and I wouldn't be able to forget them after he left. But I didn't care about that. All I cared about was right now. A little bit of time with Landon was better than no time with Landon.

"I like the sound of that," I whispered. He was close enough for me to smell his body wash. I touched my nose to his Adam's apple, and his grip on my waist tightened. He smelled so good. I wanted to lick every morsel of skin I could find. But I pulled away, hungering even more for his words. His scent and general sexiness were a feast for my senses. But his words went straight to my heart, and I wanted more.

"I went to see Val after the meeting."

"How is she?"

He smiled. "Enjoying your M&M's. Thanks for stopping by to visit her."

I smiled back. "I thought I'd make myself useful. How did the meeting go?"

"So-so."

I feigned shock. "The cuff links failed you? Well, if it's any consolation, they totally work on me. Both my knees are Jell-O, and it's entirely their fault."

They were sterling silver with some sort of black pattern in the center. And damn they were potent.

His smile widened, transforming his entire expression. "All their doing, huh? I don't get any credit?"

"Maybe a tiny bit."

In demonstration, I held my thumb and forefinger so close to each other they almost touched.

Landon set his hands at my side, trapping me. Our noses were in sniffing distance. Our mouths in kissing distance. And still he didn't kiss me.

"You were saying about the meeting?" I prompted when the tension was so thick, I felt my nipples pebble.

"They weren't happy to hear about Val. Not out of concern for her well-being, but because she wouldn't be able to oversee the project herself. I offered to manage it myself until Val feels better. It'll probably take a month to six weeks until she can resume her normal activities."

"You're not leaving next week anymore?"

I felt the change in him before he pulled away. His jaw went rigid.

"You sound disappointed."

I had the social skills of a doorknob when I was surprised or nervous. "Of course I'm not disappointed. I'm happy you're staying longer. You just took me by surprise. That's a really nice thing you're doing for your sister." Nice was putting it mildly. I didn't know anyone who'd do that. I looked at Landon with renewed admiration. "What did Val say?"

The corners of his lips twitched. "That I'm her hero. Then went on to question said heroism, wondering if she's the only reason I'm staying."

Does he mean what I think he means?

"What did you tell her?"

I rested my hands behind my back, flicking my thumbs against the counter.

"That those sounds you made last night might have swayed my decision too," he said.

"You did not tell her that!"

Launching forward, I made to pinch his stomach, but he caught my wrist. I brought my other hand forward. Rookie mistake! He trapped that one too. Cuffing both my wrists in one hand, he brought them above my head, pinning them against the cabinet.

I sucked in a breath as Landon's gaze settled on my lips. He skimmed his free hand under my top, slipped it under my bra. He drew his thumb languidly on the underside of my breast until my whole back arched. When he flicked the thumb over my nipple, I went up to my toes, desperate for his mouth. We kissed until we were both out of breath.

My kitchen had never seen such erotic action. I almost expected the legs of the wooden table to buckle under the weight of the sexual tension. My legs certainly felt like they'd give way any moment.

He let go of my hands, cupping my face with both hands, thumbs resting on my cheeks, fingers splayed on my neck. He was holding me like I was precious to him. So much energy coursed through me that I couldn't stay put. I kept fidgeting.

"I have one rule, Landon. You're not allowed to make me fall in love with you."

"You have nothing to worry about." He swallowed, his Adam's apple dipping low in his throat. "I don't think I know how to do love anymore."

"We're safe, then."

"Are we?" He smiled. "With you, I want things I haven't allowed myself to want in years, Maddie."

I traced the contour of his jaw, wondering if I should keep quiet, but decided not to. "What do you mean, you haven't *allowed* yourself to want things?"

His eyes grew sad. "Recovering after Rachel died wasn't easy. I felt lost and vulnerable, and for a long time, I figured it was safer not to get too close to anyone. It was safer not to want certain things."

"Oh, Landon."

The sadness in his gaze melted into playfulness. "But I want to spend more time with you, Maddie. I want to get to know you. All of you."

My entire body buzzed at the thought of more time with Landon, even as I knew I was endangering my heart. I hadn't been sure I could keep my heart safe when I thought I only had a few days with Landon. But a few weeks?

New resolution: I wouldn't think about the future. I had to admit, it was liberating to just live in the present without worrying how my current actions would impact the future.

If I eat a second slice of bacon, will it go straight to my hips or my belly? If I order the cheaper soap, will it dry my skin? If I spend more time with Landon, will I fall in love with him? See... those kinds of questions. They took the joy out of the moment. Some of them had merit, sure, but they were also killjoys.

"I'm taking you out on a date," he announced, shoving both hands in his pockets, as if *not* touching me required effort and he was determined to succeed. Ah, but our goals were at odds, because I *wanted* to be touched, and kissed, and ravished.

"Hmm... this is how you want to go out with me? Wearing this lovely suit and cuff links? This will make women everywhere swoon. I'm doing them a favor by keeping you all for me. They won't know what they're missing. Plus, traffic is a nightmare at this time."

His gaze snapped fire, and a smile danced on his lips. I had the feeling he saw right through my attempt to seduce him. In retrospect, it had been a little lousy. Traffic, really?

"Make no mistake, Maddie, when we come back, I'm going to sink so deep inside you that you'll forget your own name. But right now, I want to spend some time with you outside the bedroom.

Anything against that?"

"No." I was a little breathless, a lot hot. He was charming me like it was his job. Was he even aware of that? "But for the record, I didn't just have naked activities in mind when I suggested we stay in. I could take care of you. After the day you had, you could use it."

His eyes softened and he leaned in, kissing the corner of my lips. After a beat, he said, "You can take care of me anytime you want, Maddie. I'd like that. But tonight, *I* am taking care of *you*. So let's go."

As I caught a glimpse of the flowers, a small voice at the back of my mind whispered that it would be very hard not to fall in love with Landon. I quieted the voice as he took my hand, whisking me out of the house for an evening of debauchery.

Chapter Eighteen
Maddie

Landon knew how to wine and dine a woman. He'd brought me to the Four Seasons Hotel in Beverly Hills. They had an elegant restaurant set up on the patio, with twinkle lights hanging everywhere. I was soaking it all in, but truthfully, the man sitting across from me was monopolizing my attention.

"You, sir, have excellent taste," I informed him as I took a sip of my red wine, a shiraz. It went well with my steak. "How hard will it be, juggling Val's project and your merger?"

He frowned. "Very hard. I keep trying to map out a plan of attack so I can give both projects the attention they need, but it's going to be hellish."

"Well, you can count on me for helping you relax," I declared. His frown melted into a smile.

"How do you plan to do that?"

"I don't know yet, but I'm gonna draw up a serious plan."

I was going to take good care of him. So good that he wouldn't want to let me go. *Whoops*. Where had that thought come from? I gave my shiraz the evil eye.

"How long are you still going to work on

Val's yard?" he asked.

"Three weeks. Then I'm landscaping a school yard. It'll be less complicated than Val's, because it doesn't involve terracing. I'm looking forward to it."

"A school? I thought you said you liked working on residential projects."

I was pleased he remembered that little detail.

"I do, but I couldn't pass up this opportunity. It's for a private school, and if the parents like what they see, that might lead to other projects."

"Smart. Very smart."

"Thanks. That's the project I needed those permits for."

"So you handle everything? Permits, design, implementation?"

"Yes. I do work with subcontractors, though. For example, Val wants stone steps, and I'm bringing in a mason for that. If the soil requires more than the standard irrigation system, I bring in a company specializing in that. But I do try to do as much as possible myself. I'll hire a permanent staff as soon as Grace finishes law school."

"You're an amazing woman, Maddie Jennings."

"Why, thank you, Mr. Connor."

"You're hardworking, and you're devoted to your sister, two qualities I admire." He put his hand over mine on the table, squeezing lightly. "I admire everything about you."

"Now you're making me blush."

"I love it when your cheeks go all red." His

voice was lower, breathier, and it sent my mind right into the gutter.

"Landon! We're halfway through dinner. You can't make me blush already. I believe we were talking about my business."

He gave me a wolfish grin. "You're right. Have you thought about partnering with one of the subcontractors you use more often? You wouldn't have them on your payroll, but you could use the synergies."

I leaned back in my seat, playing with my wine glass. "I did think about it, but honestly, that spells headache. My ex and I had a similar arrangement. Even though we had different areas of expertise, we'd set up a company together, Eden Designs. We were sharing an office, and administrative expenses like accounting. Occasionally some of his clients used my services too. When it all went to hell, it was so much work to disentangle myself. It got messy. He fought me for every contract. The lawyer fees ate up a lot of my savings. It soured me for partnerships. I work better alone."

"Your ex was a real douchebag."

"It was weird, starting all over again. New house, new everything. Most of our friends were *his* friends, because he was from LA, so my circle of friends was suddenly very small, and meeting new people isn't easy."

"Did you think about going back to Miami?"

"No, I like it here. But when I moved to LA, I never imagined I'd have to start over twice. I hope I never have to do it again. It's exhausting."

Landon scrutinized me, but then his attention was caught by a tall man in a suit approaching us, stopping next to our table.

"Landon? I can't believe this. I didn't know you were back in LA. How long has it been?"

Landon stood up, shaking the man's hand. I stood up too.

"Stephen. Nice to see you." Pointing at me, Landon said, "This is Maddie Jennings. She's a very talented landscape architect."

Landon sounded so proud of me that I wanted to kiss him on the spot. I took in his body language, and I knew those weren't empty words. I knew it was wrong to compare Landon to my ex, but I couldn't help it. Whenever Owen introduced me to someone, he left out my occupation, and when I brought it up, he'd cringe.

"Nice to meet you, Maddie." Stephen shook my hand before focusing on Landon again. "How long are you in LA?"

"A few weeks."

"I'll call to set up a meeting. I'll leave you to enjoy your evening."

We sat again after Stephen left, finishing our steaks. Landon cradled my legs between his under the table. I loved being surrounded by him like this. After the server took away our empty plates, I rubbed my belly. "Are we having dessert? I'm dying to eat their panna cotta."

A smile played on his lips. He cradled my legs

tighter until my knees touched. "I'd rather eat you, but panna cotta will do, for now."

"You're shameless," I whispered. "You brought me out here, and now you're seducing me?"

"You're complaining?"

I opened my mouth, closed it again. "I'm hot and bothered, but I feel like I should give you an earful just because. I'm conflicted."

Without taking his eyes off me, he ordered panna cotta for both of us, then leaned forward. "How hot and bothered *are* you exactly?"

The air sizzled between us, and I considered bolting before dessert. But my stubborn side reared its head and I held my ground, even enjoying two more glasses of shiraz until we finished the panna cotta.

Landon offered me his arm when we rose to leave, and I gladly took it. I was wearing sky-high stilettos. The shoes were new and I hadn't had time to break them in, so the balls of my feet were hurting.

As we passed the row of tables, I became aware of women eye-fucking him. A lot of women.

"This is the last time you're going out with me wearing cuff links. Every woman in there wants to bang you," I whispered when we were alone in the corridor leading to the lobby.

"Bang me?" He laughed. *Oh, this amuses him, huh?* "You're a little buzzed from that wine."

"Maybe. But I know what I saw. Next time

we're going out, you're wearing some ugly sweater. A paper bag over your head would help too."

"Possessive much?"

I sucked in a breath. "I'm getting ahead of myself, sorry. I have no business being possessive."

Landon came to a halt, turning to me. He kissed me so hard, it made my mind spin. "Yes, you do. Sweetheart, the thought of you with another man drives me crazy." His eyes glinted as he ran his thumb over my lips, delicious possessiveness written all over him. "I like seeing you all worked up, but you don't have to worry about anything. You're all I want, Maddie." He kissed the corner of my mouth, whispering, "Let's go home so I can show you how much."

I'd never prayed for zero traffic more than now.

When we stepped inside my bungalow, Landon kissed me hard and walked me backward to my bedroom, until the backs of my calves hit the bed. He lowered me on it, breaking our connection. He switched on the light, remaining near the switch.

"Take off your clothes for me, Maddie."

I toed off my shoes and then climbed on the bed. I lifted the hem of my top just a little, until my belly button was visible. Landon fixed me with his gaze, as if daring me to continue. I lifted it a few inches more, as slowly as I could. He released a sharp exhale, and my hands started to shake with anticipation. Watching him watch me was a damn turn-on. I lifted it another inch, and then Landon took off his own clothes. When he was completely naked, he climbed onto the bed in front of me. He cuffed my ankles with his hands, still watching me. When I pulled off my shirt, he bit his lip. I reached under my pillow and retrieved the condom I'd hidden there... just in case.

"Unclasp your bra." Although his voice was a whisper, it still sounded like a command. I did as he said, and my breasts spilled free in front of him. Releasing one of my ankles, he reached out one arm, undid the zipper and button of my skirt, then pulled it down my legs, throwing it behind him. I felt exposed, wearing nothing but a thong. He was watching me with a lustful gaze, his eyes darting from my neck to my breasts to the triangle between my legs, then back up.

He moved over me, capturing my mouth. I sighed against his lips, my hips bucking off the bed when he cupped one breast, twisting the nipple slightly. I instinctively tried to push my thighs together. Since he was sitting right between my thighs, I merely squeezed him good. He groaned, pulling back, looking down between us. Lowering one hand, he placed his thumb right at my entrance, over the panties. A shiver of anticipation ran through my body. He dragged his thumb all the way up to my clit.

"Landon! Oh—"

He repeated the motion. I parted my thighs, giving him more access. He settled between them, lowering his head. Through a haze of lust, I felt him slide two fingers along the rim of my panties, right where my thigh met my center. I fisted the sheet when he hooked the fingers in the fabric, pushing it to one side. And then his hot mouth was on my slick flesh, and it felt so impossibly good, so impossibly intense, that I cried out shamelessly. Pushing my head up, I saw he'd lowered an arm under him. His shoulder was moving—he was touching himself. While his mouth was on me, his hand was on his erection. The sight awoke something deep inside me. Warmth billowed under my skin.

Unexpectedly, he took the thumb away from my clit, sliding his hand under my ass, lifting it up the mattress. I dug my heels in the bed, my tummy contracting as I braced myself. He sucked my clit into his mouth.

"Aaaaaah!"

My glutes stiffened, my thighs burned. My center was on fire. My entire body shook. It was as if thin, invisible threads connected my clit to every cell in my body. I thrashed and whimpered, needing my release. The tension inside me kept mounting.

The next few seconds were a little fuzzy. Landon moved, pulling away from me just as I was on the cusp. I heard him rip the package of the condom, and then he moved over me, sliding inside me as I came.

Pleasure of such intensity ripped through me that it knocked the breath out of my lungs. My inner muscles spasmed and clenched along his length. My orgasm intensified. Pleasure coursed through my entire body, making my toes curl and my fingers stretch out, almost in a spasm.

"You feel so good, Maddie. So good." His voice was an unsteady whisper, and as I came down from cloud nine, I noticed his arms were shaking slightly. He'd braced them on either side of me. Kissing my neck, he slid in and out of me. It was impossible, but I felt that with every stroke he filled me more, gave me more of himself.

"Lift your legs, wrap them around me," he said.

Blindly I hooked a leg around him, then the other, not understanding where he was going with this... until I did. As I pressed my heels on the back of his thighs, just under his ass, the angle between us changed, and he was rubbing a spot inside me he hadn't touched before. I didn't even know pleasure so intense was possible. I was putty in his hands, his body pushing mine closer to the edge with every thrust. My body strummed with tension, muscles clenching. Landon kissed me, interlacing his fingers with mine.

The next moment, my senses were overwhelmed as my entire body coiled with the orgasm. Through my own cries of pleasure, I heard Landon's and knew he was right there with me.

Chapter Nineteen
Landon

The streets were crowded on the drive to Val's house the next morning, even though it was early. The city had begun to wake up, but we made it back with enough time to spare. Maddie's crew hadn't even arrived.

"You know what? I'll bake a carrot cake for Val as a welcome home gift," Maddie said as we walked up the front porch.

"I'm gonna share a secret with you, Maddie. My sisters' telltale signs when they don't like some food. Val drinks a lot of water, so she doesn't have to eat much. Lori only takes very small bites. Hailey will say she's on a diet. So if Val didn't eat much last time…."

She shook her head. "Why didn't she just tell me she didn't like it?"

"You can't escape my siblings' flinch-inducing honesty if you share their blood. They show more tact toward the rest of the world."

"And I had to sleep with you to find out the family secret, huh?"

"Can't sell our secrets cheap."

I pulled her into my arms, kissing that sassy

smile. Then I headed upstairs to change into fresh clothes. I'd only brought two of my best suits, but I'd arrange for more to be sent from San Jose. Clothes mattered, especially when dealing with people who didn't know me. A groomed appearance set a foundation of confidence and trust, even before I introduced myself. I knew how to play that game well.

When I stepped back outside, Maddie was near the front gate, stretching her back. A sack half her size was propped on the ground next to her. She must have unloaded it from her truck all by herself. I hurried to her.

"Maddie! Wait for the guys to arrive and unload."

"Why waste the time when I can start right away?" She straightened up, making to move for the gate, but I put a hand on her waist.

"Because you'll break your back. Wait for the guys."

My voice was firm. I didn't want her to exert herself. She tilted her head to one side, pushing my hand away.

"Do you think you can give me orders just because your dick's been inside me?"

She was a spitfire. And hearing the word "dick" from her mouth turned me on.

"I'm not giving you orders. Just looking out for you."

"Right," she countered, but her expression had softened a bit. "I'm a tough girl, Landon."

"I'm not questioning that. But the laws of physics still apply to you. I'll help you unload them."

"And wrinkle this mouthwatering suit? It would completely offset the effect of the cuff links. You'll do no such thing. If you think—"

I pulled her into a kiss, eating up all her fire and sass, palming her butt and rolling her hips against mine.

I'd been semi-hard all morning, but now there was no semi about it. When I ground her against me, I could feel her nipples pebble even through her bra and work shirt. What this woman did to me was insane. My shoes sank into the earth as I scooped her up by her ass. She wound her arms around my neck, her knees pressing at my sides.

I kissed her until the sound of the front gate opening reached us. Maddie pulled back, gasping as I put her down.

"I don't want the guys to see me like this," she said.

"Why not?"

"Because I'm their boss."

I dragged my thumb across the skin around her lips, which was red from our kiss. I'd marked her as mine.

"I've messed you up," she murmured, arranging the collars of my shirt and suit. "Good luck today, Landon."

I took one of her hands and kissed her palm, holding it to my lips. I'd loved waking up next to her, feeling her warm little body next to me. I'd been cradling her in my arms and hadn't been ready to let go. I wasn't ready now either, but we had to start our day.

***

I took a cab to the office and called Adam on the way. As I'd predicted, he hated my news.

"Landon, you can't do that, man. Look, I'm sorry this is a bad time for Val, but it's not peachy around here either. Sullivan is going back on every point. He's trying to renegotiate everything, and he's aggressive. He'll have a field day when he finds out you won't be back for another six weeks."

"Adam, you're my acting CEO. Sullivan knows that."

"Yes, but I don't actually own this company, and that diminishes my decision power. Is Val's project really worth the risk of striking a bad deal with Sullivan? Or the deal falling through?"

A chill ran down my spine. Clenching my teeth, I looked out the window. I wanted to grow the company to be a force to be reckoned with. Our investors required the same. To set up the company, I'd had no choice but to take outside investment, and I'd had to give away shares in exchange. I owned 49 percent, the rest was distributed among the various investors, and they wanted larger profits. I'd brought the company as far as I possibly could have, but I couldn't bring it to the next level on my own.

I needed more funds, or a partner with access

to a wider distribution network, which was what Sullivan was bringing to the table. More funds meant an IPO or bringing in even more investors, which I didn't want because I'd have to give up even more shares and control. The partnership with Sullivan was my best option, which was why I needed the deal to go through. But this couldn't be helped.

While Adam was a close friend, he didn't understand how deep family ties went in the Connor clan. Explaining myself further wasn't going to change things, and I didn't care to do it anyway. Ultimately, I was in charge. Adam had to do what I decided.

"I'm needed here, Adam. I'm officially not on vacation anymore, so I can be contacted at any hour after today. I'm taking the time to reacquaint myself with Val's company. I can give you ten minutes right now to discuss any urgent matters."

Two things became clear within a few hours in Val's shoes. One: she was more efficient than 90 percent of the people I knew. Two: she didn't delegate jack shit. She oversaw everything from executive decisions to small operative details. Nothing escaped her sharp mind, or pen. Almost everything needed her approval.

"We need approval for the shipments—"

"The samples will arrive today. We need you in the conference room at two."

"The budget still needs changing."

"When is Val coming back?"

"She hasn't replied to our e-mails. That hasn't—"

I jumped in. "And she won't be replying for the time being."

I felt like I was on a baseball field, fielding balls left and right, with several hitting me straight in the face while I was busy with others. Val's daily to-do list was busy enough for two people to hack away at it until their eyes watered. In the rare moments when I was alone in the office, I went over the budget for the department store line, but the constant interruptions made it impossible to concentrate. Val led an open-door policy I did not appreciate.

Her assistant stepped in just as I'd started making notes.

"Mr. Connor, we need you down in shipping. We—"

"No."

"I'm sorry?"

"Look—Angelica, that's your name, right?"

"Yeah."

"I will not be available for the next two hours."

Her face drained of color. "But—"

"No ifs or buts. I will be here in the office, but I don't want anyone to disturb me."

"Val called."

Jesus. My sister was still in the hospital.

"Right. Until I tell you differently, you will not be taking my sister's calls. I will also need you to prepare a briefing for me. Include every major topic along the value chain."

Angelica looked at me like I was mad, but she nodded and left the office. I closed the door behind her, taking a deep breath. I needed to draw up a plan, a damn good one. And unlike Val, I needed silence to think things through.

The offices hadn't been here when I was with the company. We had fewer employees, so we didn't need an entire building anyway. Val was smart to move everything here when the company grew. It was far enough from her house to make commuting a pain, but land was cheap, so she'd bought it, saving a lot on rent.

I sat behind the desk, which Val had positioned in the south corner of the room. I could as easily glance at the door and out the window. Maddie's garden stretched outside. Even from here, it looked like the calm-inducing oasis Val described. I rose from my seat, grabbed the laptop, a pen, and some papers, and headed out of the office.

A few minutes later, I stepped inside the small park. It was amazing. A wide cobblestone path snaked through the center, and several narrower ones sprung to the sides. Everywhere I looked, it was green, with the occasional speck of color. I didn't know the names of the trees, but I recognized a few palm trees and ferns. I snapped a photo of it and sent it to Maddie, along with a text.

Landon: This is amazing!

I figured she wouldn't see it until later,

because Maddie didn't keep the phone with her when she worked. She answered within seconds.

Maddie: There's a bench behind that big fern.

Landon: Thanks.

I laughed when I found the bench, wondering how I could already miss Maddie. Did she miss me? Maybe she'd kept her phone with her because she'd hoped to hear from me, even though it was more likely that she was waiting for a business call. This morning had felt like a slice of someone else's life: waking up next to her, our closeness, her cute determination to smooth the hell out of my shirt and suit. How would life feel if every morning started this way?

I allowed that fantasy to take over just for a moment before diving into work.

Chapter Twenty
Maddie

Over the next few days, Val's house became a revolving door for her entire family. Will stopped by every day to check on her, Lori brought food by, and Hailey had flown in for a quick visit the day Val was brought home. Jace had visited her daily between his training sessions, and seeing a six-foot-three soccer player hover around his sister as if she were a baby was endearing to watch.

Val's yard was looking so much better. The mason was scheduled to work on the stone steps next week, and I still had some work left, but I'd planted drought-resistant plants like the California mountain lilac and California yarrow on each of the terrace levels.

I still had to plant two Jacaranda trees near the outer edges of the porch, and on Thursday morning, I went to pick them up from *Elise's Plants and Flowers.*

Elise was hands down my favorite supplier. She owned a small shop, but anything I needed, Elise could make it happen in half the time anyone else did, and at a decent price.

"Everything okay? You seem a little on edge,"

I said as she helped me load the baby Jacaranda trees in the back of my Chevy. Her raven-dark hair was piled up in a bun on top of her head, and she just looked tired.

"Yeah, I'm just… redoing my website, hoping it'll bring in more business. I just don't know how to pimp it up."

"I could give you a testimonial. Or better yet, you could include the pictures from the Murieta project." That was the one I won the Best Garden award for.

Her eyes widened. "Are you sure? I don't want to steal your laurels."

"You're not stealing anything, Elise. You really *should* list it. I bought all those flowers from you."

"Okay, I'll do it. Thanks. You sure have a knack for business, girl."

I left her shop with a smile on my face, brainstorming other possibilities for cross promoting. Elise and I were both one-woman shows, even though she did have two part-time employees. She had suggested a formal partnership a few months ago, but I didn't want that. The mere word *partnership* still brought memories of lawyers, financial messes, and feeling small. However, it was smart to use our synergies. I was bursting with excitement when I pulled into Val's driveway.

My time with Landon was limited to sharing a

morning coffee in his sister's kitchen. I was happy to spend any time with him at all, but I couldn't help wanting more. I was working up the courage to ask him to spend a night or two (or every night) at my house, but I didn't know if inviting him even deeper into my life was a good idea. I'd put defenses in place, but he seemed to demolish them with every kiss, every stolen moment together.

"What are you doing this evening?" he asked on Friday morning. I was on my second coffee. I usually didn't drink more than one, but Landon never left before I finished, which made me want to drink an entire bucket if it meant he'd stay around a little longer.

"Nothing planned yet."

I was perched on the kitchen counter, dangling my feet. Landon stepped between my thighs, nudging them farther apart.

"Keep tonight free." He looked down at me with that molten gaze of his, and it did *delicious* things to me. My fingers itched to touch him. I wasn't particular about where. But if I had a choice, it would be his ass. I wondered if I could run my hands down his back and accidentally on purpose grab it. Maybe I could pass it off as... what? Hmm... maybe I should keep my hands to myself until I came up with a good excuse to grope him in his sister's kitchen.

"And why would I do that?" I teased as my stomach whooped and cartwheeled.

"Because after the family dinner, I want us to spend time together. I haven't planned anything yet."

He dragged his nose up and down my neck. I loved when he did that. I loved everything he did to me. "I just want to spend time with you," he went on, placing open-mouthed kisses on my neck. They worked my nerve endings into a frenzy. When he slid me closer to him, wedging his hands under my ass and rolling my hips against him, I figured I had free rein to grope *his* ass too.

Damn, I loved his suits. The fabric was so thin it was almost like touching his skin. Almost. He groaned seconds into my exploration of his glutes.

"Maddie, stop, or I'll fuck you on this counter."

I weighed the cons: Val was upstairs, but common decency dictated this was not okay. Unfortunately, I hadn't completely forgotten my decency. But I could feel it melting away the longer I felt Landon's breath on my lips.

I let go of him, and he immediately took a step back. I sighed at his rumpled shirt.

"Why do you let me mess you up every morning?" I asked, smoothing the fabric as best I could.

He swallowed. "I like watching you fix me up."

"I like doing it," I admitted. I liked it a lot. It felt so couple-ish, like he was my man, and I was making sure he looked spotless before he went to work. It was a foolish dream, but I couldn't help but lose myself in it every morning, or when he sent me texts throughout the day, sharing tidbits about his work or asking about me.

When our gazes met, a bout of vulnerability crossed his features. It was so raw that I felt it in my chest. Was he having those same thoughts too? I didn't dare ask, but when he pulled me into a hot and soulful kiss, I kissed him back with all I had.

***

That evening, he arrived at six o'clock. I ran into him outside the front gate.

"Hey!" He raked his gaze longingly over me, stopping on the car keys in my hand. "You're leaving?"

"Yeah. I'm done for the day, and I don't want to be in anyone's hair."

"But we have plans tonight." The top button of his shirt was open, and he'd rolled up his sleeves again. He looked tired and pissed off.

"*After* your dinner. Text me when you're ready, and I'll drive back. I won't be far away. I'm exploring the neighborhood."

"Maddie, I'd meant for you to have dinner with us."

"Oh! But… this is a family dinner. I'm sure you have a lot to talk about."

"No state secrets, I promise."

I shifted my weight from one leg to the other, looking down at my red ballerinas. I was flattered he asked, but still didn't know if I should accept. Wouldn't the other siblings mind? They'd been warm and welcoming at the Fourth of July celebration, but this felt more intimate.

"Are you mad at me?"

I snapped my gaze up, startled. "Why would I be mad?"

"I know I've been neglecting you for the past few days. I'm sorry, I didn't mean to—"

I stepped closer, covering his mouth with my hand. "Stop, Landon. I'm not mad. You've been working. I understand."

I felt him smile against my hand before he pushed it away. "So you didn't miss me."

"I didn't say that."

"So you did?"

"I didn't say that either," I teased. He drew the contour of my mouth with his thumb, then tugged my lower lip between his teeth. I stilled, letting him continue with the ministrations. He didn't outright kiss me, just teased me until I ached for him. We were in front of Val's gate, where any neighbors or passersby could see us, and I didn't care. I was like a besotted schoolgirl when it came to Landon.

I took in his body language. He was on edge, and I wanted to take that edge off, so I kissed him with all I had. He kissed me back with fervor, as if he'd been starved for me the whole day. As if he was still starved for me and needed to kiss me as much as he needed his next breath.

"Hard day?" I asked when he moved his lips to my neck, rocking me in his arms.

"Fucking hard day. I hate people sometimes."

"Me too. That's why I work with plants and earth and stones."

"You just made this day much better, though." He laughed, then pulled back a notch. "Stay for dinner. I'd like to have you by my side."

He sounded sexy when he was determined. He still had his arms around me, and he was drawing small circles on my back. His gaze was on my lips.

"I feel like you're about to use your allure to talk me into this."

He grinned. "What gave it away? The kissing? The touching?"

"Nah, that look in your eyes. It's almost predatory."

"That's a yes?"

"It's a yes."

The corners of his mouth lifted, and he kissed both my hands before leading me right back through the gate. He looked visibly more relaxed than when he'd arrived. I smiled to myself. I didn't want to claim full credit for that, but I felt pretty confident I could at least claim 50 percent.

One word could describe dinner with the Connors: loud.

During the Fourth of July party, we'd all been scattered through the backyard, but five of the Connors plus me were gathered around the living room table. Hailey's plane had had a delay, so she'd only arrive later. Milo had scarfed food down quickly and was currently in the sitting area of the living room, earbuds plugged in his ears, eyes focused on an iPad.

Everyone was talking at the same time. My ears would pop any second now. Landon was having a blast. Clearly his earlier statement about hating people didn't apply to his family.

Val was at the head of the table, sitting in an armchair that had a support for her cast.

"I don't need a full-time caretaker, Landon," she repeated for what seemed like the millionth time. "The nurse who comes to help me bathe is enough. I've learned to maneuver the crutches. I can't move quicker anyway, unless I get a wheelchair, which I refuse to do. It's impractical with the stairs anyway. I just wish the effects of the concussion would go away faster. I still can't read without getting a massive headache, and I get tired quickly."

Will chimed in. "It's good for her to do things on her own, as much as she can."

When Landon shook his head and opened his mouth, Will turned to me. "Maddie, I'm entrusting you with a very important task. You need to get Landon to relax. He has this annoying belief that everything is his responsibility. He's gonna grow white hair soon."

Jace cornered me too. "Yeah, use those womanly wiles. We've tried everything else and failed. You're our last resort."

The skin on my neck felt red-hot, but I was determined not to cower, even though I couldn't believe he'd just used the words "womanly wiles."

"I'll do my best," I countered, keeping my face straight.

Lori glanced at Milo, but he still seemed lost in his iPad, earbuds safely on. "Jace, I forbid you to say the words 'womanly wiles' in front of Milo."

Jace glanced at his sister in mock surprise. "Why? Think he won't understand? I'm more than happy to explain. He needs to be prepared for what's out there."

"He's six," Lori said so sweetly, even *I* feared she was cooking up a revenge plan in case Jace blabbed in front of Milo.

Hailey arrived midway through dinner.

"I'm sorry I'm late. Plane took off ninety minutes too late from Seattle." She hugged Val tightly, then plopped down on Landon's other side. In between scarfing down food, she questioned him about work.

"I have everything under control," Landon said.

Hailey raised her eyebrows. "I want details, please."

Landon gave in and recounted the past week play-by-play.

"That sounds like a lot to handle," she admonished when he finished. I was on Hailey's side. I was exhausted just hearing it.

Landon waved his hand. "I can balance the workload."

Interesting. He'd admitted to me that it was going to be a nightmare, but he didn't admit it to his family. While I felt honored that he'd shared that with me, I thought that putting up this bravado wasn't having the effect he thought it had. Case in point: Jace and Will were both casting him worried looks.

"Val, I won't be able to attend dinner next Friday. We're playing in New York," Jace said.

Val pouted. "The season hasn't started yet."

"It's a friendly game. Though you wouldn't know it by the way our coach had us train. You'd think we're playing for the world championship. But I'll stop by before I leave. And I'll wink at you when they interview me."

Val pointed her finger at him. "You're just trying to rope me into watching your game."

"You're not even going to watch my game when you've got nothing else to do? Low blow, sis. Low blow."

Everyone at the table erupted in laughter.

"I'll try," Val said. "But I get a headache when I watch quick movements on a screen."

***

"In a few weeks she'll go crazy," Landon said later when we left Val's house. We climbed down the slope using the wooden trail.

"Anyone would if they were housebound. Don't worry. I'll keep an eye on her, report any mischief."

"Spying for me now, are you?"

"I'm adaptable. Dinner was so much fun. And loud. My ears are still ringing a bit. But can I just say one thing? You shouldn't put up that bravado in front of your siblings. They can see right through it, and it makes them worry."

He hesitated. "It's a reflex by now. Growing up, Val and I did whatever it took to keep any trouble from them."

I nodded, understanding where he was coming from. "I get what you're saying."

"You do?"

"Yes. Our situations were nothing alike, but I often felt like a parent for Grace. Especially on the nights our parents were performing."

We came to a stop at the foot of the wooded trail.

"The venues where they performed weren't exactly kid friendly, so we were on our own a lot from the time I was about nine."

Landon frowned. "Nine is young to be left alone. Especially with a younger sibling."

"I know, but they didn't have much choice. They're good people, but very passionate about music." I'd often wondered if they loved music more than us, but that was a really unfair judgment. They did the best they could, and that was really all any of us could do. "They provided us with enough to get by, it's just... I'd just wished they'd been more present, you know? It was the little things that added up, like Grace falling asleep waiting for them, wanting to show them something she'd drawn. Or when I wanted to talk to my mom about girl issues, but she didn't have time, so I interrogated the lady at the pharmacy. I sound ungrateful."

"You wanted love and attention," Landon said softly. "Those are normal things to want."

I blinked, shaking my head. "I don't usually talk about this." What was it about him that made me talk so freely?

"You can talk to me about anything, Maddie. I understand where you're coming from, and I like listening to you."

We were more alike than I'd thought. I felt the connection between us like a physical hook in my heart, pulling me closer to him.

"Anyway, back to you and your family. You should try being more... relaxed around them. When they ask you how it's going, try not to automatically say, 'I have everything under control.'"

"I'm that predictable?"

"No, but I'm starting to figure you out, Landon Connor. And if I can figure you out, so can they, so be upfront with them."

"I'll try." The corners of his mouth twitched. "You took Jace's trolling like a champ."

I feigned shock. "Trolling? That was serious advice. And I plan to use my womanly wiles on you tonight."

"Do you now?"

"Yep."

"What are you doing this weekend?" he murmured. "I'd like to spend it together with you, if that's possible."

"I'd love that. I have plans for tomorrow, though. In the morning, Grace and I are going to the flea market. You want to come with us?"

"I have a conference call with Adam, my acting CEO, in the morning. I had no time to talk to him today. What are you doing in the afternoon?"

"I need to paint two of my outer walls. I painted the other two a while ago, but I really need to get to it this weekend. But after that, I'm free to use my womanly wiles on you again."

"You're painting alone?"

"Yes, Grace is working at Macy's in the afternoon before her shift at the Lucky Bar."

"I'll paint with you."

I waved my hand. "Oh no. That's a messy affair."

"So? We'll be faster together."

"Landon, really. I'll deal with it." I made to walk toward the front gate, but he caught my arm, spinning me to face him. His gaze was focused, hard.

"Why are you so stubborn?"

"I'm not stubborn, but I don't want you to feel obligated to help me with stuff like that. It feels as if we're a couple."

I felt vulnerable for revealing that particular detail. I was pushing him out, and I didn't know how to stop. After my breakup, I'd been afraid to let anyone get close. I didn't want to give anyone the chance to make me feel insignificant. I tried to shrug everything off, but I suspected Landon could see right through me. He seemed wired to my emotions.

He let go of my arm, cupping my face in both hands. "We *are* a couple, Maddie. This isn't just a romp between the sheets. Yes, I want you every damn second of every damn day, but I also want to just spend time with you. Doesn't matter what we do." His thumbs caressed my cheekbones, and then he kissed me. "You're fun, loyal. You're a great woman, Maddie. You deserve someone who knows how to treat you the right way. I want to be that man for you. Here, now, I want to be that man."

He leaned in until his chest brushed my breasts, and I sucked in a breath. Landon stole the next one, sealing his mouth over mine. He kissed me gently but demandingly. I twisted my fingers through his hair. His hands and lips were wreaking havoc on my senses, but his words had reached straight to my heart. Landon was like a hurricane. He swept me off my feet completely, and even though I knew I'd be better off in the long term if I fought my feelings, I couldn't do it anymore. I wanted to take all this man had to offer, experience everything he made me feel.

Landon tore his mouth away. "Woman! Don't start with those wiles before we even leave my sister's yard."

Laughter began to bubble up my chest, but it got stuck in my throat when he cupped my breast, flicking my nipple over my dress. After work, I'd changed into a light blue cotton dress with a V neckline and short sleeves.

He lowered his hand on my right thigh,

bunching up my dress until he reached my skin. I shuddered.

"I love how your body reacts to me. It makes me want to just stroke you like this for hours."

I bucked my hips, desperate for more friction. He kissed down the side of my face, tugging at my earlobe, whispering in my ear.

"Landon! The things you make me want." How could he bring me from zero to 100 percent turned on in a few seconds? I didn't even know I was capable of that. Landon made me discover new sides of myself, though I suspected I would only ever respond to him this way. It was pitch dark in the yard, but still. I couldn't climb him here, so I did the sensible thing and took a step back.

"Shall we go?" I asked.

"Yeah, we should." I heard the smile in his voice as we left the yard. "So, we're on for painting tomorrow."

"Yes, bossy man. We're on for painting. Where do you want to go now?" I asked once we were in the car. "The view from the Griffith Observatory is really spectacular at night. Or we could go to the observation deck on city hall, and then have drinks downtown. Or we could go to a beach. Not Venice, too much going on."

"I forgot how amazing this city was."

"Oh, I'll remind you. I always think imports value LA more than the locals."

A dangerous idea popped into my mind. Would he ever consider moving back here? Could

I… persuade him? I shook my head, pushing away the selfish thought. But I found myself wishing that this thing between us could stretch beyond *here and now.*

"Well, then, LA expert. Show me what I've been missing. You choose the adventure tonight."

I glanced at him suspiciously. "You're so accommodating. No negotiations?"

"I'll prove my negotiating prowess later tonight."

"Will clothes be involved?"

"Of course." He leaned in closer. "I didn't say we'd be *wearing* those clothes."

Chapter Twenty-One
Landon

I rarely admitted that I bit off more than I could chew, even to myself. But two weeks into juggling two companies, I had to admit it. Overseeing the development of Val's project for the department store had turned into running the entire company. Since her headaches had subsided somewhat, Val was working from home a few hours a day, answering e-mails and taking phone calls, but the brunt of the work had to be done from the office. When my sister was back on her feet, I had to talk her into hiring someone as a right hand. She couldn't do the job of two people forever.

The deal with Sullivan required more of my time than I'd anticipated, which explained why I was the last person in the building, with samples of perfumes and body washes covering half of my desk, reports the other half.

A shuffling sound caught my attention, and I looked up from the samples, wondering if Val's assistant was still here after all, but was pleasantly surprised to see Maddie leaning against the doorway. I rose from my seat and headed to her.

"Beautiful, come on in. What are you doing

here? How long have you been standing there?"

"Not long. Was just admiring a CEO in action. It's a very good look. That suit and those cuff links are *yumm*. Do you have an endless supply of both?"

"Almost." Adam had sent over almost all of my clothes.

"I've come to whisk you away."

I pulled her into the office, kissing her hard. I'd spent almost every night at her house the past two weeks. Her bed was my favorite place. Her sweet smell was embedded in the sheets and the pillows. It was my own personal heaven.

"Come on, let's go," she murmured.

I glanced back at the literal mountains of work on my desk, but she tsked.

"Oh, so you think you can boss me into painting my house, but I can't take you away? That's not how it works, Mr. CEO. I give in, you give in. It's a two-way street."

I had no idea what she had in store, but I was looking forward to it. My Maddie had been a bright light among the San Jose deal spiraling out of control and developing Val's line. But coming home to Maddie and waking up next to her had made everything else manageable.

"You're feisty today! I wasn't going to say no. That mountain of work can wait until tomorrow."

Her face split into a grin. "Come on, then. We have a sunset to catch, and an evening of debauchery to take your mind off that mountain of work."

We arrived at our destination forty minutes later. The view was extraordinary, the weather as warm as mid-July could be in LA. We were higher up over the city than I'd realized. I could even spot the ocean in the distance. As far as parks went, this one was wild. We were surrounded by yellowing bushes and overgrown grass, but I preferred it to perfectly kept spaces. As a plus, we had no company.

Maddie sat down on the grass, stretching out her legs. She patted the spot next to her, but I shook my head. Instead, I sat behind her, pressing my chest against her back, cradling her legs between mine, needing to touch as much of her as possible.

"How was your day?" I asked.

"Exciting. I'm always excited when I start a new project. It's so weird being in a school and not seeing any kids around. But it's easier to work when they're on vacation. We're due to finish right before they start school. I'm going to miss working for Val, though. And I can't spy on her from a distance."

"Between Lori, Jace, and Will stopping by so often, I think that's covered. How did you discover this place?"

"I often look for wild spots in the city. For inspiration, you know, since my landscaping aims to mimic the wilderness. Natural habitats have a more relaxing effect on the human brain than perfectly manicured spaces. Obviously I can't just plant things anywhere and allow them to grow wild, because they'd get in the way. It wouldn't be practical at all.

But I like observing naturally formed clearings and such, because nature usually finds clever solutions, you know?"

I didn't know because I rarely paid attention to such things. In fact, I didn't remember the last time I'd taken the time to watch the sunset. Usually I avoided downtime at all costs. But with Maddie, all I wanted to do was carve out more of it in the weeks we had. I liked that she made me stop and pay attention to details.

"I saw an ad today from a residential housing developer. They're working on a green concept. They want to raise apartment buildings and have the surroundings look like a park. It would be a dream to work on something like that." She giggled. "Sorry, that was random. I was just excited when I saw it."

"It's an honor to hear about your dreams," I assured her. "Thank you for sharing them with me. Did you apply?"

"I did, actually. But I think I did it just because I couldn't help myself. I don't have the capacity for such a project. The area they're talking about is huge."

"A partnership sounds more appealing?" I teased.

"The idea keeps nagging, but it still sounds more like an ordeal than an opportunity."

"That's fear, Maddie, because it went wrong once. You shouldn't let that keep you from going after what you want."

"I know... you're right. I could approach

bigger projects in between residential ones. There are so many opportunities in LA, and there are so many different habitats. That's what I love about this city. When I first moved here, I traipsed through the city for hours every afternoon, determined to learn it."

I loved her determination to own her life no matter what. I almost asked her if she'd ever consider leaving LA. From what she'd shared about her ex and her move to LA, I was willing to bet every penny to my name that she wouldn't upend her life again, least of all for a man. And it wasn't fair to ask her to give anything up for me, when I wasn't sure that what I had to offer was enough to make her happy. But damn if I didn't want the right to make all of her dreams come true.

I pushed her hair to one side, kissing the back of her neck. Being near her and touching her wasn't enough. I wanted to taste her. She stilled when my tongue came in contact with her skin, letting out the sweetest moan.

"You're so good with your mouth," she whispered.

I kissed her until the rhythm of her breathing intensified and she crossed her legs on a gasp. I groaned, knowing what that meant. But I wanted to hear her say it.

"Are you wet?"

She made a small sound at the back of her throat, nodding. I tugged at her earlobe with my teeth, curious to test how far I could push her.

"Landon!" she whispered. "We can't get

naked here."

"Sweetness, I don't need to get you naked to make you come."

She was wearing denim shorts and a pink polo shirt.

Maddie swatted me away, pointing to the horizon. "Keep your hands where I can see them."

I placed one on her breast, the other between her legs, rubbing her pussy over the denim. I moved two fingers up and down, turning us both on. She swatted my hands away again.

"You're distracting me." Her voice was breathy and uneven.

"If my hands distract you, that says more about you than about me."

"We came all the way here to see the sunset. Keep those dirty thoughts for later. Much later."

I wasn't going to settle for much later. "We'll watch the sunset, Maddie. But we won't end this rendezvous without me sinking into you. You can choose where—here, the car, your house—but I *will* make love to you."

"You've got no shame," she whispered.

"Or honor," I confirmed. "Not when it comes to you."

She turned around and pressed her mouth to mine. "So that's how you're playing it, huh? Sweet-talking your way into my thong?"

She wiggled out from between my thighs, sitting next to me. I pulled her feet into my lap and took off her sandals. She groaned when I pressed my thumb into the arch of her foot.

"Oh, pulling out the big guns, huh? Giving me foot rubs?"

"You're on your feet all day."

"I see. Just to double-check, this is purely for my benefit? You're not looking for sexy rewards later on?"

"Sweetness, make no mistake, I'll *take* those rewards. But this is just for you."

She smiled at me, and I knew right then that I'd die a happy man if I could have her smile at me like that every day for the rest of our lives. We watched in silence as the sky turned a mix of pink and orange and then descended into darkness while the city lit up gradually.

After putting her sandals back on, Maddie rose to her feet so fast that she nearly lost her balance.

"Hurrying somewhere?" I teased, steadying her.

"Yep. I'm no exhibitionist, so the house it will be. Unless those were empty promises?" She jutted her chin out, challenge rising in her eyes.

"My promises are never empty, Maddie." To drive the point home, I pulled her flush against me so she could feel just how hard I was for her. Cupping her ass, I kept her in place, rubbing against her lightly. She gasped, digging her fingers into my arms.

"Oh, perfect. I can't wait for you to make good on those promises."

She blushed, licking her lips. I tugged that lip

between my teeth, making her squirm.

"I hope you liked our trip. This is my secret place, by the way, so don't go around blabbing about it," she said.

"My lips are sealed. Thanks for bringing me here."

When she rested her arms around my neck, I felt more connected to her than I'd ever felt to anyone. The realization should have scared me, but instead I held her closer. How was I going to handle not having her in my life?

Chapter Twenty-Two
Landon

Hailey dropped a bomb at the next Friday dinner.

"You didn't," I exclaimed.

"Yeah, I did. Look, you've been stretching yourself thin these past three weeks. I can even see some white hairs sprouting. I spoke to my boss and told him I need to take one month off. He went berserk, but I pulled on all my negotiation skills and convinced him to give me three weeks. So Monday morning, I'm coming to the office with you. We can split tasks."

I stared at her in bewilderment. "Okay, back up. How did you come to the conclusion that I need help?"

"Your partnership with Sullivan is rocky, and Val's project requires 200 percent of your attention. Some might even say it would have been a great idea for her to hire someone to assist her."

She slid her gaze to Val, who was suddenly very interested in her quinoa and avocado salad. Since we wanted Val to rest, we took turns preparing Friday dinner. This had been Will's contribution. Had I been too careless these past Fridays?

Complained too much? I racked my brain but didn't remember doing so.

"Hailey, I appreciate the thought, but this isn't necessary. You have your own career to focus on."

Hailey crossed her arms over her chest. "I have a lot of accrued time. It's my right to go on vacation. My boss is like all bosses—present company excluded, I hope"—she slid Val and me a cutting look—"and he doesn't like his employees to actually take time off, but there's nothing he can do about it."

A while ago Hailey confided in me that she was on track for a promotion, and I knew sharks in the consultancy world well. They wanted your sweat, blood, and full commitment. Taking this time off would work against her. But Hailey knew all this, so I needed another angle.

"You don't know the business—"

"I'm a business consultant, Landon. I tackle unknown businesses for a living. I take everything on a project-by-project basis, and I have a good system for learning the nuts and bolts quickly. And I've worked with other companies in the industry."

She held her chin up high as if daring me to question her expertise. Okay, so that had been a lousy angle. I was running out of ideas. I looked at Val for support.

"Val? You're really going to let her do this?"

Hailey sighed. "I'm an adult, Landon. I don't need permission from either of you to do what I please."

My twin sister looked miserable. "I don't want either of you putting your lives on hold for me. But Landon, you do have your plate full. I'm not making much of a dent in your workload with what I do from home. My team isn't used to working remotely with me. I know I'm not good when it comes to delegating, and your deal needs more of your attention."

Negotiations had reached a new low this week. Sullivan was reopening negotiations on every front, including unimportant details. He was wasting both our time, and that bothered me, because I couldn't see his endgame. He'd seemed a straightforward person in the beginning. I would have backed out of the deal, but I had no other way of delivering the results I'd promised to investors.

I hadn't mentioned the latest troubles with the merger to my family, though. How did they know? Had Adam called Val? I'd kill him. I looked around the table for support. It took me all of three seconds to realize I would get none. Lori, Jace, and Will were nodding appreciatively. Milo was focusing on his second serving of salad. I wished Maddie was here, even though I'd be outnumbered even with her vote of confidence.

"When I say I can take care of something, it's because I can," I said calmly.

"Jeez, you're stubborn," Lori said.

"We can out-stubborn him," Will added.

Jace chuckled. "Let's not get cocky. The stubborn streak runs deep in the Connor bloodline, but Landon takes stubbornness and determination to a whole new level. Need to tackle this somehow else. I'm thinking old-fashioned bargaining."

"I can take care of this," I repeated, but with less conviction. I remembered the conversation with Maddie from three weeks ago about not placating my siblings. I knew she was right, but knowing and doing were different things. I could start trying, though.

"You don't have to take care of things on your own anymore, Landon. We're grown up. And you're our brother, not our parent," Jace said. The table went quiet.

"I know that."

He shook his head. "Sometimes you seem to forget, which I suppose is normal since you and Val…. Well, we all know what you did for us, and we're very grateful. But you don't have to do everything on your own anymore," Jace said with so much tact that it threw me off. Tact usually wasn't a priority for him.

"She already asked for time off, Landon," Lori said. "Just relax. It will all work out."

"Okay, I… appreciate the help. But I wish you'd told me about this before making a decision."

Hailey clapped her hands, then practically shoved a finger in my face. "No way in hell. The best way to negotiate with you is to ambush you. Worked when I was a kid, and it's working now. Why change a running system?" She elbowed Lori playfully.

I laughed. Lori had invented the ambush

technique when she couldn't sway me to buy her a dalmatian. She'd promised to take care of it all on her own, but I figured she didn't know what that entailed. One night when Val and I came home from the pub, she was waiting for us in the living room, a dalmatian in her arms. She'd held the puppy to her chest, looking at me with accusing eyes.

"I hope you will find it in your cold, black heart not to put him out on the street."

Her words had sliced enough that I could remember them to this day.

Of course, I wasn't going to put him out on the street. The dalmatian stayed, and the ambush technique was born: a strategy used with success by all my siblings—sometimes even Val.

"By the way," Jace said, "where's Maddie? I got used to having her around on Friday nights."

"At the bar where her sister works. They're having a big event and Maddie is helping."

Will held up his beer to me before taking a swig. Hailey propped her elbows on the table, looking at my eyes intently.

"What?" I challenged.

"I think I see stars in your eyes," she said.

"Oh boy, here we go," Jace said. "Run while you can. I sense another ambush coming. I get that every time a fan looks too long at me."

"That's different. We're just looking out for you," Lori explained, helping herself to more salad. "What if they want to take advantage of your fame?"

"Maybe I don't mind," Jace said, and we all

laughed. I was proud of my brother. Playing soccer professionally required dedication and hard work. He'd been in love with the game since he was a little boy, watching Val and me play. Our school's soccer coach had declared Val and me to be natural talents, but when Jace went for tryouts, he didn't even make it on the team. Coach told him he'd better focus his efforts somewhere else. Instead, my brother asked me to practice with him. He was relentless in his determination. The next year, he made the team, and now he's one of the best players in the country.

Val shifted her leg on the ottoman, then swayed widely in her chair from left to right, like the pendulum of a grandfather clock.

"My butt hurts from so much sitting," she explained when we all paused to watch.

"As soon as your ribs are better, you should move around more," Jace instructed. "The muscles in that leg will atrophy anyway, but it's important to keep the rest of the body strong. That's the advice our club's doctor gives us when we have an injury. I'm going to keep pestering him to make time to check you. He's the best."

"Oh, more doctors. I'm looking forward to it," Val said dryly. Then she perked up. "Is he hot?"

Jace looked murderous. "He's not good for you. He's a manwhore and—"

Val burst out laughing. "I was just messing with you. Jeez, relax." He opened his mouth, but Val held up a hand. "I believe we were talking about Landon's love life before we got derailed." She winked at me. "Is it my imagination, or are you spending a lot of time together?"

I couldn't tell if she honestly hadn't noticed I'd only slept a few nights here in three weeks, or if she was trying to take the attention off her by shifting it on me.

"Not your imagination," I answered. Val beamed with so much honesty that I decided to give her the benefit of the doubt.

Later, I shot Adam a message as we cleared the table.

Landon: Did you talk to Val recently?

Adam: No, man, but Hailey called last week.

Landon: What exactly did you tell her?

Adam: Hell if I know. She started asking me about my dog, and by the end of the conversation I think I even told her what color Sullivan's logo had. You know how she can get. She's got that talent for talking until the cows come home, like all business consultants have.

Of course.

After dinner, I was tempted to call Maddie. We hadn't made plans for tonight because she and Grace would be at the Lucky Bar until closing time, but I missed her. Was she having fun? Was she thinking about me as often as I thought about her? I *needed* to see her.

For years, I hadn't wanted to need another being, because losing them crippled you. But when it came to Maddie, I couldn't help myself. My days here were numbered, and I didn't want to let one pass without seeing her. I was of half a mind to show up at The Lucky Bar unannounced, but decided to text her first.

Landon: Everything all right? Having fun with Grace?

Her answer came moments later.

Maddie: Inofun. Cowded

Had she typed without watching the screen? I went out on the front porch and called her.

"What was that?" I asked the moment she picked up.

"Hi, Landon. This is Grace. Sorry about my sister's blunder. She typed before I managed to whisk it away from her."

"Is she okay?"

"Oh yeah. But Jose, the bartender on shift tonight, thought he'd prank her. Made her a Bloody Mary with one of those fancy vodkas that don't burn your throat. You can't even tell it has vodka. He was… quite generous."

"Doooooon't tell him that. He'll think I'm drunk." Maddie's voice resounded through the phone, rising over the background noise.

"She still thinks she's sober," Grace informed me.

"I got that. How is she getting home?"

"I'm going to get in a cab with her, drop her off at home, and then come back. I'm serving drinks tonight, and I need to be here until the band leaves. Or… we could use your white knight services. Are they available tonight?"

"Yes," I said at the same time Maddie's voice rose to a pitch.

"You little traitor. I don't want him to see me drunk."

Grace chuckled. "Oh good. She can tell she's drunk. We're making progress. How fast can you be here?"

"Half an hour."

"Great. I'll keep her far away from the Bloody Marys in the meantime. José, if you serve her another drink, I will kill you in your sleep." She practically yelled the last sentence, making my ears ring.

After a hurried goodbye to my siblings, I hailed a cab and headed to the Lucky Bar.

The place was more packed than the last time I'd been here. I had to give it to the owner; his strategy of booking the place solid with live bands was smart. In a city with bars at every corner, he was thriving despite the competition. I found Maddie on one of the couches on the left from the bar. A wisp of a blonde was doting on her.

"Grace?" I asked when I was in hearing distance. She nodded, holding out her hand. She looked just like Maddie, but about a head shorter, and her eyes were almond-shaped rather than round.

"Nice to meet you, Landon. Our girl here's not feeling too well."

Maddie sighed, motioning with her forefinger for me to come closer. When I leaned over her, she immediately wrapped her arms around my neck. I kissed her without a second thought, tasting tomato juice and vodka on her tongue. But underneath all that heady mix was still my sweet Maddie. My sweet and inebriated Maddie. I realized just how inebriated when I had to stop her hand from snaking under my shirt.

"I'll get you home, drunk girl," I murmured after tearing my mouth from hers. Straightening up, I turned to Grace. "I'll take care of her tonight. Don't worry about a thing."

Grace sighed. "Wow, my sister is right. You have graduated from the school of perfect men."

"She says that?"

"Oh yeah. So often, I'm gonna start being jealous soon."

Maddie poked Grace's thigh. "Don't get jealous. He's mine. Not sharing him."

"Oh boy," Grace exclaimed.

I whipped my phone out and ordered an Uber. According to the timer it would be here in three minutes.

"Come on, sweet girl. Up you go." I took both her hands, helped her up. I couldn't yet determine how steady she was on her feet, but I hooked an arm around her waist just in case. Grace walked us to the entrance, and once we stepped out in the pleasant evening air, Maddie almost became a deadweight in my arms. She was silent on the way home, nestling her body against me.

Grace's words played in my mind. I was far from perfect, but knowing Maddie had so much faith in me made me want to be the man she saw. I wanted to be the man she needed. I carried her in my arms all the way to her bed.

"How was dinner?" she asked, curling on one side after I took off her shoes. I sat next to her, stroking her hair.

"Good. A bit crazy. Hailey's taking three weeks off to work with me."

Maddie did not look surprised. Instead, she tried to hide her smile in the pillow.

"You knew about this?" I asked.

"I might have accidentally on purpose outed you to your sisters."

I bit down a smile. "How do you do something accidentally on purpose?"

"Well, Val cornered me on my last morning at the house. Started pestering me with questions. I thought it was just girl talk, you know? But then Hailey called too, and I thought she might be up to something. But instead of downplaying how much you work, I laid everything out for her. I sold you out. In my defense, you seemed to need it."

Her voice came out muffled because she was hiding her face in the pillow in earnest, fiddling her toes against one another.

"I'm glad you did. I was in over my head, but I'm not used to admitting it."

She perked her head up. "You're a strange white knight. You rescue everyone else, but I think you need a rescuer yourself. Far from me to overplay my abilities, but I'm the perfect candidate. Can I apply for the position?"

"It's already yours, Maddie."

"It is? What are you doing?" she asked in alarm as I stretched next to her on the edge of the bed.

"Lying next to you. Or next to the bed. I'm gonna fall over if you don't make space for me."

"But you're not sleeping here, are you?" She sounded even more alarmed, even as she made space for me.

"Why the hell not?"

"B-because I'm not feeling well. I might barf, and that's messy and—"

"Maddie! I'm staying!"

"Oh, by all means, go all bossy and melt the pants off me when I'm down. Damn Slutty Marys."

"What?"

"I asked Jose to make me a Bloody Mary, but light on the vodka because I was helping Grace. I didn't want a Virgin Mary. That's boring. It should be illegal to have to drink nonalcoholic cocktails on a Friday night. Anyway, he did a number on me. Said I looked like I needed it."

"Did you?"

I'd thought she'd felt strangely tense, but I put it up to her not wanting Grace or me to see her drunk. I should have known there was more to it.

"A little. I'd just gotten off the phone with my parents, who said they wouldn't make it to my birthday because they've booked a gig. They didn't have time to get together for Christmas, so I was hoping they'd make it to my birthday in two weeks. I wasn't planning a big party. I'd love one, but I don't have time for that. Just a small dinner…." She was silent for a moment before adding, "I sound so silly, getting worked up over this."

"You're not silly. It's important to you."

She shrugged. "I should let it go. I just miss them so much. But I have Grace, and my friends."

"Aren't you forgetting someone?" I teased.

"Hmm. I'm friendly with the postman. Maybe I should put him on my list. Think I'm missing anyone?"

"Me." I leaned in closer, kissed her earlobe. "You have me, Maddie."

I wanted to be important to her, to be on that list of people she wouldn't hesitate to call close, to reach out to.

"Not really. I'm just borrowing you from your life in San Jose. I love our time together, but I don't want to fool myself."

Her words were true, even though I didn't want them to be.

"But you have me now."

She scrunched up her nose, looking at me intently. "Hmm. That's a vague statement. I'm pretty sure I can claim ownership of this." She cupped my cock over my pants. "But which other part of you? Your brilliant mind? Or that squeezable ass?"

"Squeezable?"

"More than that. Bite-worthy."

She moved her hand over my chest, her eyes

locked on mine.

"You have all parts of me, Maddie. You have all of me."

She smiled sheepishly, burying her face in my chest.

"Will you still be here in two weeks, for my birthday?"

"Yes, I will." And even if I wasn't, I'd fly back for the occasion. I'd fly back to spend Christmas and every other holiday she wanted with her. Truth was, I couldn't imagine a day when I wouldn't want her. Could she? "See, you'll have me too on your birthday. I'll make it a day to remember, I promise."

"Oooh, you're about to bestow more of that charm on me. By all means, go ahead."

She lifted one of my wrists, pointing to my forearm. "This should also not be legal. Do you know how hot you look with your sleeves rolled up?"

"I thought you liked the cuff links."

She scooted closer to me on the bed. Her arm was wedged between us, but I still felt her right breast press against my chest. I was barely refraining from tearing her clothes off.

"Oh, I like those too. They say *I'm in charge*, and that's hot. But this says, *I'm not afraid to get my hands dirty.*"

She licked across the vein on my inner arm, and I could feel the lick on the length of my cock.

"Maddie, fuck."

"I like when you're dirty with me." Her tone was pushing me further to the edge. She was begging for it.

"Not tonight, sweetness."

I couldn't be gentle with her tonight, and I risked her getting sick if I had my way with her. She shifted the hand wedged between us, stroking my erection until my control nearly snapped. I cuffed her wrist, bringing it to her stomach.

"He wants me." Lowering her voice to a whisper, she added, "Why doesn't your boss allow us to have some fun? He's being mean."

Maddie tried to lower her hand again, but I switched tactics. I climbed on top of her, pinning both her wrists above her head, trapping her legs between mine.

"What are you going to do now?" I teased.

Her eyes were wide, her breath frantic. "Whatever you want me to do, Landon."

Fuck, she was going to undo me. I couldn't resist this forever. But I knew what she needed. Her eyes glittered with desire, her body humming with the need for release.

I clasped her wrists firmly with one hand, brought the other to her jeans, undid her button and lowered the zipper. When I slipped my hand into her panties, I groaned. She was wet.

"Maddie, beautiful, since when are you so wet?"

"Since you carried me inside," she whispered, like it was a dirty secret. I stroked her slit up and down slowly. So damn slowly it was killing us both.

"Faster, Landon."

I kissed the corner of her mouth, went up to her cheek. She was so turned on, I knew she'd come for me in ten seconds flat. But that would be an unsatisfying release. I wanted to draw it out, coax her to a peak so high that the release would melt away all the tension she'd gathered in her body and mind today. I was going to make her forget all about it by giving her the kind of pleasure she could feel in her bones.

"No," I said.

She tried to push herself against my palm, but I took my hand away.

"No," she whimpered. "Don't stop."

"You said you liked it when I was in charge."

She stilled, and I brought my hand down her center again.

"This is me being in charge, Maddie."

She pinched her eyes shut. I was shaking from the effort of not giving in to my instincts. I needed to be inside her badly, but tonight was all about her. I stroked her even slower than before.

Her legs began to shake first, then her belly. I held her in my arms while her entire body convulsed, riding out her orgasm. She cried my name over and over again, until she was spent.

Then I moved, pulled her shirt over her head, then her jeans down, kissing her legs.

"What are you doing?" she asked.

I smiled against the skin of her upper thigh. "I'm going on a search for those birthmarks again."

She laughed. "Missed some spots on your last

search, huh?"

"Doesn't hurt to double-check."

"Well, you *are* a thorough man."

She took off her bra, and I pulled down her panties too. I kissed her breasts, teasing her nipples with my tongue. She opened her legs wide for me. Her complete trust and surrender nearly undid me. I sucked on her clit, sliding two fingers inside her and curving them. She dug her heels into the mattress, shimmying her hips.

"All of this is mine, Maddie."

"Only yours."

I moved between her legs, teasing her clit.

She cried out, and her thighs were shaking a little. "Landon, it's too soon. I don't know if I can get there again."

"You will. For me, you will."

She came apart soon after. Then I moved next to her, cradling her to me. She was still panting softly when she lowered a hand to my zipper. I caught it, bringing it up to my lips.

"I'm not going to make love to you tonight, Maddie. I'll just hold you."

She sighed, scooting over until she was half lying on top of me. Her body was relaxed. I couldn't feel one ounce of tension anymore.

"You put me first."

"You deserve nothing less."

"You're so good at dismantling my walls, Landon. Brick by brick. You're very, *very* thorough."

I chuckled, holding her even closer. I knew

what she meant. She was blasting through mine.

Chapter Twenty-Three
Maddie

My head seemed to weigh a thousand pounds when I woke up. Thankfully, the curtains were drawn together. My heart filled with joy at the realization that Landon must have done it. Voices filtered in from the living room through the cracked door. I recognized Will's and Lori's voices in addition to Landon's. What were they doing here? I sat up, assessing my condition. I felt relentless pounding at the back of my head and along my temples, but no nausea. I was wearing an old shirt and yoga pants Landon had helped me change into last night. I rose from the bed and discovered I was steady on my feet.

Landon pushed the door open wider. "Thought I heard you move. How do you feel?"

"Headache," I mumbled. "Are Lori and Will here?"

"We came to the rescue," Lori called. Landon smiled, taking my hand and leading me to the living room.

Lori and Will were sitting next to each other on my couch. Lori pointed to the plastic bottle on my revolving bookcase, which also served as a coffee table. The greenish liquid inside the bottle gave me the creeps. In my experience, no green drink tasted better than it looked.

"That's the Connors' secret hangover cure," she explained. "Very efficient."

Will pitched in. "As a tester, I vouch for it one hundred percent."

"Well, if even someone with a badge vouches for it, I'm sold. Thanks." I sat on the chair opposite them, still eying the liquid with suspicion. "What are you two doing here? Where's Milo?"

"Milo has a playdate," Lori said. "Landon called to ask me for the cure's recipe. I like you too much to allow my dearest brother to poison you, so I made it myself. Landon's heart is in the right place, but his skills in the kitchen are not. Will was having breakfast with me, so he tagged along."

I felt so much gratitude toward the three Connors under my roof, doting on me. Landon grabbed the bottle and headed to the kitchen. Moments later, he returned and handed me my favorite cup, the one that said "Every Day Feels Like Monday Without Coffee." The greenish liquid looked a little more appealing.

"Thanks."

"Do you want anything else? I'll go get it," Landon said.

"No, I'm good."

Lori sighed, then nudged Will. "Watch. Learn."

"Are you implying I don't know how to treat a woman?" he asked.

"A sister can never be too careful."

"You mean too nagging."

I grinned at Landon and fake whispered, "Do you think they remember we're here?"

Landon kissed my forehead, whispering back, "Oh yeah. They just don't care."

I brought my mouth to his ear and whispered for real, "Would you mind if I invite your family for my birthday dinner?"

Even though I'd gone to their Fourth of July party and even to some Friday night dinners, I didn't want to cross any boundaries.

"Not at all," he said out loud.

I cleared my throat. "Will, Lori, my birthday is in two weeks, on that Tuesday. If you have time, I'd love if you stopped by. I'll call everyone else today."

Lori frowned. "That's the day our cousin Sebastian is visiting with his family."

"They can come too," I said. "The more, the merrier. I'll probably have to find a new location, though."

Lori sat up straighter. "I can take over the organization. You know, since I plan events for a living."

"Excellent idea," Landon said.

"What? No, you don't have to go to all that trouble. I can handle it."

"Baby, let Lori oversee this. Look how excited she is. You can handle *me* in all that spare time you get."

"And that's our clue that we've overstayed our

welcome." Lori rose to her feet. "Will and I will be going. I'll call to talk about the birthday details. Take care of your girl, Landon."

My cheeks warmed. Truthfully, my entire body did. I liked the sound of that. I liked it very much.

"Thanks for stopping by. And for helping with the party. You can still back out anytime," I said as I walked them to the door. Landon was by my side, his hand firmly on my back. Once his siblings were gone, he led me to the couch, then shoved the cup in my hands.

"The sooner you drink it, the better."

I pouted. "Why can't it be pink?"

"You don't trust me?"

"Oh, but I do."

"Take a sip. First one is the hardest."

Hardest might be an understatement. It was terrible… and then it wasn't. It left a bittersweet aftertaste, but I focused on the sweet part and took gulp after gulp until I emptied it.

"That's my girl," Landon said as I plunked the cup on the floor and then lifted my feet up on the couch. I'd barely noticed Landon move when I felt his hands at the back of my head, pressing his fingers into my throbbing skull.

"Ooooh, this is good. So good." It felt even better when he peppered gentle kisses at the top of my head.

"Are you up for breakfast yet?" he asked.

"Yeah, but I really want you to keep doing

that."

I remembered last night crystal clear, even with the Slutty Marys on board. He'd been so loving.

When my stomach started to rumble, he said, "We've got to get some food into you, sweetness."

"Okay. I already feel better."

"Told you that cure is magic." He left my side to mill around my kitchen. "I'll make you some toast, and I saw jam in one of your cupboards the other day. How does that sound for breakfast?"

"Great."

I loved seeing him as comfortable in my house as if it were his own. When he brought me a plate with toast, he also held out my phone to me.

"Your phone keeps making noise."

I took the plate and the phone, discovering messages from Grace.

Grace: Morning. How's your head? Do you still have Advil or should I bring you by some? Thought I'd message since I don't know how your tolerance for noises is this morning.

Maddie: I'm all set up, don't worry.

Landon sat on the couch, pulling my legs in his lap, scooting closer to me until my ass touched his outer thigh. Hmmm... if I shifted a little, I could even press my crotch against him. I wondered if I could do it without him catching on? He looked so delicious that I wanted to climb him.

He put the toast between us. Sharing a breakfast plate felt so intimate, and I'd become used to our coupley tendencies. A knot settled in my stomach. Nope, I would not go down this road. I was determined to focus on what Landon and I had now, not waste time with pesky questions about the future.

"What are you thinking about?" he asked. "You look like you're fighting with yourself."

Wow. I was an open book for him. How had that happened? Still, I didn't feel brave enough to admit I even entertained thoughts of more than *just for now.* We both knew the score. I was just extra sensitive this morning because... well, because Landon was here treating me like I was precious to him. He really had to stop being so Landon-ish.

"Come on, I know it's about me," he teased. I sighed, deciding to admit to a lesser sin.

"I was thinking that you look so delicious that I want to climb you. Am I shameless or what?"

"Not at all. That's just solid proof that you can't resist me."

I liked how in stride he took this. I set the empty plate on the coffee table, then shifted onto the couch until I straddled him.

"I'm torn. I want to tell you how great you are, but I'm afraid it'll go to your head," I said. He skimmed a hand up my arm, resting it at the base of my neck. "You're so amazing, Landon. Perfect."

He stilled. "Don't say that." I'd been expecting more cocky answers. Instead, his eyes were vulnerable, almost sad. "I lost too much for that to be true."

"You just don't see what I see," I said, aching

for him.

He fisted my shirt as I kissed his jaw, moving closer to his ear.

"I want to become the man you see."

"You already are." I nuzzled his neck, inching closer. He smelled amazing. Like wood, leather, and *man.* "You're kind and caring and the greatest man I know. And you make me so happy, Landon."

"I do?"

"Yeah. Happier than I've ever been."

Surprise flitted across his features, which I thought was completely unacceptable. It was my duty to convince him.

"You give me foot rubs, cover my culinary mishaps, *and* you brought me flowers. The list is endless." In a lower voice, I admitted, "You make me feel appreciated."

"You deserve to be appreciated, Maddie. Don't for one second think you don't."

"Well, I suppose when someone keeps making you feel small, you start believing that's how things should be."

"Just so you know, if I ever run into your ex, I'll punch him. On principle. With no explanations."

"See, that's just more proof that you're a great man," I said lightly, climbing into his lap, running my hands over his broad shoulders and the lean muscles in his arms.

***

Landon

I threaded my fingers through her hair. I needed more of her. I'd never get enough of her. Maddie's fingers worked the buttons of my shirt, undoing them as I kissed her with all I had. I had no idea when we'd moved to the bedroom. I was lost in her, and I wanted to lose myself even more. I wanted to show her how important she was to me.

I peeled her clothes off, one item at a time, stroking her. When we were both naked, I lowered her on the bed, straddling her. My erection was touching just below her breasts. She slid her hand up and down the length a few times, squeezing me good and tight. Her hair was splayed on the white sheet, her skin flushed. I spread my palm on her chest, inching to one breast, dragging my thumb in a circle around her nipple. She licked her lips, her chest rising and falling with a deep breath.

"You're so beautiful, Maddie."

I kept moving my thumb around her nipple, feeling her quiver, lightly in the beginning, then stronger. Briefly I wondered if I could bring her to climax just by touching her breasts, but I knew I wouldn't be testing the theory today, maybe never. When it came to Maddie, I was always greedy for more. I wanted to feel her all around me. Be inside her, kiss her, touch as much of her skin as possible.

Gripping me at the base, she lifted her head, her intent obvious, but I was too far away for her to be able to take me in her mouth. Looking up at me, she gave me a wicked wink before squeezing her arms under my thighs, sliding under me until her head was right in front of my cock. I squeezed her shoulders between my thighs, and her eyes flared. She had given me complete control over her.

"Look at me, Maddie."

I needed the sweetness of eye contact. I wanted us to watch each other as we pushed past yet another boundary, moved deeper into intimacy. I wanted her to know how utterly and completely she owned me right now. I wanted to own her the same way.

When our gazes locked, she clamped her mouth around me. Watching her trust me like this was the most beautiful thing, a damn privilege. The way she opened up beckoned to me to do the same. I wanted to give her everything I had. But I didn't know if I could, or if it would be enough. When I was close to climax, I pulled back.

"I need to be inside you." I put on a condom before driving into her. She felt slick and tight. I braced my forearms at her sides, then slid in and out of her until we both climaxed.

"Wow," she exclaimed a while later, lacing her arms around my neck. I loved being in the circle of her arms.

"Sounds about right." I kissed the tip of her nose while she tried to wiggle out from under me. "Where are you going? Stay here."

"Nope. I have big plans for you today." She

tried to wiggle out some more, but I pinned her against the mattress.

"And what are those plans?"

"Let me go and I'll tell you."

"That's not how it works, sweetheart. I'm in charge here."

She licked her lips, and I felt her nipples harden against my chest. Maddie was driving me crazy. I might have fooled myself into thinking I was in charge, but the truth was Maddie had all the power. I lowered one hand between our bodies, strumming her clit. She gasped. I kissed one corner of her mouth, then the other.

"So, are you going to talk?"

"You terrible man. If you must know, I want to do something for you to relax. Something nice."

"You already give me everything I need, Maddie. Coming home to you? Waking up next to you? Those are the best parts of my day."

"That's lovely to hear." Her voice caught, and she paused for a moment, clearing her throat. "But I was thinking something more proactive. Like a hot bath or a massage. And then something outdoors. It's the end of July. Best time in LA, if you ask me."

"I have another proposition for relaxing. I want this. You." I lowered my head and flicked my tongue around her nipple until she bucked her hips.

"You're taking advantage of my goodwill," she muttered between moans. "But since I'm enjoying it so much, I might let you get away with it."

"Let me?" I placed open-mouthed kisses on

her chest, looking her straight in the eyes. "You need to be reminded who is in charge here, sweetness."

"Is that so? Well, I'm looking forward to being reminded." She flashed me a bright, beautiful smile.

I'll miss that smile. All of her. I'd go to war for that smile.

Chapter Twenty-Four
Landon

There was no other way to put it: Hailey was whip-smart. She proved it every minute of the next week. I'd never worked with her before, and part of me wondered if I'd be able to see her as a business partner instead of my little sister. I shouldn't have worried. She was keeping everyone on their toes, and had also asked me not to call her "sister" in front of the employees. She only acknowledged our shared bloodline behind closed doors (neither of us was a fan of Val's open-door policy).

She slid inside the office while I was on a conference call with Sullivan and sat on the floor, spreading small bottles and files before her. We'd brought in a second desk for her, but in the week she'd been here, I rarely saw her sit behind it.

"Sullivan, this is clearly not working out," I said. I was standing behind Val's desk, too worked up to sit. "If we don't finalize negotiations by the end of the week, we'll go our separate ways." I wasn't bluffing. I knew that investors would be uneasy, but ultimately Sullivan was wasting everyone's time.

"Due diligence is important," Sullivan countered.

"Due diligence was completed before I left. That's *why* I left. Clearly, if you have so many doubts, it means we're not a good fit." We were a good fit. I knew it wouldn't be easy to find another partner who complemented our capabilities so well, but Sullivan's work ethic in this process made me think we were better off without him anyway. "That's my final word. Have a good evening."

I ended the call, running a hand through my hair, and finally sat on my chair.

"My feet are killing me," Hailey mumbled, kicking off her shoes.

"Those are killing you." I pointed to her shoes.

"Hey! The heels are only two inches, and I love them. What do you think Sullivan will do?"

"Honestly, I don't know. But at this point, I think we'd be better off without him, even if the investors will be at my throat."

She pointed to the small bottles on the floor. "I brought the final samples. They were the winners with the focus groups we've conducted."

"You mean *you* conducted. Hailey? Thanks for being here."

"Awww, and you thought you could do all this without me."

"You won't let me forget this for years, will you?"

"Be serious. I'll hold it over your head forever."

I could see her doing that. One thing was still

nagging at me.

"Are your sure taking this time off won't count against you for the promotion?"

Hailey took a deep breath. "I've been passed by already."

"What? When did that happen? Why didn't you tell me?"

"Because it still stings?"

"You deserved that promotion. You'd brought in more revenue than anyone in your office, and you had the highest efficiency rate. What was their feedback?"

"Nothing useful. So I decided I'm not going to break my back for them anymore. Do you know how many birthday parties and Christmases I missed because I was working overtime to meet deadlines, make our clients happy?"

I knew all too well.

"I've missed every single one of Milo's school events. From now on, I'm only going to bend backward for the family. Anyone else is just not worth it."

"I'm sorry, Hailey."

"Lesson learned. I'll move on as soon as I find a job that pays well enough. That's the problem with consulting. They pay in gold for your sweat and blood, and the salaries on the rest of the market don't keep up."

"If you need a job—"

She wiggled her finger at me. "Don't you dare offer me one. I'm so disappointed with consulting right now that I'd be tempted to take it."

"You say that like it's a bad thing."

"I'd never know if you're offering because I deserve it or just because I'm your sister."

I groaned. "Hailey, I know how capable you are."

"Look, I appreciate the offer, but I don't want to move to San Jose anyway."

I opened my mouth to argue some more, but my phone lit up with an incoming message.

Grace: It's all set.

Landon: Perfect.

I'd gotten her number from Maddie, and together with her and my sister, we were planning Maddie's birthday. Lori was doing the actual planning; Grace and I just came up with ideas.

"Who are you texting?" Hailey asked.

"Grace."

My sister beamed, stretching out her legs on the floor.

"Lori told me the three of you are planning Maddie's birthday. That's so sweet, Landon. Val and I made a bet with Pippa and Summer that we'll have a Connor wedding soon on our hands."

Pippa and Summer were two of our Bennett cousins. I loved them to bits, but wished they weren't giving my sisters dangerous ideas.

"I hope you don't plan to let Maddie go," Hailey said.

When I didn't respond, she said, "I swear I'll throw this at you if you give up the chance to be happy." She grabbed one of her shoes. "Look at this heel. It can do a lot of damage. And I love these shoes, so this should tell you how strongly I feel about this."

"It's complicated, Hailey."

"Because you live in different cities?"

"Not just that. You wouldn't understand."

"Yeah, I do understand. You lost Rachel. If there is anyone who understands fear of attachment, it's us. We all lost Mom and Dad. We've been trying to tell you this all along."

I was too stunned for a moment to even think, let alone answer. I'd always hung on to the foolish hope that Val and I had managed to shield our younger siblings from that bone-deep insecurity that came with losing the people you loved and depended on.

"I'm sorry, I didn't mean to minimize your—"

She shook her head. "This is not about us. It's about you. Since Maddie, you smile again, Landon. I mean real smiles, the kind that reaches your eyes. And you're good together. Lori told me how cute you were that morning when she and Will stopped by. Maddie makes you happy."

"Very," I admitted. Hailey waited, but I volunteered no other information.

Eventually, she sighed dramatically. "If you keep up the one-word answers, you're giving us no choice but to choreograph a CSI."

"Crime Scene Investigation?" I asked in

confusion, thinking about the show.

"Connor Secret Intervention."

"What is that?"

"It wouldn't be secret if I told you the details. But you have been warned."

I glanced at the time. It was six o'clock. I still had documents to go through, and the samples, but I could do that tomorrow.

"Let's call this a day," I suggested.

"I agree 100 percent. So what are you planning for Maddie's birthday?" Hailey asked, putting on her shoes as I rose from my seat. "Lori won't tell me a thing."

"Like I'd tell you. It would get back right to Maddie."

"Are you implying I have a big mouth?"

I extended my hand, helping her to her feet. "Hailey, I love you, but you're the reason surprise birthday parties aren't a thing in our family."

"Once. I ruined it once."

We'd planned a surprise party for Lori when she turned sixteen, but two days before, the jig was up.

"Don't forget Will's graduation gift."

Hailey gaped at me. "I only did that to save him from spending all his money on a motorcycle. What was I supposed to do?"

"Come up with something more inventive than 'Hey, Will, don't buy a motorcycle. That's our gift'?"

"I panicked, okay?"

"I'll sleep better at night if you don't know."

Hailey and I said goodbye in the elevator. She was heading to the garage for her car. I was taking a cab. I hadn't rented a car because I liked to use the time on commute to respond to e-mails. Adam had sent me a list of companies we could consider for a partnership if Sullivan pulled out of the deal. My mind wasn't on the partnership, though. I was fixating on my conversation with Hailey about Maddie. Going back to San Jose meant no more Maddie. I couldn't wrap my mind around that idea.

When the cab pulled in front of her house, I saw her perched on a ladder, fixing something on the roof.

I paid the cabbie quickly, then called out to her, "Maddie? What are you doing up there?"

"A shingle is giving me trouble. I need to fix it, but I can't reach it, damn it. I'm going to have to climb on the roof completely."

"Baby, I'll fix that for you. Get back down here."

"It's okay. Can you hold the ladder?"

"Baby," I warned as I gripped the metal ladder with both hands. "You can't climb on that roof. I'm taller. I can reach it from the ladder. Get down here."

Instead of listening, Maddie climbed up to the last step of the ladder, propping her palms on the roof. I was half in a mind to grab her and bring her down, but her balance was precarious already. I held the ladder tight, tasting bile at the back of my throat when she perched one foot on her roof. When she pushed off the other foot, she lost her balance.

"Shit!" she exclaimed, groping at the roof with both hands as she slid downward. She tried to stop her slide by gripping the ladder, but she was moving too fast to catch it.

I caught her legs when she was in my reach, stopping her fall, but the force of impact messed up my balance and I stumbled backward. We both sprawled on the ground.

"Shit! Ouch!" Maddie exclaimed. As soon as I was on my feet, I helped her up, inspecting her for any damage.

"Are you hurt?"

"No. Just a few scratches."

"Why didn't you listen? I told you it was dangerous to climb on that goddamned roof," I yelled.

"Don't yell at me. Don't you *dare* yell at me," she yelled back.

"You could've really hurt yourself."

"Well, I didn't. What's the big deal? I slipped. Isn't the first time and won't be the last one. A shingle is broken, and I needed to fix it."

I dragged both hands down my face, willing myself to calm down. "I'm sorry I yelled. I just—I panicked. I thought you were hurt."

Maddie crossed her arms over her chest, but her expression softened. "I'm not hurt, Landon. Thank you for catching me." She looked up to the roof. "I need to get back up. I want to fix that shingle today."

"You're joking, right? I'm not letting you go up there."

"I'm not asking for permission."

"I told you I can fix it." I felt my temper flare again.

"I don't want to get used to relying on you for stuff, okay?"

Her words slayed me. I pulled her into a hug. "Baby...."

"I sure sound like a baby now. I'm sorry, Landon, I don't know why I'm getting so worked up."

"Maddie, let me do this for you, okay?"

She nodded, snuggling closer to me. "And I had this great plan tonight to lure out what you're planning for my birthday," she said into my neck, making me chuckle. "I kind of blew that chance away, huh?"

In the beginning, Grace and I had wanted to include Maddie in the planning, then decided a surprise was better. I could just imagine her smile on that day.

"You can try," I said on a wink. "I'm going up on the roof. You work on those persuasion skills while I fix your shingle."

I didn't want this woman to ever worry about a shingle again. I wanted to fix every shingle, paint every wall for her. I had a crystal-clear vision of our life together right at that moment. I sure as hell didn't want to let her go, but I had no idea how to hold on.

Chapter Twenty-Five
Maddie

The Monday before my birthday, I was cooking in the sun, dragging a sack of fertilizer across the school grounds, when my phone buzzed. I took refuge under the shade of a large California oak tree before answering.

"Maddie Jennings speaking," I said into my phone.

"Hi, Ms. Jennings. This is David Hooper, from Hooper Properties."

I recognized the name. It was the housing developer who was looking for landscape developers for his green residential project. I'd applied a few weeks back, but I wasn't expecting a call so soon.

"I love your portfolio, but I hit a roadblock in your application, and I'm hoping it's a typo. In the comment section, you mentioned it would take you two months longer than I asked for to complete the project."

"Yes, that's correct. Unfortunately, that's the capacity I have."

"I see. Well, if your situation changes, give me a call. I'd love to work with you."

"Sure. Thank you for the call, Mr. Hooper."

I couldn't help the pang of disappointment after the call disconnected. Sure, I'd known my personnel capacity would prevent me from winning this project, but hearing it out loud still stung. I thought about working with Elise again. Landon *was* right. I shouldn't allow the failed partnership with Owen to keep me back from following my dreams. Easier said than done, but I resolved to give this more thought after my birthday.

Right now, I saw Leta Hendricks, the school's principal, crossing the yard. I'd asked her here today to show her our progress, ask if she wanted any changes. The boys I'd hired for this project and I had worked a few weeks on it already. We still had ten days left, but I wanted her opinion before we completed it.

"This is amazing, Maddie. The parents will be very happy," she announced. "I love what you did with that cluster of palm trees and with the arch with bougainvillea. It's even better than what I imagined when you described it. And they blend nicely with the sycamore trees."

"Of course. That's what I wanted. I fell in love with this space as soon I saw them."

The California sycamore trees were on the property before there was a school here. They gave the entire space a traditional air, even if the school was relatively new.

Since she was impressed, now was the best time to ask the principal for a favor. I took in her coiffed salt-and-pepper hair, the old-school cut of her jacket and skirt. Leta looked exactly like I'd imagined the principal of a private school would look. But despite her strict appearance, she was friendly.

"I'd love to stop by on the first day of school, if that's okay with you, and show the parents and kids around."

"Sure. We'd love to have you here."

I didn't doubt Leta would refer the parents to me if they asked, but I wanted to be more proactive. Nothing beat being there in person. I normally wasn't a fan of pitching myself to people, but this opportunity was golden. I couldn't pass it up.

"Thank you."

"Well, I'll leave you to get back to work."

After she left, my stomach started grumbling, reminding me it was lunchtime. The boys had packed lunch with them, but I went to the burrito place across the street. I missed my lunches with Landon.

While I ate, I mentally reviewed my work calendar for the year. I was booked almost solid until the end of October. Even though LA had nice weather most of the time, people didn't give redoing their yard much thought in winter, and I had to go the extra mile to secure projects. I wondered if project rotation was the same in San Jose, then shook my head. Why was I even entertaining those thoughts? I knew the score.

But I was missing Landon already.

**

The next morning, I woke up buzzing with anticipation. I patted the bed next to me, even though I knew it would be empty, but I'd harbored the hope that Landon had snuck in during the night. A girl could dream.

The buzz of anticipation intensified. Grace had been teasing me relentlessly about the plans she'd concocted with Landon and Lori, but neither was sharing any details. *Bastards.* I'd get my revenge on them first chance I got. Well, on Grace anyway. I wasn't sure how that would work out with Lori or Landon. He was leaving in one week. Val had declared that she'd be fit to return to work by then. My eyes began to sting, and I blinked a few times. I couldn't tear up on my birthday.

I reached for my phone. It was almost eight o'clock in the morning. I hadn't slept so long on a weekday in years, but Landon had persuaded me to take the day off.

My phone rang the second the clock turned eight. I grinned as Landon's name appeared on screen.

"Most people wait until later with the birthday calls. Common decency and all that."

"I'm not most people. And I have no decency when it comes to you," Landon said. "Happy birthday, Maddie."

"Thank you. Are you going to tell me the plans for today?"

"Nah, but my helper will be there soon."

I wiggled my ass. "Grace or Lori?"

"Grace."

"I can't believe you've been plotting with my sister *and* your sister. And that you've used all those tricks to convince me to take the day off."

"I don't remember you complaining at the time."

I felt my cheeks burn. His tricks fell into two categories: racy and downright sinful. Of course I hadn't complained.

"You really have no decency. I don't know why I keep you around."

Landon laughed softly. "I can't wait to see you later. Have fun today."

"Fun doing what? Come on, just a little hint."

As if on cue, the bell rang. Landon must have heard it too, because he said, "That's your hint. See you later, Maddie."

"See you."

I scrambled out of bed, looking for my jeans. An idea struck me. What if Landon was at the door, and he'd just been messing with me? My heart went pitter-patter at the thought. The knock at the front door became more insistent.

When I swung it open, my smile faltered just a bit.

"What's that?" Grace's voice dripped with accusation.

I hung my head in shame and owned up to my sins. "I'd gotten it into my mind that Landon was messing with me saying I'll only see him later."

"I'd be mad, but it's understandable. I'd be

disappointed too if I was expecting that hunk and all I got was little old me."

I pulled her into a hug. "I'm not disappointed, you little schemer."

"Happy birthday, sis." Pulling back, she added, "I will be your guide today. You have fifteen minutes to get dressed."

Curiosity and panic warred inside me. Curiosity regarding our plan for the day, and panic that I only had fifteen minutes to shower and dress. Fourteen minutes later, I did a full turn in front of Grace.

"Acceptable?"

She nodded. "Let's go."

My phone rang nonstop while Grace drove us through the city. Friends and old clients called, then my parents.

"We're here," Grace announced while I was bidding Mom goodbye. She pulled the car into a parking space on a narrow street lined with restaurants and shops. We were going shopping? I loved shopping. I didn't need anything in particular, but that had never kept me from indulging. I loved pretty things.

I finished the conversation with Mom as Grace took my hand, guiding me onto the main street. Only when I shoved my phone into my purse did I realize we were on Rodeo Drive, also known as one of the most expensive shopping streets in LA.

"Rodeo Drive is a bit out of my budget, don't you think?"

She winked. "Luckily, you're the birthday girl so you're not paying. Landon's treat. He asked me what you liked to do, and I brought up shopping."

I opened my mouth to argue, but she held up her finger.

"Any complaints, direct them to Landon. I'm just your guide. But just so you know, you're not leaving here without at least a dress and shoes."

"I can't believe it!"

We came to a stop in front of a store displaying fabulous evening gowns. They looked exorbitant. I felt myself melting as we admired them. It was a hot day even for August standards. Grace pushed open the door to the store. It even smelled expensive.

A perfectly coiffed blonde vendor greeted us.

"How may I help you?" she asked.

"We're looking for an evening gown. It's my sister's birthday, and we're having a party tonight."

"Of course. Shall I give you a tour? You can tell me which dresses you want to try on, and I'll bring the right size to the changing room."

I tried on dress after dress after dress, excitement bubbling inside me. I couldn't decide which one was my favorite. The black one with a plunging neckline? The dark blue one with little ribbons up my back? I thought Landon would particularly like that one. Undressing me would be like unwrapping a gift. I toyed with the idea of sending Landon snapshots, but I wanted to surprise him. Then I had an even better idea. I took a picture of myself in between changing dresses, when I wore nothing but underwear. He replied after I'd already slipped into a new dress.

Landon: Maddie...You don't want to do this. Teasing me is a dangerous game.

I licked my lips, anticipation firing me up.

Maddie: You've teased me about my birthday. This is your punishment.

Landon: I'll collect my reward tonight.

I clenched my thighs, letting out a long breath. Right. This was not the moment to get turned on, with the vendor and Grace waiting for me to come out of the changing room. Damn Landon. How could he affect me even from a distance?

"If something doesn't fit you perfectly, we're happy to modify it. We have a seamstress here, and she'll have it ready for you in a few hours," the vendor called from behind the curtain separating the changing room from the store.

"Okay."

I still had one more to try. A white one that looked like something out of a fairy tale. The bodice was tight, with a delicate motif of pink magnolias. The skirt was light chiffon, flowing into an A-shape to the floor. Both Grace and the vendor sighed when I walked out wearing it.

"This is the one," Grace exclaimed. But my stomach tightened as I looked at my reflection. I looked like a bride trying on her wedding gown. The dress was definitely beautiful enough to pass as a wedding dress. And the man was perfect enough to marry.

I shook my head, dispelling the fantasy. I wasn't going to marry Landon. He was never going to ask. This wasn't what this was. He'd said right from the beginning that he didn't know how to *do love*. Why had my thoughts even wandered in that direction?

Because Landon was the only man who'd made me feel special. He'd done the legwork to find out what I liked, just to please me. Landon had made me feel special ever since he'd walked me home the night after we danced. Every kiss and touch made me feel special.

I loved him. I could admit that to myself, at least. There was no hiding from my own feelings when I fantasized about being Landon's bride just because I was trying on a white dress.

"No, I have another favorite," I said eventually. My voice didn't sound quite right, but I hoped neither Grace nor the vendor could pick up on it. "I'm trying on the blue one again."

I bolted back inside the changing room, pulling the curtain. I changed out of the dress without looking in the mirror. But my mind came up with more pesky thoughts.

Could I move to San Jose? I'd followed a man once, and it hadn't worked well for me. Could I start over in another city? For Landon? Grace was all grown-up, so she didn't need me here physically, and I could work as a landscaper anywhere. I had savings to cover Grace's tuition fees even in case business was rocky in the beginning.

Even though I'd built my business here, I didn't have many repeat clients. People didn't remodel their gardens often. Recommendations brought in a big chunk of business, and most clients recommended me to their friends in LA, so I'd be starting over. I couldn't believe I was even contemplating starting over. But Landon was worth the risk. The big question was, would Landon want me to move at all? I was afraid his answer would be "no."

"I want this one," I said when I came out wearing the blue one again. "But it needs tucking in at the waist."

The vendor nodded. "I'm going to get our seamstress."

"This is so expensive, though," I muttered to Grace once the vendor was out of earshot.

My sister didn't miss a beat. "Not for Landon. Let the man buy you what he wants. He was as excited as a kid when we planned this. He's the only man I've ever heard sound happy about spending money on clothes."

Oh, how well I could imagine that enthusiasm. Grace was right. It would make Landon happy. And wasn't that what I wanted? Also, the dress *was* gorgeous.

"You're right. You're absolutely right."

The vendor reappeared with the seamstress. It took her all of ten minutes to set up her needles.

"I can have it ready for you in two hours," she said.

"We can be back for it in two and a half," Grace said, making me wonder what else she and Landon had planned for me.

We shopped till we dropped. I bought two pairs of shoes and a bag, as well as a number of tops and jeans. While I was trying on my last pair of shoes, I caught Grace looking wistfully at the racks of merchandise.

"What?" I asked.

"Landon said I should buy something for myself too, but I feel like I'd be taking advantage."

My heart soared. He'd even thought of Grace.

"Well, the joke's on you, little sis. You're not leaving here without a pair of shoes."

Manicures and pedicures were on the list too. I'd asked Grace if they were a gift from Landon too, and she'd replied, "No! That's my gift, because you're the best sister ever."

By the time we returned to my bungalow, I wanted to take a nap, but I still had work to do. I had to wash my hair and style it, and apply makeup. We popped open a small bottle of champagne while we did each other's makeup.

We took a cab to the location, and I was so excited, it was ridiculous. We drove into West Hollywood and pulled in front of a white building lined with wood poles at regular intervals. The simplicity was chic and elegant. The rooftop was glass-encased, and I could see people milling around. The name of the restaurant, Sinful, made me smile.

Landon came out the front door the next second, giving Grace and me a wide smile.

"Here is the birthday girl," my sister announced unnecessarily.

"Happy birthday, Maddie," said Landon.

"Thank you for today." I did a full turn so he could admire me. My blonde hair was styled in a chic updo, with a few curled strands falling from it to reach my shoulders. The dark blue dress didn't have a plunging neckline, but it did show enough cleavage to spark someone's imagination. The ribbons on the back were my favorite part. The skirt reached down to my toes. I moved my leg through the thigh-high gap, showcasing the shoes—black, sky-high heels, and a thin strap I'd wrapped around each of my ankles. Landon might not know shoes, but he recognized *hot as hell* when he saw it. His eyes turned molten.

Grace cleared her throat. "Shall we go upstairs, lovebirds?"

I smiled sheepishly, taking Landon's arm as Grace led the way through the building. We went up a narrow spiral staircase. I held my dress up in my free hand, afraid I'd step on it.

"Who is here?" I asked when we reached the upper floor, tapping my foot to the rhythm of the music blaring through the loudspeakers. The room was dimly lit, with an inviting atmosphere. The glass wall at the other side of the room showed a beautiful view of LA at night.

"You'll see," Landon said, kissing the side of my head.

Grace beamed. "Landon and Lori asked me to make a list of the friends you'd like to see."

I'd been expecting Dylan and Alena, and even Emma and Robbie, who'd driven over from Desert Hot Springs. But I definitely wasn't expecting my best friends from college, Jenny and Wilma, and even Sarah and Lydia, with whom I'd shared an apartment back in Miami.

The Connor clan was sitting at a round table, near the glass wall. Val still had the cast on her leg, but her ribs had healed, at least. Lori strode straight to us, flinging her arms around me.

"Happy birthday," she chanted. "What do you think?"

"This is incredible. Thank you."

"Now, I don't want to take all the credit, Grace and Landon helped. But it was mostly me," she said with sass.

"Well, this is great. Where is Milo?"

"I arranged a sleepover with one of his friends so I didn't have to leave too soon."

I went on to say hi to everyone, smiling from ear to ear the entire time.

Jenny monopolized me right after I made the rounds, dragging me to the bar. The menu was full of cinematic-themed cocktails. I ordered a *Casablanca*, and Jenny a *Cleopatra*. She was rocking a little black dress, not looking one day older than in our college days.

"Girl, I thought I'd melt on the spot when Landon called. You've found yourself a keeper," she said. I sighed sadly, sipping my drink. I knew that, of course. The question was how to keep him?

I hadn't had a big bash in years, not since I moved to LA, anyway. Life had gotten in the way, and I'd always had a small celebration, but this was the way a birthday should be celebrated. In style.

I found my way to the Connor table soon enough. Lori and Hailey were sitting with Val. Landon, Jace, and Will were scattered around the room. The Connor girls were knockouts tonight. Val was wearing a tunic-style red dress with a black leather belt around her middle. One leg was bared, the other concealed by the white cast. Hailey had styled her dark hair in a frilly bun, with curled strands falling in ringlets around her face. I was jealous of her killer red shoes with silver heels. It was only when I saw her sitting between Lori and Val that I realized she was the only sister who didn't have green eyes. Hers were dark, like chocolate. Lori rocked a white, short dress with a lovely lace pattern, her blonde hair pulled into a French braid.

"Girls, I come bringing cocktails," I announced, setting the tray with four glasses on the wooden table.

"My favorite words ever," Hailey exclaimed.

We all helped ourselves to a glass, and as we clinked them, Val said, "To the wonderful Maddie, who's made our brother happier than I've ever seen him."

"Hear, hear," Hailey said. "I can vouch for that, and I've been keeping an eye on him at the office."

"Girls, stop. You're making me blush."

Val, who was sitting nearest, covered my hand with hers. "You're good for him, Maddie. And looking at you, all happy and gooey, I'd say he's good for you too."

Lori was picking at her fingernails, a suspicious smile playing on her lips. "Just saying, but I want to plan a Connor wedding soon. Considering the state of things, you're the most likely candidates."

Damn. My imagination didn't need more ammunition. It was in a dangerous place tonight as it was. The cocktails weren't helping.

When Landon pulled me in the darkest corner of the dance floor a while later, my emotions were running high. If that was how he did birthdays, I wondered how he'd make a proposal. I bet it would be epic. I sighed. Tonight, Landon had opened the floodgates. Dreams and hopes were coming through. I was powerless to stop them, and that scared me a little.

"What are you thinking about? Must be something real good. Look at the smile," he said.

"It's top secret," I teased.

"Is that so?"

I nodded confidently, even though my pulse skittered. I was afraid he'd see straight into my heart.

"I happen to know a few techniques to make

you spill secrets," he said.

He touched my upper lip with his forefinger, pressing on the bow. He pulled me to him, swiping his tongue where he'd touched before, in a slow, sensual movement. I felt his lick straight between my thighs. He captured my mouth with his, kissing me until my toes curled and I wanted to climb him. Oh goodness, his kisses weren't helping me close those floodgates. Not at all.

"What you did today for me was so thoughtful. Thanks," I said. "I'm just happy."

"I'm glad to hear that. I love making you happy."

He flashed me that dreamy smile I adored. I reached out and pulled him in for another kiss, needing his lips again.

Landon touched my arms, my back, then lowered one hand down my back. There was a small, inviting slit between the last ribbon and the base of my spine. Landon found it and slipped two fingers there, as if what was on display wasn't enough and he needed to touch more of me. I melted against him, moaning into his mouth when I felt his erection against my belly. Landon rocked me to the rhythm of the music, resting his mouth on my neck.

"I can't wait to take you home, make you mine," he said when the song was over. His voice was gruff. His breath was coming out in hot bursts that lit me up too. He looked at me as if he wanted to claim me right here on the dance floor. I swear I could feel my panties melting under the heat in his gaze.

I trailed my fingers on his chest. The white shirt was stretched over his taut muscles. I could trace his dents and ridges in my sleep by now.

"Maddie, don't tempt me."

I knew his words were supposed to warn me, but his voice sounded like pure sex, making me wanton. But I decided to behave. I didn't want to tempt him to the point where he'd whisk me away. I was detecting that possessive glint in his eyes that meant he wasn't far from throwing me over his shoulder, and I hadn't even cut the cake.

Chapter Twenty-Six
Landon

Lori and Grace had pulled off a great party. Maddie was having fun, and I couldn't keep my eyes off her. Those ribbons down her back begged to be pulled open, and she was taunting me relentlessly.

Shortly before eight, my cousin Sebastian Bennett arrived with his wife and two of his kids. If I wasn't mistaken, they were three years old.

I went to get Maddie, who was at the bar with Grace.

"Maddie, remember I told you my cousin and his family would stop by?"

"Yes. They're here?"

"They just arrived." I guided her to them, drawing small circles with my hand on the small of her back. She sucked in a breath when I touched bare skin through that slit under the ribbon.

"Maddie, this is my cousin Sebastian and his wife, Ava."

Sebastian shook her hand. "Happy birthday, Maddie. Sorry to crash your party, but we haven't seen this lot in a while. Thought it'd be a shame to pass through LA and not catch up. We'll only be staying for an hour. These two get cranky when their bedtime passes."

"Don't hurry. I'm happy to see you here," Maddie said.

She shook hands with Ava, then crouched until she was level with the two boys.

"And what might your names be? I'm Maddie."

Both of the boys looked up at Ava. She pushed a strand of her blonde hair away from her face before answering.

"Seamus and Peter. They're very shy."

"They're twins?" Maddie asked with excitement, straightening up.

I chuckled. "Not identical, but yes, twins. There's a strong twin gene in our family."

"You must have your hands full all of the time," Maddie said, looking between my cousin and his wife.

"Oh, we've got two more at home. They're with their grandparents," Sebastian supplied. "Four in total. For now."

Ava snapped her head in his direction, eyes wide. "For now? Husband of mine, I think four will do."

I bit back a smile. "Don't be so harsh on him, Ava. We come from big families."

Sebastian pulled her closer, kissing her temple. "I'm not worried. I always wear you down."

"He does," Ava whispered conspiratorially to Maddie, then grinned. "I wish I could say otherwise, but when Sebastian wants something, boy oh boy, is my man persuasive. He even got me to agree to name this little one Seamus."

"Took me four kids to finally convince you to use the name," Sebastian said. "Still, I did it."

Maddie was grinning at them. "Well, come on in."

We walked with them toward the bar. Midway, Seamus wiggled his hand free from Ava's grip. He could barely keep his balance, but he broke into a run, as if determined to test his legs. Maddie ran after him, scooping him up in her arms before he pelted headfirst into a wall.

"We've got this," I assured Ava and Sebastian. "You two have a drink. We'll bring Seamus back."

Maddie was talking in a soft voice when I approached them.

"That's a wall, little one. Hard and solid. Nothing good can come out of running into it, I promise. That's an experience you can forgo."

She brought him right in front of the wall, putting his small hand on the surface.

"See?"

She'd be a great mother one day. Something stirred in me, and the longer I watched her, the stronger it grew. When she walked with him toward me, the vision of a family became all too real. Our family.

"Seamus is adorable," she informed me, kissing his forehead. "Pity I can't keep him."

I almost asked, "Do you want to keep me?" But that was a conversation for another day. I didn't want to put her on the spot on her birthday. Seamus was playing with her hair as if it was the most fascinating thing in the world. I agreed with him. She was fascinating. And she had become the center of my world.

"You know what? I'll ask the restaurant to bring out the cake now, so these two angels see it too," she said.

"I'll take care of that." I kissed her lips, then headed to one of the servers, making arrangements. Fifteen minutes later, we all gathered around Maddie, singing "Happy Birthday." When she blew out the candles, I made a wish of my own.

The party went on until well after midnight, and I barely kept myself in check around Maddie. But the moment we were inside her house, I backed her against the nearest wall, kissing her temple, descending to her earlobe. I traced her jaw before finally settling at the corner of her mouth. She was shuddering in my arms, and I hadn't even kissed her.

"I've dreamed about doing this the entire day." I kissed her bottom lip, biting gently in the center. Maddie pushed her thighs together.

"You did?" Her voice was uncharacteristically small and shy. I wanted to erase her doubts.

"Yes. You have no idea how often I think about you. I can't get enough of you. You're so precious to me. I don't want to ever stop kissing you, to stop feeling everything you make me feel."

"Then don't stop."

I'd never felt as close to her as I felt tonight, as if we were connected on every level. Our emotions were tied together; our bodies yearned to be united. I undid the ribbons on her back and pushed her dress down to her feet, kissing her skin. She was wearing a red lace thong and matching bra, with the clasp at the back. Turning her around, I unclasped her bra, then swiped my tongue along her spine, running my hands down her sides. Her skin erupted in goose bumps under my touch. I didn't stop when I reached her ass. I ran my fingers down the red lace between her ass cheeks, then bunched the fabric between my fingers, tugged and let it go. A little *snap* resounded when it made contact with her skin.

She shoved her hands against the wall, curling her fingers as if wanting to dig them in. The sight sent a zing of lust right through me. I instantly hardened. She had a perfect ass. Two round globes. I sank my teeth lightly in one, kneading the other in my hand.

"Landon," she gasped, clenching her thighs.

"Turn around." When she did, I smiled and rose until I was level with her breasts.

Her nipples were already tight. I kissed around one, then the other, pushing a hand up her thigh. She parted her legs, giving me access. I cupped her pussy over her panties and rolled one nipple between my lips at the same time. She arched her hips, tugging at my hair.

"Landon, please, I need your fingers inside me. Please. Now."

Smiling against her breasts, I slipped my fingers into her panties, sliding one inside her. I loved that she told me what she needed without my coaxing.

She transformed into a wild thing right in front of my eyes. *My Maddie.* This side of her was just for me. *She* was made for me, and no one else. Her breathing became shallow as I slid the finger in and out, and she cried out my name when I slid in a second one. When I pressed the heel of my palm against her clit, she clenched around my fingers. My control snapped, replaced by a blind need for her.

"I'm going to fuck you against this wall, Maddie."

Looking down, I saw she was already unbuttoning my pants, lowering my zipper. I kissed up her breasts, her neck, nipping at her skin. A wild desire to mark her hit me. To somehow leave an imprint on her. I wanted her sweetness, her passion, her pleasure. Her future.

"Yes. Do it."

"And then I will carry you to bed and make love to you the entire night."

"Yes, do that too. I love your plans. You always have the best plans."

She shuddered slightly in my arms, looking up at me with wide, trusting eyes. I took out a condom, gloved up, and then touched her clit, watching her succumb to the sensation until she bucked her hips, riding my hand, taking her own pleasure.

I lifted her by the ass and slid her onto me

before she'd ridden out her orgasm. She cried my name, and my eyes nearly rolled into my head. She was so tight around me I couldn't even breathe from the intensity of it.

"You—oh this feels…. It's different than before," she murmured, moving an arm up my shoulder and around my neck.

"It's different every time," I murmured back. Every time was *more*. More than I could say, more than I could admit. She pulled me closer to her, as if sensing how much I needed her warmth. Realizing the strength of our connection made my world tilt on its axis. I drove into her so wildly, I thought I'd split her in two, but I couldn't hold back.

With every thrust she clamped tighter around me, her breath came out shakier, her moans louder. I wanted this every night, every morning. Maddie owned me in every way possible.

My balls tightened, heat zipping from them, spreading in my entire body. I was too close to the edge, and I wanted this to last longer. I wanted her to come again. Slowing down, I buried my head in her neck, inhaling deeply, moving my pelvis so I was pressing against her clit. She fisted my hair, her teeth grazing my shoulder.

Pulling out of her, I carried her to the bedroom, laid her on the bed, and climbed on top of her. I loved her slowly, gently, needing this to last the entire night. When I came too close, I stilled, leaning to kiss her shoulders, her arms.

When she started clenching around me in

quick, rhythmic spasms, energy coiled through my entire body. The muscles in my abdomen contracted, as if someone pulled a hook behind my navel. I exploded when she gasped out my name.

I kept her tightly to me afterward, rocking her in my arms. She fell asleep quickly, but I was wide-awake. My mind was spinning, mapping out solutions so I could keep Maddie in my life. She was curled in a fetal position across the bed, facing me and using my chest as a pillow. Even sleeping, she had a wide, satisfied smile. Knowing I was responsible for that happiness made me feel whole. A strand of hair fell over her face, and she scrunched up her nose. I quickly pushed it away so the tickling wouldn't wake her.

"I didn't think I could fall in love again, Maddie. But you made me fall for you. I love you, sweetness."

Chapter Twenty-Seven
Landon

The next day started bad enough, with the worst traffic jam I'd experienced since returning to LA.

It turned even worse when Adam called. I typically didn't like talking on the phone in a cab, but it looked like I'd be stuck in traffic for a while longer. Better put the time to good use.

"Finally figured out what Sullivan's been up to," Adam said the second I picked up. "He's been talking to our board, convincing them to sell."

My mind went blank as the full meaning of his words hit me.

"What? He doesn't have the funds to buy us out. Our company's valuation is larger than his."

"Yes, but he's been in talks with a private equity fund to come up with the rest of the cash. I did some digging. Apparently, they approached him after you left for LA."

That bastard! I forced my temper under control. I needed my head cool.

"How did you find out?" I asked.

"Bowman came forward today, told me about Sullivan's proposal. Very generous."

Bowman was the head of our board.

"Let me guess. They're in favor of selling?"

"Yes. You know they've wanted you to sell the company for some time. We reached a peak two years ago, and you don't want to do an IPO. They only agreed to wait because you promised the cooperation with Sullivan."

I felt the ground sliding from beneath my feet. He was 100 percent right. If Sullivan could convince the board to sell, they could force me to do so, even if I was the CEO and owned 49 percent. The role of the board was to protect the interest of stakeholders. I was one of those stakeholders; the investors who held the other 51 percent made up the rest.

"The board isn't happy that you've been away for so long. They doubt your commitment to the company."

"I've given the company everything for years. Now I take a few weeks for my family and suddenly they doubt my commitment? This is just an excuse. They've been nagging me to sell for two years."

I undid the top button of my shirt, but that didn't make breathing any easier.

"I can't believe we didn't get wind of this until now."

Adam cursed. "Sullivan is sly, I'll give him that. I didn't even know he was talking to the board outside our meetings."

My absence had simplified everything.

"I've called an emergency meeting with the board, but you have to be here, Landon. You're the only one who can convince them that selling isn't the only option."

"I know." I pressed my free palm against my temple. A dull ache was forming there. "What time is the meeting?"

"Six o'clock."

"Okay. I'll whip up a plan and call you later."

I called Hailey next, explaining everything. I hated that the situation had escalated so far out of my control.

"This is insane. But Adam's right. You need to confront your board and convince them. I like Adam, but he doesn't have your charisma, your charm. It's good that he knows that. I can handle things here, and Val's cast comes off in a few days. You do what you have to do. If we can help in any way, just say the word."

***

Maddie

I arrived at the school later than usual. Damn traffic. My boys hadn't arrived yet. None of their trucks was in front of the gate, but I did see a cab. Was the principal paying us a visit? She did say she'd like to check on our progress this week.

I slipped through the gates, intending to go straight inside the school building, but came to a halt when I saw Landon pacing near the corner where I'd been storing supplies.

I hurried to him, my insides coiling with

dread. "What are you doing here? Is Val okay?"

"Nothing happened to Val. I came here to see you. I received a call from Adam this morning."

He rattled off terms like "sale," "hostile takeover," and "board." Panic rose in my throat. My spine stiffened. "How can they take your company away from you? It's yours."

"Forty-nine percent is mine. The rest belongs to other investors. The board acts in the interest of all stakeholders, so if they think it's in the stakeholders' best interest to sell the company, they can overpower me."

"Forcing you to sell?"

"Essentially, yes."

I covered my mouth with both hands. "So what can you do?"

"Talk to the board myself, convince them otherwise. They didn't like that I was gone so long. I have to head back."

"You're leaving right now?" My brain short-circuited. "Oh, no! But I had this big goodbye dinner planned. I mean, of course you have to go talk to your board."

Landon set his jaw, rolling back his shoulders. "You'd arranged a goodbye dinner?"

"Of course. Oh, Landon. I'm so not prepared for this. Obviously I knew we only had a limited time, but God, that goodbye dinner was going to be epic."

I was rambling. I didn't know what to say, except that I had to keep talking. I was afraid I'd cry otherwise. I'd planned to talk to him about our options during that dinner. I searched his expression for any sign that he didn't want this to be over, that he wished for us to work to stay together. He said nothing. In all fairness, he had more important things on his mind now, like saving his company.

"When is your flight?" I asked.

"I haven't looked, but I'm heading straight to the airport, hopping on the first flight."

I retrieved my phone from my back pocket and pulled up a browser, searching for flights. I needed to concentrate on a task, any task, and I was glad for the excuse not to look straight at him.

"Okay, so there is a flight in one hour, but you won't even make it to LAX until then. The other leaves in three hours. Do you want me to book a ticket for you?"

He cleared his throat, and I peeked up. His brows were knitted together. I couldn't read his expression.

"I'll buy it straight at the airport."

"Okay." I shoved the phone back in my pocket and crossed my arms over my chest. "Good luck. I'll keep my fingers crossed for you. Wear your best cuff links." My heartbeat was thundering in my ears now. I wondered if Landon could hear it too.

"I don't think that'll have much of an effect. I wear them too often."

"Nah, no one's immune to them, trust me."

I mustered up a smile, and Landon rewarded me with one of his own, even if it was strained. I couldn't imagine mine looked any better. A loud honking sound startled me.

"That cab in front is for you?" I asked, just now remembering it.

He nodded. "Yeah. I wanted to wait and talk to you first, face-to-face. I didn't want to do it over the phone."

"Thanks. Well, don't leave him waiting longer. And good luck."

Damn it, Maddie! You already wished him good luck. My brain was running in a loop.

He stepped forward, kissing my cheek. My cheek! That was it? After everything, we ended with a kiss on the cheek?

I wanted to wrap my arms around him, tell him everything would be all right, that he'd get to keep his company. But I was too frozen to do more than return his chaste peck.

I walked him to the cab, my legs feeling like they belonged to someone else. As he climbed in the back seat, I barely caught myself before wishing him good luck a third time.

Chapter Twenty-Eight
Landon

Just before I boarded the plane, Adam sent me all the details on the buying offer. I read the entire document during the flight, but I couldn't concentrate. My mind was on Maddie. I hadn't waited for her to say goodbye. I'd waited because I was looking for a reason to fight for us. Instead she talked about goodbye dinners, and how she'd known we had limited time together.

Had our closeness been just wishful thinking on my part? I'd imagined a future with her, a family—all those things I hadn't let myself wish for anymore. My chest ached at the realization that I'd been alone in wanting all those things.

As the plane started the descent, I tried to push away all thoughts of Maddie. Hard as this was, I had to focus.

After landing, I went directly to the office. I knew the board could move fast when it wanted to. Entering the building through the garage, I went directly to the private elevator that led up to my office. As I strode through the corridor, anger simmered through me. This was my company. My building.

Voices reached my ears as I approached the meeting room. I hovered a few seconds in front of the door, attempting to cool down. It didn't work. My anger had wired into a nasty headache. When I pushed the door open, the buzz died almost instantly.

"Landon, you made it," Bowman, the chairman of the board, said. His tone clearly conveyed that he'd hoped I wouldn't.

"Yes. Yes, I did." I surveyed the room, my gaze lingering on each of the twelve board members. Adam and I had agreed that he wouldn't attend this meeting. "Don't look so disappointed. When someone threatens my company, I don't waste any time."

"We weren't—" Bowman begins, but I held up one hand and he fell silent.

"Let's not pretend. It will make this much quicker." I took my seat at the head of the table.

"We are just considering the offer. No one's made any decision, yet," Delacroix explained. He was one of the mentors I respected most.

"So that six of you already voted for selling is a rumor?" I asked in a measured tone. A shiver went around the table. No one answered, which was answer enough.

"Have you looked at the offer?" Bowman asked.

"Briefly, on the flight."

"We suggest you look closer. The offering price is more than fair," Delacroix continued.

"If I were interested in selling, I would look closer, yes. But I'm not interested."

Delacroix and Bowman exchanged a glance. The rest of the board was unusually silent.

Eventually Delacroix spoke again. "If I may, Landon, you've brought this company to a point so high, one none of us here imagined. But you can't take it higher by yourself. The partnership with Sullivan was a good interim solution. The synergies would have allowed for exponential growth. But the endgame of a software company of this type, especially when you have so much investor capital, is going public or selling. You know that. I drafted the first business plan with you. You had projected to sell the company three years ago."

"Business plans can change," I said dryly.

Delacroix spoke again. "You could move on to other endeavors. Think about what you could do with all that capital. We're talking north of a billion."

"I know how much the company is worth." I leaned back in my chair. The pounding in my temple became more pronounced, and the fact that I'd only slept a few hours last night was taking its toll. I was prone to making rash decisions, and lashing out at people when I was tired. Add people pushing my buttons to that and you had a recipe for disaster.

"Clearly we're at odds here," I said as calmly as I could muster. "I know I can still grow the company, bring in higher profits for all shareholders, without selling or going public. We'll meet again next week, and I'll present you with the options." It was

Wednesday, which gave me a few days to come up with a plan. "If I get wind that any of you contacted Sullivan, I will be going for blood. Understood?"

No one spoke. They usually didn't when I was in my ruthless mode, and now I was beyond even that. Exhausted and livid, I left the meeting room. I wanted to go straight home, but first I stopped by Adam's office. My assistant, Debbie, was in there too. The door was ajar, and she jumped to her feet when she saw me.

"How did it go?" There were finger markings on her cheeks, as if she'd pressed her hands to her face for a long time.

"I've bought us a few days to come up with a plan."

"Do you want me to order from your favorite Chinese restaurant? I can have them deliver it when you get home," Debbie said.

"I'll order for myself," I told Debbie and then left the office. My headache didn't subside on the drive home, but I was sure it would once I'd cooled down in my loft.

Fresh, clean air greeted me when I stepped inside. Debbie must have had the place cleaned while I was away. I could still smell a hint of lemon in the air from the cleaning products. Wheeling my bag inside the living room, I dropped on the couch, leaning my head on the headrest, closing my eyes. It had been a day from hell. I couldn't help thinking how the end of the day would have been if I were still in LA. Maddie and I would probably be in her bungalow, or on Val's porch, laughing at something my sister said. Or I'd be training Milo.

The urge to hear Maddie's voice was so strong that I barely stopped myself from calling her. She wasn't mine to call. This morning it hadn't seemed like she wanted me to call her again. She'd offered to book me a plane ticket, as if my leaving was no big deal. I'd been such a fool, letting myself hope, envisioning our life together.

Blinking my eyes open, I intended to head to the kitchen and order something from one of the takeout menus pinned to the fridge door. Instead, I took a long look around the living room. It felt like a stranger's house, even though I'd lived here for four years. A specialized company took care of decorating this place, and it had felt like home. It was still a home, but it didn't feel like *my* home anymore.

One hour later, after I'd eaten and showered, I still felt out of place. I went to bed convinced I'd see things differently in the morning, but after three hours of relentless tossing and turning, I booked myself into a hotel, packed a bag, and left. I needed my mind clear to deal with the crisis, and I couldn't afford a sleepless night, or channeling my energy into discovering why I felt out of place in my own condo, even though deep down I knew the answer.

I was missing Maddie.

***

Maddie

Why, oh why, did the fair have to be this week?

I was in no mood to be around people. But I'd put my kicking-ass pants on and come to the House & Garden Remodeling Fair after finishing my workday at the school. I'd hoped to pick up some contacts, maybe even some new clients.

"Ms. Jennings, this looks very promising," an older man said, tucking my business card in his pocket. "My wife's been talking about letting a professional handle our garden for a while now."

"Tell her to give me a call. I'll give her all the details." I shook his hand and nodded. I'd been doing a lot of nodding and shaking hands for the past few hours, and this day was a long way from over. I had to drop by some potted flowers for Val's porch after the fair ended.

I felt like I was on autopilot, and I didn't like it one bit. But I couldn't help the way I felt, which was as if a piece of me was missing. Since Wednesday morning, I'd been going through the motions. Grace had slept at my house on Wednesday and Thursday nights, and she promised to drop by tonight too.

I needed girl time and lots and lots of love to nurse my heartbreak, which meant my sister had her hands full with me. Luckily she didn't mind. On the contrary, she enabled my craving for girly activities, such as painting nails. So far I'd painted them red, pink, light pink, dark pink, and neon green before deciding on a French manicure.

I didn't think changing the color of my nails another fifty times would stop me from missing Landon like crazy, but I persevered. My heart grew heavy every time I thought about how fast he'd cut me out of his life. Meanwhile, here I was, wondering what was wrong with me that made it so easy for the people I loved to walk out on me.

I sighed, knowing I couldn't dwell on any of that now. I was here to make contacts and kick ass. So ass I kicked. I still had a lot of fairgoers to plow through, so I went to the restroom to freshen up a bit. I'd chewed my lipstick off, and my concealer wasn't concealing much anymore. I smeared on some more of the latter and dabbed with my finger to even it out. Yeah... that wasn't a lost cause or anything. My lack of sleep was showing.

I'd never been a troubled sleeper, but that had been before Landon. Problem number one: My bed was empty. I'd gotten used to that mountain of a man sprawled on it, and using his hard chest as my pillow. Or his arm. Or his abs. I didn't mind any part of him, really.

Just feeling the heat of his skin and the rhythm of his pulse had filled me with a *peaceful* happiness. He'd made me feel so loved and cherished. Sometimes he'd decided sleep was overrated and had his wicked way with me in the middle of the night. That had filled me with *giddy* happiness.

Everything Landon did made me happy. Except leaving, of course.

Since he'd left, I'd discovered my trusty old pillow just didn't cut the mustard anymore. I even missed the sound of his breathing filling my room. I'd woken up several times each night, convinced he was next to me. When I'd realized he wasn't, taking the next breath physically ached, squarely in my chest. I hoped it would dull in time.

I took another look in the mirror and gave up on the whole concealer business. I could kick ass without it too.

One hour later, I had the pleasant surprise of running into Elise from the flower shop.

"Fancy seeing you here," I said, kissing her cheek. Like me, she had a stack of papers and brochures.

"Thought I'd try and nab a few customers."

"Great minds think alike."

"Not easy, though. Most people don't think about their garden until they're halfway through remodeling their house."

"Depends how you sell them the idea." I glanced at her brochures, then at mine, which had pictures of some of my best work, all of which contained plants I'd procured from her. "Let's stick together. I use your stuff all the time anyway."

She smiled. "I won't say no to that."

We spent the rest of the afternoon together, chatting up customers. We were more efficient together, that was clear.

"Elise, are you still interested in a partnership?" I asked.

"Hell yes."

"Okay. I've given this a lot of thought. Let's meet next week and talk about the details."

"I'd love that."

When she'd suggested a partnership months ago, I couldn't even wrap my mind around it, too weary after the fiasco with Eden Designs. Now I was seeing things in a different light. I wanted to take the risk. Landon's influence, no doubt. The man had changed me in more ways than one.

Despite everything, I smiled to myself.

Chapter Twenty-Nine
Landon

Over the next few days, I chose to work from the hotel's executive lounge. Going into the office would have meant spending half my time fielding questions from the employees about the future of the company, the security of their jobs. Word about the potential buyout had spread like wildfire.

On Thursday, I descended to the hotel's restaurant, and over breakfast mentally brainstormed the best way to handle this.

Scrolling through my e-mails, I noticed that each board member had sent me an e-mail, stating their case—meaning, why selling was the better option. Regardless of my current beef with them, I had chosen them based on their intelligence and business acumen, so I decided I'd assess their cases fairly, then build my argument.

Grudgingly, I started reading through my board members' correspondence, jotting down notes. It was clear by the repetitiveness of their wording that they'd discussed this at length. After plowing through them, I took one of the hotel's notepads and a pen. I always worked better with a pen and paper in hand.

The board was right in one aspect: I had envisioned letting go of DBC Payment Solutions when I drew up the original business plan, but work had been my refuge for the past years. Had I clung to it for all the wrong reasons? Was it time to let it go? I spent the entire day making notes.

On Friday, I began to build a compelling presentation. Aside from the geographical expansion, the company could also grow by moving vertically into other close industries. Both options were equally complex. Expansion was work so grueling that I still had scars from the years when we were just starting out in Europe.

I ran a frustrated hand through my hair, looking at the ten pages of notes and the presentation slides. It was dark outside already. Between six coffees and zero food, the day had gone by. For the past four years, I'd relished challenges, and the chance to have even more work to throw myself in. But now my heart wasn't in it anymore.

Hell, I didn't want to continue living the way I had. Holed up in my office, working every waking moment. There was more to life than that. The time I spent in LA with my family and Maddie had made me realize what I was missing out on.

God, I missed Maddie. Bits and moments of our time together flashed in my mind. There was no way I had imagined our connection. She'd trusted me more every day, given more of herself to me every day. What Maddie and I had was beautiful and real. She meant everything to me. But why had she acted that way before I left?

Sure, my news had caught her by surprise. I replayed our conversation in my mind. I had spoken in detail about the problem here, but not about us. I'd been expecting a signal from her before approaching the subject, but what if she'd been waiting for one from me too? Was I overanalyzing this?

I had no idea, but I did know one thing. If there was a chance that Maddie wanted a future for us, I was going to grab it with both hands. Was I grasping at straws? Maybe, but the ache in my chest eased at the mere possibility that I could still keep Maddie in my life.

My phone buzzed, and I kept my fingers crossed that it wouldn't be Adam. I had no answers for him. It was Will. I looked around the business lounge before answering. I was alone.

"Hey! How is it going?" he asked.

"Not good."

I heard the chatter in his background and realized it was the first Friday dinner I wasn't attending in almost two months. I'd seen everyone at Maddie's birthday party, but my gut still twisted.

"We're having beef stroganoff. Adam told Val you're working from home, so she ordered the same for you from some restaurant near you. But the delivery guy just called her to say you're not home. Where are you?"

I smiled. Of course Val would try to dote on

me even from a distance. I imagined Adam's chagrin at being questioned by Val about my whereabouts.

"I booked into a hotel. I can concentrate better."

"That makes no sense," Val said, which clued me in that Will had me on loudspeaker.

Hailey chimed in next. "By the way, my pep talk about not letting Maddie go was worth jack shit, huh?"

I cleared my throat. "Lori, this would be a good time for you to note all this language is bad for Milo."

"No, Milo is watching his favorite show on the iPad. With earbuds, so we don't have to censor the conversation," Lori said.

The clan was as thorough as always.

"So?" Hailey pressed.

"What makes you say that?" I countered.

One of my sisters sighed dramatically. I thought it sounded like Lori.

"She came to bring by some flowers for my porch just now, and she looked like she couldn't wait to grab hold of sweatpants and ice cream," Val continued.

"Sweatpants and ice cream?" I repeated, more confused than before.

"Girl code for nursing a heartbreak," Lori explained.

Fuck! I'd hurt her? That was the last thing I'd wanted.

"That's a giant leap of judgment," Jace said,

speaking for the first time.

"No it's not," Lori said.

"She looked like she hadn't slept much," Val continued.

"I swear she seemed thinner too," Lori added. "Or maybe that's just because she was pale."

"Those are signs she's missing you. You two are so good for each other, Landon," Hailey said. "You belong together."

"I know. You're right," I agreed.

"Yes!" Hailey exclaimed. "Can you please say the words 'you're right' loud and clear? Just this once. They're music to my ears."

"You've just given them ammunition to hold over our heads for years," Will informed me.

"A lifetime," Hailey corrected. "And you're wearing a badass badge, Will. How can you be afraid of us?"

"Simple. Badge doesn't work on you," Will replied.

"Landon, do you want me to send the delivery guy to the hotel with the stroganoff?" Val asked.

"Yeah, do that. I'm texting you the address right now."

After I finished typing and sending, I brought the phone to my ear again. "Listen, everyone. Thanks for calling me, but I have to—"

"Yeah, yeah, we're letting you go back in your cave and brood," Lori said. "But your brooding period has an expiration date, just so you know."

After I clicked off the phone, I tried

scribbling on my notebook again, but ended up pushing it away and shutting off my laptop. I knew I had to schedule that board meeting soon, but I wouldn't be reaching any conclusions tonight, that much was clear. Energy rushed through me as I contemplated my future with Maddie instead. I didn't have all the answers to how I could make things work, but I loved her. I loved her, and I wanted to fight for our future.

***

Maddie

I was exhausted when I got home. I'd given out close to one hundred business cards and brochures, and fifteen of the receivers seemed serious about redoing their gardens.

I was happy that I was finally home, even though my house was full of memories. I saw Landon everywhere: in my kitchen, my living room, my bedroom. But I still had some wound licking to do, and my home was the place for that. All that ass kicking had taken a toll on me, sapping all my energy. And dropping off the potted flowers at Val's had been a sad affair. I was ready to try out a new nail polish.

I'd promised Grace I'd wait for her before I tested a new color, so I decided to take a bath first. I lay in the tub, covered in bubbles, and massaged my feet, which were protesting after a day of wearing heels. I even lit up a few candles and set them on the edge of the tub. Plugging in my earbuds, I carefully set my phone on the tiled floor next to the tub and sat back to relax.

Midway through my bathtub extravaganza, I thought I heard my doorbell ring but decided I must have imagined it. Grace had a key. Only when the water cooled did I leave the tub. Since my sister hadn't arrived yet, I decided to hunt down some goodies at the store and make us dinner.

When I opened my front door, I nearly knocked over the beautiful flower arrangement. My heart stilled. I bent at the waist, picking it up. There was no card, but I only knew one person who could have sent this.

Days of silence and now he was sending me flowers? What did this mean? I set the arrangement on the coffee table in my living room, trying to calm my racing pulse. I lost that battle when a text message popped up on my phone.

Landon: I miss your voice. I miss you like crazy. Is this a good time to talk?

There was a real risk that I'd start rambling again if I heard his voice. Sure, he wasn't in front of me to distract me with those sinful eyes or lips of his, but even so, who knew what I might spew out. But I'd missed his voice too. I missed all the ways in which he made my life better. I missed making him happy, and I wanted to hear what he had to say, so I typed back *Yes*.

My screen flashed right away with an incoming call from him. I plopped my ass on the floor, crossed my legs in front of me, and took the call.

"Hey, beautiful."

"Hi, Landon. I got your flowers. You did send them, right?"

"I don't know. You think anyone else is missing you like crazy?"

"I have to check my long list of suitors," I said dryly. "How are things with the takeover?"

"I'm making plans now. They'll be on the right track soon."

"That's great."

"How are you, Maddie? I've been hearing some worrying reports."

I gulped. "What?"

"Val called me after you dropped by her house. She insists you look as if you don't sleep much. Lori swears you're thinner. Hailey insists those are signs you miss me."

I loved that the Connor sisters were worrying for me, but I was still going to murder them for breaking girl code and telling him. Then again, what did I expect? He was their brother, and the Connor clan was tight. If this had been about Grace, I'd spy for her like it was my job.

"Maddie, I don't like how I handled things when I left. I'm sorry about that. I'm sorry I hurt you."

"You did," I said quietly. "But I didn't do any better either. I was so awkward.... I didn't know what to say."

"What we have is real and beautiful, and I feel so connected to you that I can't stop thinking about you every moment. About us. You're part of me."

"Really?" I whispered.

"Yes, really."

I didn't know what to say to that, so I said the first thing that popped into my mind. "I miss you so much that I don't know what to do with myself."

"I'm coming to LA next week," he announced, and I swear my entire body responded to his statement. Energy coiled through me. I felt like a live wire.

"For how long?"

"I'm thinking Thursday to Sunday. Do you have time for dinner on Thursday?"

"Sure. I can do dinner."

"It's a date."

My heart tripled in size. I was so thrilled that I'd be seeing him, and so hopeful that it didn't even occur to me to ask what the dinner was about. Only after hanging up the phone did I wonder if it was about our future or getting closure. I wasn't sure my poor heart could handle the latter.

I admired the flowers on my coffee table some more. He wouldn't have sent flowers if he wanted closure, or called and said all those sweet things. I smiled, deciding to allow myself to feel hopeful.

Chapter Thirty
Maddie

On Thursday evening, I put on one of my fancier dresses, dark pink and bandage style, and paired it with black heels. I was equal parts giddy and nervous. Landon had sent me flowers every day. *Every day.*

I arrived twenty minutes too early at the restaurant where we were meeting. Some might say I was overeager. Some. Not me. I had too much energy to wait in my car, so I headed inside the restaurant. A petite blonde in a black uniform stood behind a *Wait to be Seated* sign.

"Hi! I arrived a bit early, but I'd like to be seated in case the table is free already. Reservation under Landon Connor, I think."

"Mr. Connor arrived already. I'll show you to your table."

I grinned as I followed the waitress. So I wasn't the only one who was impatient. She led me to the far back of the room. I took in the splendid view of the ocean through the large windows. When I saw Landon, my breath caught.

"Someone will be taking your order shortly," the waitress informed me before heading to the front.

Landon stood up as I approached, flashing me a huge smile. His green eyes were molten and one-day stubble covered his jaw and cheeks.

"You look beautiful, Maddie."

"Thanks."

He kissed my hand, then pulled me into a hug, holding me tight, as if he didn't want to let go. I didn't want him to let go either. But he did let go and held out the chair for me, which was when I realized the chairs weren't opposite each other but on adjacent sides. I was sure the idea behind that was so that both of us could enjoy the view of the ocean through the windows, but I saw it as an opportunity for accidental-on-purpose touching.

He took my hand in his, pressed it to his cheek. "I've missed you, Maddie. Since I got into that cab, I've been missing you like crazy. I couldn't even stand being in my condo. I felt like I didn't belong there, and I don't. I belong with you. I love you so much, Maddie."

I covered my mouth with my free hand, swallowing a small sob. Next thing I knew, my vision became blurry as tears sprang in my eyes.

"These are happy tears," I whispered. "I promise."

Landon moved his chair right next to mine and wrapped me in his arms. I thought I might explode from the sheer emotion building up inside me.

"I love you more than I can say, Landon." My

voice shook, but I repeated the words again and again. And then his mouth was on mine, and I brought my hands to his face. I was so greedy for him that I didn't know where to touch him first. Somewhere in the back of my mind, I remembered we were in a public place, so the touching had to adhere to standards of common decency. He loved me. This wonderful man loved me.

"I missed your lips," he whispered, holding me in his arms. I rested my nose in the crook of his neck. "Your skin. All of you. I wasn't looking for love, but you're part of me now. We belong together."

At that, I pulled out of his arms, straightening up. "Yes. I gave this some serious thought. I'll move to San Jose. I'll start my landscaping business there, or maybe even work for a local company for a time."

If anyone had told me a few months ago that I'd be uttering these words, I wouldn't have believed it. Last time I moved for love, things ended in a fiasco. I never thought I'd take such a risk again, but Landon had changed me. I was ready to start over for him. I could build my business there. Since I'd been ready to partner with Elise, maybe I could start with a partner there from the get-go. I certainly had the portfolio and awards credentials to be an appealing business partner.

"You'd do that for me? For us? My sweet Maddie. It means a lot to me that you'd consider it."

He smiled, kissing the tip of my nose. *Hmm…. Why isn't he jumping up and down with joy, or whatever the manly equivalent is for that?*

A waiter arrived at our table, pad and pen in hands. "May I take your order?"

"We haven't looked at the menu yet, but bring us some sparkling water and champagne."

I took the champagne as a good omen. Landon scooted his chair back into its place once the waiter left.

"Why did you move away? I could get away with feeling you up much easier," I said.

"That's exactly why I moved. You're distracting me."

"From?" I challenged, batting my eyelashes.

"Telling you that I've decided to sell DBC Payment Solutions."

It took me a second to realize what he meant. "Wait, you're selling your company?"

He nodded, looking genuinely thrilled about it.

"But you went back because you wanted to stop the sale," I said slowly, not quite understanding.

"We're not selling it to Sullivan or any of his associates. I won't hand over my employees to dishonest people. But others have expressed interest in acquiring us in the past. We're reaching out to them."

"You never mentioned you wanted to sell it."

"In the initial business plan, I did envision selling it about one or two years ago, but for the past four years, I wanted to lose myself in my work. The truth is, I held on to the company for too long, and now it's time to let go."

I understood what he meant. If we were alone, I'd lace my arms around his neck and kiss him with all I had. But I stayed put, because I didn't think I could keep it decent this time.

"Are you sure?"

"Absolutely. I'll be flying back and forth until we kick off the sale, but in the meantime, think you can make a place for me in your bungalow?"

"I don't know. What do I get in return?" I teased.

He leaned in so close that our noses were almost touching. "I promise to hold you every night. Make your coffee in the morning." He veered left, brushing my cheek with his, bringing his lips to my ear. "I'll sink so deep into you every night that you'll still *feel* me when you leave the house in the morning."

Pulling back, I pouted, pretending his words hadn't tugged at my heartstrings *and* made me all hot and bothered.

"Think you can sweeten the deal, Mr. Connor?"

He kissed my hand. "I will love you with my whole heart, Maddie. Every day."

The need to be alone with him slammed into me. Landon's gaze fell to my lips, and when he rested his hand on my thigh under the table, I felt my need mirrored in his grip.

The waiter appeared, carrying the tray with soda and champagne.

"Are you ready to order appetizers? Or do you want to move on directly to the main course?"

I wanted neither. All I wanted was Landon. The thinly disguised desire in his eyes only stoked my fire.

Without taking his eyes off me, he said, "I'm afraid something came up, and we have to leave right away. We'll take the champagne with us."

***

We barely made it past the threshold of my house before we started undressing each other. My dress landed on the floor of the living room, my bra and panties in the hall. Landon's clothes became a heap next to the bed.

"I love you, baby." He peppered kisses on my shoulder, fondling my right breast, then the left one. "I've missed them."

"I knew it," I teased. "You made all those life-changing decisions for my girls."

He licked a nipple and gripped my ass in his hands. "Don't be modest. This beauty sealed the deal for me. Begs for a little biting." He spun me around and I felt him lower himself. I laughed when he bit my right ass cheek.

I turned around, lavishing him with attention. I started kissing his torso, insisting on the defined squares of his abs, then tracing the V-shaped obliques with my tongue, feeling his erection against my clavicle.

The look in his eyes when I stroked his hard-on was so intense that heat rushed between my legs. Gripping him at the base, I squeezed him tight, and as I moved my fist up to the tip, I licked every inch of him my hand freed up. When I reached the tip, I took my hand away completely, swiped my tongue across the head. I was rewarded with a heavy and masculine groan, and his thighs quivered almost imperceptibly.

I wanted to take him in my mouth, but Landon hoisted me up, effortlessly laying me on the bed on my back, thighs spread wide.

Settling between my legs, he eyed my center, licking his lips. Then he dragged his thumb from my clit right down to the entrance. My entire body shuddered. He slid on protection and rubbed his length along my clit, until my thighs were shaking.

Then he entered me. I cried out as he filled me, inch by inch, stretching me. He held my gaze, brought a hand to my face, touching my cheek gently, kissing my chin, the tip of my nose.

"I love you, Landon."

He started sliding in and out of me slowly, never breaking eye contact. We were both coming apart at the seams. Every inch of my body was on fire. When a burst of pleasure coursed through me, every muscle tightened, my breath caught, my ears were ringing. I felt our connection growing deeper with every thrust until I was completely lost in him.

I laced my arms around his neck, touched my forehead to his. So many emotions bubbled up inside me that they overwhelmed me. He was back in my arms. He was mine to keep and to make happy. Oh, I had *such* great plans to make that happen.

"What are you thinking about?" he asked after a beat.

I smiled sheepishly. "That I will shower you with love every day."

"I like the sound of that."

"Fair warning, I might go overboard and smother you."

"That's really not possible."

"Ah, that gives me so much leverage. You're never going to win another negotiation." He tugged with his teeth at my lower lip while his fingers feathered the sides of my breasts.

"I look forward to proving the opposite, my love."

Chapter Thirty-One
Landon

I held my hand around Maddie's shoulders as we headed toward Val's house the next evening for Friday dinner. I kissed the side of her head and nuzzled her temple with my nose. I couldn't stop touching her—wouldn't stop. She was mine, and I planned to take advantage of that every waking minute. I loved the way Maddie leaned into me, her warm, soft curves fitting perfectly against me. I would never get enough of her, and I couldn't wait for her to be my wife. If it were up to me, I'd pop the question right now, marry her at the nearest city hall. But I wanted to do everything the right way: the proposal, the big wedding, let her have her dream dress. I wanted to fulfill every dream of hers for the rest of our lives.

I couldn't help imagining the clan's reactions when I broke the news of my return to LA. I'd simply told them I was visiting, and they hadn't pushed for more. The door swung open before I'd even knocked.

"I'm so happy to see you! Both of you!" Val grinned, looking between Maddie and me. Her cast had been removed, but she was still using one crutch because the muscles in one leg had atrophied somewhat. "When did this happen?"

"Yesterday."

Val cocked a brow. "You flew in yesterday? And didn't tell us?"

Maddie tilted her head, narrowing her eyes at me. "You were pretty confident you'd spend the night with me, huh?"

"What can I say? I knew I had strong arguments."

Maddie huffed. She was adorable. I focused on my sister again.

"So, are you going to let us in or what?"

"No, I'm considering keeping you out there as punishment that you flew in incognito. But you brought Maddie, so you're forgiven."

Dinner was delicious and loud. Business as usual at the Connor table.

Before dessert, I cleared my throat. "I have a few announcements to make."

"Obviously you two are back together," Hailey remarked.

I took Maddie's hand, pressed it to my lips.

"Yes, we are. The second thing is this: I'm selling DBC Payment Solutions and moving back to LA."

The table fell into a stunned silence for a few seconds before everyone started talking at the same time.

"Wow, that's unexpected—"

"When exactly are you moving back?"

"When did you decide to sell?"

I explained everything in a few quick words. Once I'd realized I didn't want to continue living the way I'd had and that I was ready to let go of the company and the past, I hadn't agonized over the decision to sell. It was time.

"Welcome home, brother," Jace said. "That'll give us more leverage when these three"—he pointed at our sisters—"decide to band together."

Lori rolled her eyes, muttering, "*Men.*"

I grinned. I loved being back, knowing I'd be here for weekly dinners, bickering with my siblings like we'd done since we'd been kids. I was sure we'd be doing the same well into our retirement.

Most of all, I was grateful my Maddie was right next to me. I still hadn't let go of her hand, and I felt like holding it a while longer.

She shook her head, laughing. "Jace, sorry to break it to you, but I'm tipping the balance in the girls' favor."

I whipped my head to her. "No you're not. You're on my side."

"I won't automatically take your side. Only when I'm convinced it's the right thing."

"Ouch," Will exclaimed.

I glared at Maddie. She returned my glare, even though her cheeks were turning a delicious pink. I would have pressed the point further, but I didn't want her switching sides *before* I'd brought up my next point.

"So, since you know I'm selling the company, you know I'll have a lot of spare cash in the near future," I began. Maddie squeezed my hand. Out of the corner of my eye, I saw she was suppressing a smile.

"You could buy yourself a decent car," Will suggested. "You know, not *sensible*."

I cocked a brow. "Since when is a Mercedes sensible?"

"Since you can afford a Maserati."

"I'll stick to what I know," I informed him.

"So what are you going to do with all that wad of cash exactly?" Val asked. Ah, how I enjoyed keeping her on the edge. I could tell she was wondering how she'd missed all this. Truthfully, I was surprised they didn't know about the sale. I had to give Adam more credit. But even Adam didn't know about my plans. I'd only shared them with my Maddie.

"I will set up an investment fund."

"Smart," Jace said. "What will you invest in? Real estate? The stock exchange?"

"Start-ups?" Will followed.

I shook my head. "I'm keeping my options open. I have my eyes on a very promising cosmetics company."

I was looking directly at Val now. She opened her mouth, closed it again.

"No, no, no," she croaked finally. "We—it's your money, Landon." She looked around the table helplessly. "Back me up."

The rest of my siblings seemed as stunned as Val, but I was banking on them being less stubborn and proud. And if they were, I'd pull on my creativity. The stubborn streak was strong in the Connor clan.

"This extends to everyone, by the way. You need funding, tell me before you go to a bank or external investors."

"The purpose of an investment fund is profits," Jace said. "You don't owe any of us anything, and we're not kids anymore. You and Val did more than your fair share raising us."

I sat up straighter. "That's not what this is. An investment fund *invests* in worthwhile ventures, like our family's future. As your older brother—"

Val held up a hand. "You can't play the older brother card on me. We're twins."

"Still fifteen minutes older than you," I reminded her. "And still 500 percent more stubborn than you."

Val shook her head, but I saw the small smile playing on her lips. The development of the line for the department store chain was progressing well, but if she took my offer, she could expand sooner.

"At least wait until we finish dessert to start attacking my defenses," she said.

Maddie laughed, smiling at me. "Come on, Val. Your brother is a man of opportunity. He sees an opening, he takes it."

"By the way, the offer extends to you too, Maddie."

She gasped, squeezing my hand. When I told her about my plans, I'd skipped the part where I could invest in *her* business. Now, when she'd openly agreed that my fund was a great idea, was the best time to bring it up.

"We don't have to discuss specifics now. I just wanted everything out in the open, give you all food for thought," I said.

"That was sneaky," Maddie commented a few minutes later as we headed to the kitchen. We'd offered to bring the dessert to the table.

"I disagree. It was smart. Just think about it, babe."

She took the tiramisu out of the fridge, setting the tray on the counter. I was supposed to take out the plates, but instead I pushed her hair to the side, kissing the back of her neck. She shuddered, her skin instantly turning to goose bumps.

"Landon, stop."

"Why, you don't like it?" I teased.

"I like it too much, you terrible man. Stop." She fidgeted as if trying to break free, but her attempt was so halfhearted, it only made me smile. But I did stop and spun her around to face me.

"We need to talk about you not being on my side."

She pinched her nose, poking my chest with one finger. "If I see Neanderthal attitude, I have to call you out on it."

I grabbed her wrist, kissed her finger. "You

didn't seem to mind that attitude this morning."

She'd tried to tease me this morning, walking half-naked around the kitchen. Emphasis on tried. I loved her so hard on that counter, it creaked with our movements.

"I can't believe you're using that as bargaining chip. You're even more terrible than I thought. First you get me to fall in love, now you show your true colors. Typical. You almost demolished my kitchen this morning." She was so adorable that I had a hard time keeping a straight face.

"About that…. I like your bungalow, but it's small. I want to build a big house on that lot of land we both love so much. Could you draw up a plan?"

"I'd love to, but it's been years since I worked on anything other than outdoor spaces. I can recommend a top-notch architect."

"But you'll help? I want you to plan it just the way you want it. It will be our home."

"Our home?" she asked quietly.

"Yes, Maddie. *Our* home. I want you to be my wife. And—"

I stopped, but too late.

"Landon," she whispered, her eyes wide.

There went my grand plan to wait and do it with a ring and right atmosphere and everything. "I want to spend the rest of my life with you, Maddie. Will you marry me?"

"Of course I will. I love you."

"I'll wait for as long as you want, but… I'd really like our life together to start soon."

She sneaked her arms around my torso. I hugged her tight, then even tighter as she said, "You don't have to wait at all, Landon. I love you. I can't wait to be your wife."

Epilogue
Three months later
Maddie

Out of all the things I imagined doing on my wedding day, taking a pregnancy test wasn't on the list.

My period was three weeks late. In the beginning I'd chalked it up to my stress level going through the roof with the wedding preparations. A week ago I started feeling nauseous in the mornings. I'd put it up to more nerves. But today I'd almost fainted while having my hair done. I'd sent Grace to buy a test right away.

The wedding was taking place in one of the finest beach hotels in the Los Angeles area. Landon and I each had separate rooms to dress in. He'd arranged for an entire team of hair and makeup artists to come here for me, and they'd worked their magic for hours. They were all gone now, though. It was just Grace and me.

"Maddie, come on! I'm dying here," Grace exclaimed from the other side of the bathroom door. I blinked at the test, then blinked some more. Grace had bought me one of those that displayed "pregnant" or "not pregnant."

Mine showed "pregnant." I tried to blink back the tears of joy but couldn't. My entire body was alive with happiness. I'd hoped from the first signs, even though it was unplanned. The test didn't say how far along I was, but I was almost certain I could trace the date baby Connor was conceived to the evening Landon signed the papers for selling his company. It was a good thing construction on the new house had started already.

I opened the door, holding the test with the display toward Grace. She shrieked, jumping up and down.

"I'm going to be an aunt! Congratulations." She hugged me tight, then pulled back abruptly.

"You can't cry, Maddie. Your makeup—"

"I need to tell Landon."

"Now?"

"Yes, now. I want him to know before we say our vows."

"Okay. I'm going after the makeup lady. She said she'd drink a coffee in the lobby before leaving. You go to Landon's room. But you only have ten minutes, tops. Then I need you back here so we can fix your makeup and get you dressed. I looked over the schedule Lori set up. There is no time for sexy activities. Or fixing post-sexy-activities hair." My hair was styled in a half updo, with loose waves under an intricately twisted bun. No way would I risk that getting messed up.

Nodding, I fastened the white silk robe tighter around me, pocketed the test, and dashed out of the room.

Landon's room was one floor below. As our wedding planner, Lori had decreed we couldn't be on the same floor. What if we bumped into each other? Bad luck seeing the bride in her dress before the altar and all that. I suddenly hoped I wouldn't run into Lori. She and Grace were scary today.

I could barely contain my grin when I knocked on Landon's door. It swung open the next second... and I came face-to-face with Lori.

"What are you doing here?" she whispered. "Landon can't see you."

"I'm not wearing my wedding dress. And I need to talk to him."

"Is everything okay? Your makeup—"

"Lori, who's at the door?" Landon's voice came from inside.

"Maddie," I said loudly before Lori could channel Grace too much.

Landon appeared at the door in a blink. He was further along the dressing process than I was, already wearing his sleek black tux, his white shirt underneath. His green eyes stood out. God, was my man handsome. I wondered how many seconds it would take to peel it off him. Grace's warning rang in my ears. Hmm, I could climb him even with the tux on, but could I risk wrinkling the shirt? Nope. No time.

"Maddie, what's wrong?" he asked as I stepped inside.

"Nothing. I just need to talk to you real

quick." I looked at Lori. "Ten minutes, I promise. I know we're on a schedule."

"Okay. I'll wait for you in your room. Actually, I'll go find the makeup lady."

The corners of my mouth twitched. "Grace is already on it."

Lori took off with a nod. Once we were alone, my heart leaped into my throat. Traitorous little organ. How was I supposed to keep my voice even now?

I didn't trust myself not to blubber while saying the words, so I took his hand and led him to the couch.

Then I retrieved the test from my pocket, holding it for him to read.

"We're going to have a baby." His voice broke on the last word. And then there were no more words. He brought his mouth down to mine and kissed me fiercely. I pulled him to me, needing to feel him flush against me.

"You have no idea how happy you just made me, Maddie."

Oh, I did know. That's why I'd wanted to tell him now.

He lowered a hand to my belly. "I will love both of you so much."

I had no doubt, because no one had more love to give than Landon. I still couldn't believe this was my life, that this wonderful man would soon become my husband, and that a little bundle of joy was already on his or her way.

"Are you hoping it's a boy or a girl?" I asked, running my hands through his hair.

Since his face and hair were the only places I could touch him without ruining the wedding outfit, I planned to take thorough advantage. I settled more comfortably between the armrest and the backrest.

"I don't have a preference. I just want it to be healthy." On a frown, he added, "Is all that physical work you do safe for both of you?"

Oh boy. We had nine long months ahead of us if he was already flexing his protective muscles. I loved that side of him, but I couldn't own up to that. I had the good sense to keep that tidbit of information to myself. Besides, Elise and I had formalized our business partnership last month. We were already in talks with David Hooper about a future residential project he had in mind.

"Yes, yes it is. But if you want to make sure I relax, might I suggest date nights?"

"Sure."

Well, that was easy.

"Breakfast in bed?"

"Anything you want, Maddie."

Now *that* was such a dangerous statement to make, really. He probably thought I'd exercise self-restraint or at least common decency in my requests. I planned on zero decency. He could forget restraint altogether.

He leaned in for another kiss. It was even fiercer than the first one. Hotter. Deeper.

I felt his hand skim up my thigh, and we both

groaned when he reached the lacy frills of my panties.

Grace's warning flew out of my mind, as did our time constraints. But a loud knock at the door brought both back into focus. We scrambled to our feet, trying not to look too guilty.

"Who do you think it is? I vote Grace," I whispered.

Landon considered this for a few seconds. "Nah, I'm sure it's Lori."

It turned out to be Hailey. She was wearing a beautiful red silk dress, her hair hanging in waves on one side.

"You two are lucky *I* showed up here. You owe me for saving you from Lori and Grace."

I barely managed to wave at Landon before she whisked me away.

My room erupted in cheers when Hailey and I entered. Val and Lori were grinning from ear to ear.

Grace gave me a sheepish smile. "Sorry, I had to tell them."

"You had to, huh?"

Grace winked. "You try surviving a Connor ambush."

They pulled me into a group hug, which lasted exactly ten seconds before Lori cried, "Time's up. Her makeup needs retouching."

Yep, hugs were timed too. The makeup artist, Sheila, was waiting in the same spot she'd applied my cosmetics first, next to the vanity in the corner of the room.

While she focused on my face, she interrogated the girls.

"None of you are married?" she asked. They answered in a chorus of "No."

Sheila chuckled. "Wedding season is open now. Bet you'll all follow in Maddie's steps."

I peeked open one eye, looked at the Connor girls and my sister.

"Well, it won't be me," Lori said. "I've got Milo to focus on. No place for another man."

"That's lousy logic," Val said. I grinned, secretly agreeing with her.

"When's the last time you were on a date?" Hailey asked.

Lori sighed. "Years. Years! But don't tell Landon that. I *might* have misled him to think otherwise because he was nagging."

I caught Lori looking at my engagement ring longingly. *Mental note: What Lori says is not what Lori wants.*

"Are the other brothers as handsome as the groom?" Sheila asked while reapplying my mascara.

"Oh, they are," Hailey said. "We might be biased, but…."

Grace looked up from her phone, where I bet she was checking the schedule. "I'm not biased. And I can vouch for that. This family has great genes."

Sheila smiled, finally releasing me. "Well, my job's done here. But I bet I'll be back for a new wedding in no time at all. I've seen that happen so many times. First one in a group gets married, then the rest fall like dominoes."

"Okay, time to dress the bride," Grace announced.

I smiled the entire time the girls helped me in my dress. I couldn't stop touching it. It was so pretty, a trumpet silhouette with a sweetheart neckline covered in Chantilly lace. It was fitted around my body and flared out midthigh.

My nerves kicked in when I stepped out on the terrace where the ceremony was taking place. It was a perfect day. Sunny, warm, with a gentle breeze coming in from the ocean cooling my skin.

Our guests were already sitting on the white chairs arranged in straight rows. The sheer number of guests was huge, given how many cousins the Connors had. The entire Bennett clan had flown in from San Francisco.

I swept my gaze over to the wedding arch adorned with flowers and a white veil, and the man waiting beneath it. The anxiety melted away. When we made eye contact, he was all I saw.

My parents had flown in for the occasion, and Dad gave me to Landon, who kissed my hand, murmuring, "I love you, beautiful."

The pastor welcomed everyone, starting the ceremony. Landon held my gaze the entire time. My heart was bursting with love for this handsome man standing before me, ready to tie his life to mine. The wind had ruffled Landon's black hair, and I pushed two strands away from his forehead before we exchanged rings.

"And now the vows," the pastor announced.

Landon held my hands firmly in his, joy dancing in his green eyes.

"Maddie, my vows to you are not just a promise, but a privilege. I vow to love and respect you my entire life."

"I vow to be worthy of your love," I replied.

"I promise to care for you and spoil you every day." He kissed my hands, and emotion rose in my throat.

"Landon, I promise to be your best friend, your partner, your ally, your lover."

"I promise to be right next to you when you chase your dreams."

"I promise to be your biggest supporter."

"I promise to out-stubborn you even when you give me your best."

I grinned. "I promise to let you *think* you won an argument once in a while."

The guests laughed, and even the pastor chuckled. We were both misty-eyed as he declared us husband and wife, and then Landon kissed me softly.

"I can't wait to make you happy for the rest of our lives, lovely wife," he whispered.

"I can't wait to return the favor, husband of mine."

We turned to face our guests, and I caught a glimpse of Lori watching us with tears in her eyes.

She dabbed at the corners, smiling and whispering, "I love weddings."

I smiled back, making a mental note to be sneaky when the time came to gather all the single ladies and throw my bouquet. I planned to throw it in Lori's direction.

Other Books by Layla Hagen

The Bennett Family Series

Book 1: Your Irresistible Love (Sebastian & Ava)

Sebastian Bennett is a determined man. It's the secret behind the business empire he built from scratch. Under his rule, Bennett Enterprises dominates the jewelry industry. Despite being ruthless in his work, family comes first for him, and he'd do anything for his parents and eight siblings— even if they drive him crazy sometimes. . . like when they keep nagging him to get married already.

Sebastian doesn't believe in love, until he brings in external marketing consultant Ava to oversee the next collection launch. She's beautiful, funny, and just as stubborn as he is. Not only is he obsessed with her delicious curves, but he also finds himself willing to do anything to make her smile. He's determined to have Ava, even if she's completely off limits.

Ava Lindt has one job to do at Bennett Enterprises: make the next collection launch unforgettable. Daydreaming about the hot CEO is definitely not on her to-do list. Neither is doing said

CEO. The consultancy she works for has a strict policy—no fraternizing with clients. She won't risk her job. Besides, Ava knows better than to trust men with her heart.

But their sizzling chemistry spirals into a deep connection that takes both of them by surprise. Sebastian blows through her defenses one sweet kiss and sinful touch at a time. When Ava's time as a consultant in his company comes to an end, will Sebastian fight for the woman he loves or will he end up losing her?

AVAILABLE ON ALL RETAILERS.

Book 2: Your Captivating Love (Logan & Nadine)
Book 3: Your Forever Love (Pippa & Eric)
Book 4: Your Inescapable Love (Max & Emilia)
Book 5: Your Tempting Love (Christopher & Victoria)
Book 6: Your Alluring Love (Alice & Nate)
Book 7: Your Fierce Love (Blake & Clara)
Book 8: Your One True Love (Daniel & Caroline)
Book 9: Your Endless Love (Summer & Alex)

The Lost Series

Lost in Us (James & Serena)
Found in U (Jessica & Parker)
Caught in Us (Dani & Damon)

***

Standalone USA TODAY BESTSELLER
Withering Hope

Aimee's wedding is supposed to turn out perfect. Her dress, her fiancé and the location—the idyllic holiday ranch in Brazil—are perfect.

But all Aimee's plans come crashing down when the private jet that's taking her from the U.S. to the ranch—where her fiancé awaits her—defects mid-flight and the pilot is forced to perform an emergency landing in the heart of the Amazon rainforest.

With no way to reach civilization, being rescued is Aimee and Tristan's—the pilot—only hope. A slim one that slowly withers away, desperation taking its place. Because death wanders in the jungle under many forms: starvation, diseases. Beasts.

As Aimee and Tristan fight to find ways to survive, they grow closer. Together they discover that facing old, inner agonies carved by painful pasts takes just as much courage, if not even more, than facing the rainforest.

Despite her devotion to her fiancé, Aimee can't hide her feelings for Tristan—the man for whom she's slowly becoming everything. You can hide many things in the rainforest. But not lies. Or love.

Withering Hope is the story of a man who desperately needs forgiveness and the woman who brings him hope. It is a story in which hope births wings and blooms into a love that is as beautiful and intense as it is forbidden.

AVAILABLE ON ALL RETAILERS.

***

Anything For You
Copyright © 2018 Layla Hagen
Published by Layla Hagen

Published: Layla Hagen 2018
Cover: RBA Designs

***
Acknowledgements

Publishing a book takes a village! A big THANK YOU to everyone accompanying me on this journey. To my family, thank you for supporting me, believing in me, and being there for me every single day. I could not have done this without you.

CPSIA information can be obtained
at www.ICGtesting.com
Printed in the USA
BVHW03s1607250418
514392BV00023B/928/P

9 781635 765069